Finding Richard

By Mitch Davis

For Chuck and Jim.

Beginnings lead to endings

And endings start anew

The flesh he wears in this life

Is just an anteroom

One

Richard's breathing was heavy and each exhale produced a thin cloud of vapor that trailed behind him as he peddled through the night air. Farm country surrounded him for as far as his eyes could see, the landscape dully illuminated by the light of a full moon hanging in a cloudless November sky. He had been on the long stretch of country road for an hour and ten minutes already. Another hour and 20 minutes separated him from the thing he needed most. The only sounds he could hear were raspy, wet rushes of air coming in and out of his burning lungs, and the metal on metal clicking created when the bike's left pedal hit the kick stand on every up stroke.

He was heading into the wind again. The frigid blast swept tears from his eyes and stung his face like wasps. Clear, thick mucous ran slowly and steadily from his nose, over his upper lip and into his panting mouth. The gooey liquid had a salty taste he had grown accustomed to, so he swallowed it.

The look on Richard's face was understandable given the viscously cold air, his burning lungs and exhausted muscles, all of which were caused by riding his bicycle 26 miles at night in 12 degree weather. But his expression held something more than discomfort; it was fearfully and painfully contorted, like a man who had been stabbed once and watched helplessly as his assailant's knife sank into his flesh again and again.

His eyes darted left and right and then straight ahead, scanning for movement. Straining forward up a long hill he tried hard to clear his mind of the bad things and focus on the two good things he cared most about at the moment, coffee and cigarettes. It would be a while before he reached the café, so he decided to stop and light up. He had to wait for the coffee, but not the cigarettes. Stopping close to the gravel shoulder, his legs straddled the bike. Again he turned his head in frantic, jerky movements to the left and right and to his backside, like a sentry surveying his defensive perimeter. Once he was certain there was no immediate threat he unzipped his coat and reached inside to his left shirt pocket as he had been doing for 29 years. He pulled out a cigarette, lit it and took a long draw. The soothing smoke eased the tension in his haggard body. He closed his eyes and tilted his head back as the nicotine began to do its work. He took another long draw before opening his eyes and taking in the expanse of darkness and pinpricks of light hanging above him. The night sky was still and cold, as if it was dead or had never been alive. The sight awed him, but also made him feel small and alone. He thought about God and wondered where he was at the moment. A chill ran through his body, forcing him to look back down to earth. As far off into the distance as he could see the landscape offered nothing but barren fields lined with the skeletons of trees.

Richard took another long draw from his cigarette and exhaled slowly. He removed his gloves, cupped his hands around his mouth and blew. The warmth from his breath lasted only a moment until the cold set in again. Wincing from the pain, he stuffed his hands into his coat pockets and continued puffing with the cigarette hanging from his lips.

"THEY'RE HERE," the voice said, echoing softly like distant thunder. It did not startle Richard; he had heard it many times. It was the warning that caught his attention. Someone or something was present.

"THEY'RE COMING FOR HIM," the voice proclaimed.

He closed his eyes tight, but shutting them wasn't enough; he covered them with his hand like a frightened child trying to overcome his temptation to peek, fearing what he might see.

"Go away", Richard said, weakly. "Please go away."

"THEY'RE COMING!" the voice repeated.

"Go away!" he yelled.

The evildoers had begun hunting Richard long ago. Decades of battle against them had worn him ragged and he often succumbed to their attacks, retreating and begging to be left alone. But the scars of battle ran long and deep and were a constant reminder that retreat had gained him nothing but fear and pain.

Cowards don't win, he growled silently. *Cowards retreat and lose*! Richard loathed cowardice, and he was sick and tired of being a victim. He had had enough. The evildoers would feel his wrath, and they would feel it tonight. His anger rose like steam in a pressure cooker and his teeth sank into his lower lip like it was chewing gum. He felt the flesh give way, and soon after the metallic taste of blood filled his mouth - a bitter reminder that he was at war. Richard tore his hand from his eyes and threw his half-smoked cigarette to the ground, ready to do battle.

"Come on! Show yourselves you evildoers! Show yourselves!" he screamed.

As if responding to his challenge, a loud snap followed by the sound of cracking brush burst forth from the tree line to his right. Richard whipped his upper body around and froze like a rabbit that had just spotted a wolf. Adrenaline coursed through his veins and his hands began to shake. His heart felt like it would pound its way through his chest as he scanned the dark abyss of gnarled trees and underbrush.

"Show yourselves!" he shouted again, jerking his head to the left and right, expecting something to lunge at him. Nothing came.

Emboldened now, Richard dismounted his bike like a soldier off his warhorse. He dropped to his knees and scratched frantically at the gravel shoulder until he uncovered three golf ball-sized rocks.

"Evildoers! Filthy evildoers!"

He stood up and raised one rock above his head, ready to hurl it at anything that moved.

"Come on! What are you waiting for? I'm right here!"

Another loud crash was followed by the sound of large branches breaking like twigs beneath the weight of the thing that was out there. Richard stepped back, but as soon as he did his anger rose again. He stepped forward defiantly, swiveling his toe into the gravel like a ninth inning pitcher. He cocked his arm and launched the rock as hard as he could in the direction of the thrashing. It disappeared without making even the smallest sound, as if it had been swallowed by the darkness. He took another rock and held it at the ready as he scanned the tree line. His breathing was quick and shallow and he could no longer feel the cold.

"Come on!" his fearless voice echoed off the hard earth.

Another crash came from just inside the tree line. Richard saw the faint outline of a large, dark figure. It began to move, its dense form the only thing not blurred in his field of vision. He knew the things eyes were locked on him.

"THEY'RE HERE," the grim voice said with finality.

Richard dropped the two remaining rocks he held in his hands. Reaching franticly for his bike, he set it upright and pushed forward several yards before mounting the seat. His feet found the pedals and he began pumping as fast as he could go. But his desire for speed outweighed his agility and one of his feet slipped off a pedal, causing the bike to swerve onto the gravel shoulder just a few yards from where he had started. As the bike went down Richard spread his hands outward to break the fall. Gravel dug deep into his palms and knees as he skidded across the shoulder and into the ditch. He rolled a few feet, stopping with a thud as he hit the bottom. For a moment he lay dazed and motionless. But fear quickly took over, clearing his fogged mind. He jumped to his feet as if a bolt of lighting had nipped his heels. Limping, he moved quickly up the incline to the shoulder where his bike lay. He didn't want to look back, but his survival instinct forced him to do it. As he reached down to grab the handlebars he looked over his shoulder to see the large, dark figure emerge from the tree line.

"No!" spittle flew from his mouth as he screamed. "God, please! Not like this!"

He pushed forward and hopped onto the bike. The front wheel wobbled on a bent rim as he peddled harder and harder. Turning his head again he saw the apparition lurch forward in powerful leaps as it pursued him. Richard was unaware of anything except his desperate need to move faster than the thing that was closing in on him. His taught muscles straining to overcome the sluggish hunk of metal and rubber, his legs pumped the pedals hard enough to cause chunks of gravel to spit from underneath the bike's rear tire until it made contact with the pavement. The deafening screech of rubber skidding on asphalt startled Richard, and for a moment he was surprised to think that he was pumping the bike's pedals hard enough to produce such a sound. He was surprised even more when he learned that the sound had come from a barreling Ford F-150 truck that swerved around him, coming within inches of crushing him beneath its massive weight. Undaunted, Richard peddled hard down the middle of the road. He considered the near miss with the truck to be inconsequential compared to the near certainty of being brutally dismembered by the thing that was after him.

Richard did not stop for another cigarette break. He peddled hard for the next hour and twenty minutes, his legs aching and his lungs burning as he gasped for air. He doubted he would make it. His legs began to give out as he struggled to the crest of a steep hill. Exhausted, he coasted for the first time since the ordeal with the evildoer. Looking to his left and saw the lights from Belford's gas station cutting through the trees like a beacon. The brightly lit pumps and building were the first of many along the main street that ran through the middle of the town of Ripley. It felt like the entrance to a safe haven, a place where there would be no monsters, and where hot coffee flowed abundantly. His pace slowed and he breathed easier as he rode past Belford's, then past a small red brick building on which hung a huge sign with the word HARDWARE emblazoned in black letters. He peddled past a weathered looking post office, a tavern, a craft store and other buildings bordering the street. The details blurred when he spotted the radiant light emanating from the sign outside the Blue Moon Café. It pulled him forward like a tractor beam from a space ship.

Having secured his bike to a street sign outside the café, he opened the door and stepped inside. He scanned the room from his vantage point in front of the cash register, stopping to look intently at two customers sitting at the counter. They met Richard's gaze, unsure why he was looking at them like they had just stepped out of a dark alley holding brass knuckles and nun chucks. One of the customers tried breaking the tension with a forced smile. Richard did not smile back. Instead, he unzipped his coat and moved to the back of the restaurant.

The man at the table was leaning forward with his head down and arms crossed, resting on the tabletop. His shoulders were hunched, as if bearing an immense weight. The corners of his mouth were downturned in a sort of permanent scowl, and the pallid skin around his eyes was etched with deep lines. Thin, gray-white hair dropped in a straight line past bony cheeks and a weak chin and rested atop his shoulders. Black suspenders supported baggy black pants and hung loosely over a dingy white long sleeve shirt. The clothing hung on his emaciated frame like sack clothe on a scarecrow.

Richard stopped for a moment to look at the man. He was slight and unsubstantial, as if a small gust of wind could blow him away. Moving to the table Richard sat, looking at the top of the man's still downturned head. Moments went by before the man responded to Richard's presence and slowly looked up. His eyes were a jarringly brilliant blue with flashes of grey and green that lit his weathered face. His eyes were incongruent with the rest of his body, like luminous windows of stained glass hung on the exterior of a crumbling shack. They danced with brightly colored light that hinted at raw power and a cold, calculating intellect. The man looked at Richard like a strict parent looks at an unruly child, his gaze holding contempt and resolve. Richard willed himself to not look away. He felt a chill run through his body as the man's piercing eyes and mouth turned up slightly at the corners in a subtle smirk.

"You're late," said the man.

"I know, I'm sorry…I was going to leave earlier, but--"

"I don't give a damn about what you were going to do," the man fired back, his intense stare cutting deeply into Richard. "I do my part, and I damn well expect that you'll do yours. Why does this continue to happen?"

Before Richard could answer the man broke eye contact, picked up his coffee cup and blurted, "Never mind, let's get on with it. What have you got?"

Richard reached into his coat pocket and retrieved a wad of crumpled papers, a lighter, and a bottle of nasal spray and dumped it in the middle of the table. Just then a waitress stepped up to the table. "Hi hun, how we doin' tonight?" she asked, in a folksy northern Wisconsin accent.

"Fine," answered Richard without looking up.

"Would you like to try some pie? We have an apple fresh out o' the oven, and it's still warm."

"No thanks."

"Well, what can I get ya then?"

"Just coffee. And can I have the pot?"

"No problem hun, I'll be right back." She left to retrieve Richard's favorite drink.

Reaching for the wad of paper, Richard unraveled it into three separate but very crumpled sheets. Smoothing each one on the table he paused to review his notes.

Leaning towards the man he said in a whisper, "What I found out is that Francis Tadley has been acting badly."

Amused by the ingenious rhyme, Richard let out a loud, jovial laugh that caught the attention of more than a few customers.

"Shhh!" the man replied in a low but forceful tone. "Maintain your composure or the others will know!"

The smile disappeared from Richard's face as he sank back in his seat, looking away from the man's accusing gaze.

Serious now, Richard continued. "He did what you said he would do. He's a pretender and an evildoer. He sent out information about us two times this week."

"What kind of information?"

"I'm not, I, I mean I can't..." Richard stammered.

"Damn it, what kind of information?" the man yelled and slammed his fist against the table hard enough to rattle the salt and pepper shakers.

"I, I didn't get to see up close, but I know he sent letters. He definitely sent letters."

"Of course there were letters Richard! Francis Tadley is the mailman for God's sake! What did you expect him to deliver, sail boats? I swear, sometimes you haven't got the sense God gave a donut."

Seeing the waitress return with a coffee pot, the man stopped abruptly. She placed a cup in front of Richard and started pouring.

"Hun," she said, "remember what we talked about when you were here the last time?"

"I'm not doing anything wrong," Richard said, avoiding eye contact.

"You can stay as long as you behave yourself, OK?" she added empathetically.

Richard nodded his head in acknowledgement, picked up the cup and took a big sip.

"We'll behave ourselves," said the man in a mocking tone. "Now, kindly leave us so we can continue our conversation quietly."

The waitress turned and left.

"Listen," the man stated firmly. "These people intend to do us harm. Do you understand that?"

"Yes," Richard said, gulping more coffee.

"Then what do you intend to do about it?"

Richard said nothing. He took another long drink from his cup, picked up the coffee pot and poured the life-giving brown liquid until it flowed over the cup and onto the table. He didn't bother cleaning up before putting the cup to his lips for another gulp. His hand involuntarily moved back and forth in a slow tremble, spilling even more coffee.

The man shook his head disapprovingly. "You need to get some of those documents. You have to find a way to get some of those documents!"

"Alright," Richard said, his tone lacking conviction.

"What? I can't hear you!"

"Alright!" Richard shouted. "I'll get the letters! I'll get the letters to prove that Francis Tadley is an evildoer!"

Stunned at first, the man's scowl slowly turned to a gray-toothed, mischievous grin. His eyes glowed like embers. "Now that's what I'm talking about! That's the stuff! Don't let the bastards get the best of you. That's my boy!"

Richard and the man continued their conversation for another few minutes, and the people at tables closest to them pretended not to notice. "He thinks I don't know, but I do. I know what he's up to!" said Richard emphatically, the muscles in his neck contracting involuntarily, pulling his lower lip down and jerking his head to the left. The convulsions happened two more times, one immediately after the other.

Just then the waitress stepped up to the table. The eyes of most of the patrons were on her.

"Hun, I'm sorry to have to do this, but I need to ask you to leave. You're starting to upset the customers. I'm sorry sweetie, that's just the way it is. OK?"

Still agitated by the thought of Francis Tadley, Richard looked directly into her eyes for the first time.

"We're just working some things out! Other people in here are talking. Why can't we?"

"Hun," she said, pointing to the other side of the table, "you've been talking as if someone else is sitting with you. But that chair has been empty since you walked in here."

Two

Conversation ceased in the Blue Moon café. One customer who was intently watching the drama unfold accidentally dropped her fork, which clanked loudly against her plate and then fell to the floor, breaking the otherwise tense silence. Customers quietly prodded their food, pretending to be busy deciding what bite to take next. Most of them were mentally preparing to make a run for the door, half expecting that the wacko in the corner would finally lose it and pull out a gun.

Richard stared blankly at the empty chair, his trembling hand poised over his cup. A few awkward moments went by before his chin dropped to his chest and he began rubbing his skull to extinguish the fire that burned inside his head. He moaned in confusion and desperation. Then as if he had just awoken from a dream, Richard lifted his head and fixed his lifeless eyes on some far off place that only he could see. "What do I owe you?" he asked, his voice devoid of emotion.

"This one's on the house hun," the waitress said, stepping back and signaling to Richard that it was time to leave.

He stood up, put on his stocking cap and zipped his coat. Without uttering a word he walked, head down, past the waitress and through the silent, staring crowd to the front door.

***

The scenery from the sidewalk on the corner of Florence Street and Sunset Avenue in Cutter's Mill was particularly striking. Florence boasted rows of solidly built four globe streetlamps on both sides of the street. Each one radiated soft white light and illuminated century old oak and maple trees, which looked like grand granite columns rising upward and then reaching across the expanse of road to intertwine at their tops. The mass of tangled, leafless branches created a canopy and formed a perfectly rounded tunnel over the street, as if someone had painstakingly located and then trimmed each protruding branch that would otherwise have interrupted the smooth, circular passage. The trees stood beside cobblestone sidewalks, which gave passersby a place to walk and gaze upon the neatly manicured lawns and stately Victorian-style homes that were built when the grand old trees were still saplings.

The home on the northwest corner of Florence and Sunset was larger than most in that part of the neighborhood. The front porch stretched the length of the eight-bedroom house and opened to a wide stairway at its middle. Its thick, ornately designed support columns sitting atop gray clapboard flooring. In summer people often relaxed in the wicker chairs looking out over the front yard, or played board games at the two small tables located to the left and right of the main entrance. Four windows adorned the front of the house beneath the porch awning, and four were located above. White trim around the second story windows offset the teal colored siding like picture frames hung neatly upon a wall. The windows beneath the awning issued a warm light from inside the house, and every so often revealed the subtle movements of people. Carefully raked piles of leaves covered the front yard, waiting to be bagged and sent to the curb. Alpha House was the only residential care facility in Cutters Mill, Wisconsin for people with mental disabilities, and it looked like it belonged on the cover of "Home and Garden" magazine. But the building's meticulously groomed exterior was in stark contrast to the illness and dysfunction in the lives of the people who lived there.

It was 7:38 PM and Carl Maznik was getting ready to leave the office. The Alpha House director usually left work around 6:00 PM. But tonight he stayed late to put finishing touches on a forty-minute presentation he was preparing to give at an upcoming conference.

Carl's talk would help healthcare workers to better understand patients with mental disorders.

Scanning his notes he spoke as if an audience was before him. "Schizophrenia is a disorder of the mind," he began. "And its victims are often unable to distinguish realty from a disorienting and sometimes terrifying world of illusions. The illness can create false sensory experiences unlike any other mental disorder. The afflicted sense things that aren't real. They see, hear, smell, and taste things and experience physical sensations that exist only in the mind. The disorder is so traumatic that many of its victims are unable to cope. It is estimated that 40% of people with schizophrenia attempt suicide at least once in their lives. Males with schizophrenia attempt suicide at a much higher rate, approximately 60%.

"Many theories exist about the causes of schizophrenia, but there are no conclusive answers. Most mental health professionals believe that malfunctioning neurotransmitters in the brain are the root cause. Currently, there is no cure for the illness. Some people are able to control their symptoms with medication, while others have limited success. Roughly one third of its victims recover completely, one third are sick off and on, and one third stay chronically ill. Nobody knows why.

"One patient, who we'll call Buddy, falls into the category of the chronically ill. Buddy was diagnosed with Acute Paranoid Schizophrenia at the age of fourteen, and he is now forty-four years old. Buddy suffers from consistent and prolonged auditory and mild visual hallucinations, although visual hallucinations in schizophrenics are rare. At least two beings or voices, as he calls them, live inside his head. And he knows them by name. The voices regularly taunt Buddy to a point that causes him to feel great despair. He is unable to turn them off, and their harassing seems constant.

"His illness is marked by paranoid delusions. When he is awake he is tormented by thoughts that people are scheming against him or want to do him harm. At one point in the past he had a delusion that he was targeted for assassination by the federal government because he knew the truth about their supposed involvement in genetic experimentation with humans. He also has delusions of grandeur. He believes that he has been commissioned by God to expose the activities of evildoers. And evildoers are basically anyone he mistrusts, which is quite a long list of people. To put it bluntly, he has spent most of his life feeling that the rest of the world is out to get him.

"The medications prescribed to people with schizophrenia often have side effects. One of the most common is known as tardive dyskinesia, which causes trembling of the hands and involuntary spasms in the arms, legs and neck. Buddy suffers from these symptoms as well as general lethargy, and he often says the medications make him feel numb or zombie-like.

"He has been arrested numerous times for charges ranging from disturbing the peace to public urination, assault, and other offenses. Some time ago he lost his driver's license for leaving the scene of an accident. Now he gets around on a bicycle. The longest he's been able to hold a job is a year and a half. He's been kicked out of restaurants, stores, and other public places all over the county, and he has been committed to the psychiatric ward at Broward hospital four times in the past eight years. Each stay at the hospital was triggered by an assault that, in his mind, was self-defense against a person he thought was trying to harm him – an evildoer.

"When Buddy is asleep, if he actually is able to fall asleep, he often dreams that someone is operating on his brain. Most times the operation is a frontal lobotomy." Carl reached up to stroke his forehead, imagining the horror frontal lobotomy patients must have felt. "Buddy believes they use what he calls a 'German instrument' to perform the operation, which he describes as a large metal box with lots of wires and tubes protruding from it. There are times when he is convinced that the frontal lobe of his brain has actually been removed. Other times he isn't sure and simply asks people if they think he's had a lobotomy. Either way he knows something is wrong with his brain, but he doesn't attribute it to an illness called schizophrenia. I for one am amazed at the bravery it takes to go through each day knowing that neither sleep or consciousness will provide an escape from that kind horror."

Carl shook his head in affirmation of what he was planning to say during his presentation. He clicked the little computer disc icon on his screen to save the document before shutting down the computer for the night. This was Carl's ninth year as Alpha House Director, and he loved his job very much. He felt a solemn pride in knowing that he helped improve the lives of people with mental disabilities. He only wished that he could have done more to help his severely autistic sister before she was killed in a traffic accident at the age of nineteen. She was the main reason he decided to make a career in the mental health field.

Carl was a great big lovable teddy bear of a man. He had a barrel shaped chest and arms the size of most people's legs. He wore short sleeve shirts all year long because his massive but lean body generated so much heat that long sleeve shirts and sweaters were uncomfortable to wear. Laugh lines accented his deep brown puppy dog eyes. Closely cropped light brown hair, big ears and freckled cheeks framed his face and gave him the look of a large ill-featured child. Carl's size was intimidating, but his gentle ways and genuine love for people immediately disarmed anyone he met. Carl was a hugger. He only shook hands with people the first time they met. After that each meeting began with a warm embrace.

Carl reached into his pocket and retrieved the key that opened his locked desk drawer. He squeezed it in his hand as if resisting the motion of placing it in the lock. He swallowed hard and closed his eyes, trying to wash away the feeling welling up inside him. The feeling had caused him to reach for the key many times before, and each time seemed more automatic and required less conscious thought. Holding it created an unbearable sense of anticipation and intensified his desire.

He opened his hand to look at the small brass object. His mouth went bone dry, as if it had been stuffed with cotton balls. The sensation was like watching someone slowly pour cold clear water into a tall glass that would sooth his parched throat, if only he reached out to grab it. The need was both physical and emotional and he couldn't resist. His body and mind ached for it.

Carl opened the drawer and grabbed a pale orange pill bottle. He didn't pause at all before opening it and dumping three small white tablets into his hand and popping them in his mouth. One sip of water was all it took to wash them down. It would be only a few minutes before they began to do their work, but just knowing they were in his system caused him to exhale in relief.

Carl had been addicted to prescription painkillers for more than four years. Initially, back pain caused him to start taking the pills, which he had easy access to as director of a mental health facility. He handled the ordering of all prescription drugs for Alpha House and could easily get as much as he wanted without anyone taking notice. Over the course of time the need to take them for back pain was replaced by the need to take them to make it through the day, to stop his body and the little voice in his head from begging for them. Carl knew it was wrong, but he had lost the ability to resist long ago. Life without them was simply unbearable.

He had become adept at keeping his addiction out of the sight of others. Carl had always been laid back and happy so nobody, including his wife and children, seemed to notice the pills' intensifying effects on those characteristics. They did take notice of other side effects, such as his tendency to drop things or to fall asleep easily. But they laughingly attributed them to Carl getting older. Carl was happy to play along in order to mask the real problem. His addiction was his secret, and it would remain his secret.

***

Richard grabbed a bar of soap from the dish on top of the bathroom sink. He lathered up and scrubbed his hands, trying especially hard to remove the cigarette smoke stains on the index and second fingers of his right hand. The deeply imbedded dark brown stains made the tips of his fingers look like smoked sausages. None of the residue washed off. He leaned over and splashed cold water on his face. Suddenly, he stood upright without drying.

"HE'S GOING TO LOOK AT HIMSELF IN THE MIRROR FOR A WHILE," a female voice said in a casual tone.

"LOOK AT HIS EYES," said a young boy's voice. "HIS EYES LOOK LIKE THEY BELONG ON AN OLD HOUND DOG, ALL DROOPY AND BAGGY."

Richard reached up and felt the deep crevices etched into the corners of the eyes staring back at him and the puffy, sagging skin hanging beneath. Dropping his hand he stepped back and stared at the man in the mirror. His vision seemed strangely disconnected from the part of his brain that told him that the face he was looking at was his. He observed the man standing in front of him as one might observe an animal caged behind bars in a zoo, casually looking at its features and trying to understand its nature. He saw a weathered face, reddened and chapped by wind and cold. But the scars were the most prominent feature. They were not caused by physical wounds, but by mental and emotional wounds which were displayed in physical form through an open gaping mouth, which drooped down at the corners, disheveled sandy colored hair that while trimmed, seemed never to have been combed, and long brown nose hairs, which had not been trimmed and protruded out in wiry tufts. Then there were the eyes. The eyes were anxious and unknowing, like the eyes of a man standing before a jury and waiting to hear a verdict that would alter the rest of his life.

"LOSER! WORTHLESS MOUND OF FLESH!" the female screamed.

"TAINTED!" yelled the boy.

"THEY KNOW! THEY ALL KNOW!"

"IT'S NOT WORTH IT. HE SHOULD END IT NOW WHILE THERE'S STILL TIME."

"HE KNOWS! HE'S SEEN IT! IT'S A GERMAN INSTRUMENT!" they yelled in unison.

Their words fired at him like bullets from a gun. They came in torrents, one over another but distinctly separate and audible. Each one felt like a shot to the stomach, piercing his flesh and ripping his insides. Richard held his head with both hands and squeezed hard trying to choke them out, but they kept taunting him.

"WHY DOESN'T HE JUST GIVE IN?"

"HE SHOULDN'T GIVE IN! HE SHOULD FIGHT LIKE A SISSY BOY!"

"SOMEONE'S FEELING PERNICIOUS! SOMEONE'S FEELING PERNICIOUS!" yelled the boy with the tone of a schoolyard bully trying to intimidate a frightened child.

Author, as he came to be known, had lived inside Richard's mind for thirty years, since Richard was fourteen years old. They shared their mother's womb for almost nine months, but his twin bother died just before she gave birth and Richard was left without him. For years he missed the brother his mother had told him about, but he often felt his presence when he was feeling scared or alone. Then one day, Author spoke. "I am Author," he began. "I live with you. I am Author."

Richard knew that his parents had chosen the name Andrew for his twin bother. He never questioned Author about why he referred to himself by another name.

Author began commenting about even the smallest details of Richard's life. "THAT SHIRT YOU ARE WEARING LOOKS DIFFERENT."

"YOU HAVE A NICELY SHAPED NOSE."

"MRS. DRYER IS CRAZY. THE SQUARE ROOT OF FORTY-NINE ISN'T SEVEN. THINK ABOUT IT."

"HUMMINGBIRDS ARE FREAKS OF NATURE."

At first Richard was pleased to listen to Author's comments. But when Melissa came to live with him things changed. Author and Melissa began talking with each other about Richard as if he wasn't there.

"HE CAN'T PLAY BASEBALL LIKE THE OTHER CHILDREN. HE'S WEAK AND TIMID!"

"HE GOT PICKED LAST AGAIN. LOOK AT HIM; HE'S SO SAD AND DEJECTED. THE POOR BABY."

Melissa Sue Anderson played the character of Mary Ingalls in the television drama "Little House on the Prairie". As a child, Richard never missed an episode. He adored her blonde hair and sky blue eyes, how pretty she always looked in the dresses her mother had made. He wanted more than anything to sit with her by a creek or walk hand in hand through the storybook setting of Walnut Grove as her television boyfriend often did.

Now she lived in his head. He reasoned that his love for her had in some strange way granted her permission to be there. But she was not the person he thought she was. She had turned Author against him, and he regretted ever having adored her.

"HE'S FEELING BADLY ABOUT HIMSELF AGAIN. THE THING AT THE CAFÉ UPSET HIM," Melissa said.

"YES, HE'S GOING TO BE BROODING ABOUT THAT FOR A WHILE," Author responded.

Richard grabbed a towel hanging next to the sink and wiped the water from his face. He gazed into the mirror and watched as his neck muscles twitched and his head jerked sideways in response.

Exhausted and grief-stricken his eyes began to well with tears.

"OH LOOK, HE'S CRYING," Melissa said, in mock empathy. "THAT'S TOO BAD, THE POOR THING. HE REALLY SHOULD HAVE SOME HAPPINESS IN HIS LIFE."

Author joined in. "YES, BUT HE THINKS MR. LAZARUS IS PUSHING HIM TO DO THINGS HE'S NOT COMFORTABLE WITH."

Richard looked frantically around the bathroom to see if Mr. Lazarus had shown up as he had at the Blue Moon Café. Except for the voices he was alone.

"BUT, IN HIS HEART HE KNOWS THAT MR. LAZARUS IS ONLY DOING WHAT'S BEST FOR HIM."

The incident at the café flashed in Richard's mind; Lazarus, the evildoer Francis Tadley, the humiliation brought on by those at the café who were obviously colluding with Tadley. He clenched his fists. "Shut up!" he screamed. "Leave me alone! Stop tormenting me!"

Richard drew back his fist and punched the angry and terrified face staring back at him in the mirror. Large shards of broken glass fell to the sink and shattered into smaller pieces.

For a moment there was silence as he stood there looking at his fragmented reflection. Blood dripped from his hand, creating deep red splashes in the white porcelain sink. Suddenly Richard's legs buckled and he fell to his knees, his head hanging down and his hands wrapped around his chest in a desperate but inadequate attempt at a self-soothing embrace. Slow, anguished sobs gently thrust his slouched body backwards and forwards. Tears fell, and with them his desire to go on. His energy ebbed away, dimming like a flashlight issuing its last remaining bit of radiance. His sobs slowly turned to whimpers, and eventually his body had no force left in it to do anything but breathe.

He had been in this place many times before, and it was hardest of all. This was the place where he had to decide if he wanted go on or end it. He had thought about death and hoped that it might bring comfort and peace, like falling into a sleep so deep and complete that his senses would no longer function. For a moment the feeling washed over him like the tender and reassuring whisper of a mother to her child as she cradles him in the warmth and softness of her body. That feeling, which made death seem so inviting, also reminded him of the reason he had the feeling to begin with – his mother. She had always loved him dearly, and she would be heartbroken if he chose to take his own life. He had known for some time that the decision to stay or go was not really his. He thought about what his father had said about death after hearing about the suicide of a mentally ill patient at Broward hospital. "The good Lord brought us into this world," he had said. "He should be the one to take us out of here and bring us home."

Richard believed his father's words. But times like this always pushed him to the edge, and his need to know what lay beyond this life was more than mere curiosity. It seemed that death might be his only hope for peace. But he would not have that today.

Richard grabbed the edge of the sink and pulled himself up. He stood for a moment before turning on the water and letting it run over the cuts on his bloodied knuckles. Opening the broken medicine cabinet door, he found some cotton gauze and medical tape and dressed the wound.

"He'll be having a cigarette soon," Author said, his voice monotone and devoid of emotion. "He always does when he feels even the tiniest bit of pressure."

"Yup. Here he goes," Melissa added.

Richard stepped out of the bathroom, grabbed his coat, stocking cap and cigarettes and headed for the door.

***

Carl scratched his head with bratwurst-sized fingers as he checked off the last item on his to-do list and closed his work folder. Setting his pen down, he closed his eyes and sat still to enjoy the feeling of warmth and serenity caused by the tiny white pills. After a few moments he opened his eyes and glanced through the window that looked out to the back yard.

"There's Buddy now," he said to himself, watching Richard puff away at the designated smoking table. Carl put on his coat, closed up his office and walked outside. As he neared the table Richard stood to greet him. True to form, Carl wrapped his huge arms around Richard. "How you doin' buddy?" he asked.

"OK," Richard replied.

"What happened to your hand?"

"The mirror in the bathroom broke and I cut myself. I'll pay for a new mirror."

"Are you alright? Do you want to talk about it?"

"No, I'll be alright."

Carl nodded his head, sensing it would be good to change the subject. "Hey, I've got one for you," he said, lightening the mood. "A lady and her baby get on a bus. The bus driver looks at the lady and then her baby and screams. 'Wow, that's the ugliest child I've ever seen in my life!'

"'Well I never!' the lady says, visibly upset. She marches to the back of the bus and sits down. A man sitting near her notices she is upset and asks, 'Are you OK, ma'am?' The lady replies, 'No I'm not! That bus driver just insulted me.' Then the man says, 'Well, we can't have that! You go back up there and give that bus driver a piece of your mind, and I'll stay here and watch your monkey.'"

Richard burst with laughter. Carl followed him, holding his stomach while he bellowed. Richard knew what was coming next. Carl's laugh was always punctuated with a loud, throaty snort at the end. Most people would be embarrassed, but not Carl. It was one of his trademarks. Richard laughed even harder as Carl snorted away. He really loved that man. He was a bright spot in his life.

The laughter subsided after a few seconds and Carl switched the subject again.

"Hey, I'd like you to help with a little cleaning and organizing before the Bureau of Mental Health audit this Friday," Carl said. "Can you do that?"

"OK, what time do you want me to start?"

"How about right after you get back from work tomorrow, say around 4:30?"

"OK," replied Richard. The hand holding his cigarette trembled as he took another puff, burning it down to the filter.

"One more thing; I got a call from the Blue Moon Café in Ripley. The waitress there said she had to ask you to leave because you were causing some sort of commotion. Is that right?"

Richard paused. He didn't like letting Carl down, and he didn't want to think about what had happened at the café. "Yeah," he responded, his voice flat again.

"Well, what happened?"

"I guess I got a little too loud and some of the customers didn't like it."

"This seems to happen a lot," Carl said, stopping to think. "In fact I believe this is the third time in the past few months" he added, trying not to sound too accusatory.

"I know. I'm sorry."

"Were the voices bothering you?"

"Ah, Yeah, I guess so." Richard said, leaving out the exchange with Mr. Lazarus.

"What were they saying?"

"I don't remember. It doesn't matter anyway because I won't be going there anymore," he said, hoping to end the conversation.

"We need to continue working on how to control what you do and say in response to the voices," Carl added, getting up from the table.

"I know." Richard rubbed his arm and winced. "I'll see you tomorrow Carl."

"Try and get some sleep tonight and we'll talk more about it in the morning."

"They were in my room again last night."

"Who was in your room?" Carl asked, already knowing but giving Richard the opportunity to talk about it.

"They tried going in through my temple this time, but I stopped them. I woke up and stopped them."

Carl set his hand gently on Richard's shoulder. "I'm sorry you had to go through that, buddy. Would you like something to help you sleep tonight?"

"No, I'll be alright. I just need to keep my eyes open."

Carl patted him on the shoulder. "OK. Well, I hope you have a good night. I'll see you tomorrow, OK?"

"OK Carl. You have a good night too."

Carl reached into his pocket to retrieve his car keys, but he lost hold of them and they dropped to the ground. He chuckled as he bent down to pick them up. "Getting old!" he cried. Carl walked away and rounded the corner to the front of the building where his car was parked.

Richard lit another cigarette.

Three

It was 7:45 AM and Connie Trapoli was making her rounds on the shop floor at Colbourne Enterprises. Her first priority was to ensure that all workstations were set up to support the day's activities. Colbourne provided contract assembly operations for simple mechanical and electrical products. Connie had been the first shift supervisor for eleven years. She and three other supervisors handled shop floor operations, while four front office workers managed the other functions required to run the business. The remaining twenty-seven of the company's thirty-five employees were mentally or physically handicapped people who assembled and packed products for Colbourne's customers.

The large single story concrete block building where Colbourne was located was situated among other similar looking buildings in a drab looking industrial park just outside of Cutters Mill. The small gravel parking lot held only a few cars. Most employees arrived by bus or bicycle or were dropped off by family members or friends. Two bright red metal doors on the right side of the building stood out from the dirty, tan colored walls facing the parking lot. The door to the far right led to the front office, which held a small counter near the front, four work cubicles and an assortment of office equipment. The door to the left led to the shop, which took up most of the space in the forty thousand square foot facility.

The time clock and timecard holder were located on the wall to the right, just inside the shop door. Richard reached to the upper left corner of the rack to retrieve his time card. "Buell, Richard A.," he said, reading quietly to himself.

He stuck the card in the top of the time card machine, which made a clunking noise as it stamped the date and time of his arrival. He put the card back in its assigned spot, grabbed his thermos and walked to the break area were several people sat eating and drinking. As they did most mornings, Eddie and Thomas stopped eating, and in hoarse, gruff voices typical of those with Down syndrome yelled, "Good morning Richard!"

Richard felt obliged to return the greeting because he knew his co-workers were only trying to be nice. But he wished they could do it without attracting the attention of everyone in the break room.

"Hi," he replied, without making eye contact.

He took off his stocking cap, stuck it in his coat pocket and hung his coat on an already packed coat rack. He sat down at the table farthest from Eddie and Thomas, unscrewed the cup on top of the thermos bottle and, with trembling hands, filled it with coffee.

Richard didn't like being close to people. Closeness meant the possibility of conversation, and that's the last thing he wanted. All he wanted was to be left alone. But at this particular moment he had no choice about being close to others because company rules prohibited him from having coffee anywhere but the break room or the picnic table outside, and there wasn't time to go outside. This morning, like most mornings, the break room was full of people. He sat with his head down, trying not to make eye contact with the four others sitting with him at the table. He was only a few sips into his cup when one of the new guys, whose name he couldn't remember, said in a voice that sounded like it came from a small child, "My dad is gonna buy me a dog to play with. What kind of dog do you got Richard?"

"I don't have a dog," Richard replied begrudgingly, careful not make eye contact.

"You don't have a dog! Everyone should have a dog! You should ask your dad if he could buy you a dog. Then we could talk about our dogs," his co-worker said, emphasizing the word *dog* at the end of each sentence.

Richard breathed a heavy sigh and was thinking of ways to end the annoying conversation when Connie stepped into the break room.

"Good morning everyone!" she said in a very spirited tone.

"Good morning Connie!" everyone except Richard replied in ragged unison.

"Well, we had a good day yesterday," Connie continued. "And you should all be very proud of the work we did. Let's all congratulate Cole and Magdalena for exceeding their unit goal by twenty five!"

Hand claps and whistles filled the room.

"Also, give yourselves a hand for another day with no accidents or unresolved disagreements."

This time someone bellowed, "Yes! Yes! Yes!" punctuating the applause and whistles.

"Remember, it's OK to disagree as long as we work it out respectfully."

"Wuby and I got mad at eachotha yetherday, but we mathe up," said Manuel, his big smile revealing two missing front teeth.

"I know, and you both handled it very well," said Connie, hoping that others would want to earn the same sort of acknowledgement. Bickering among employees about even the smallest things was commonplace at Colbourne, and Connie spent more time than she wanted playing mediator.

"OK, let's go over today's work stations. Now listen up so we only have to do this once. The following people will be on the same workstations they were on yesterday. John and Taylor, you're on workstation A. Courtney and Thomas are on B, and Loretta, Tony, and Richard are on D." Connie flipped over a sheet on her clipboard and continued. "The following people will be on new workstations. As always you need to wait for instructions from me or Stephanie before you do anything, and Stephanie should be here shortly," she said, glancing at her watch. "OK, here are the assignments. Cole, Jose, and Manuel are on workstation C, Eddie and Magdalena are on F, and Ruby and Margaret are on E."

Connie lowered the clipboard and looked at the attentive faces around the room. She had earned their respect. Everyone knew that she was firm when it came to work rules, but she was also exceedingly compassionate and fair. "Are there any questions?" she asked.

"Can I go to the bathroom?"

"Yes, in a minute you may go to the bathroom Courtney, but please remember to raise your hand so we can be respectful to others who may have a question."

Eddie raised his hand and waved it back and forth.

"Yes Eddie."

"Will you marry me?" he asked, giggling while everyone else heartily laughed at the question they knew he was prone to ask.

"You know I'm already married. And besides you'll have to get in line behind Tony, because he asked me to marry him last week."

Everyone including Richard laughed this time.

"OK, are you ready for our morning song?"

"Yes!" everyone yelled in a loud and passionate reply.

Connie held her hands in front of her like a choir director. She waved them back and forth in syncopated rhythm with her counting. "One-two-three-!" On count four everyone joined Connie in singing in a military styled cadence.

"Well here we go! We're at it again! We're movin' out! We're movin' in! We're standin' tall! We're lookin' good! We oughta' be in Hollywood!"

Everyone clapped and cheered until Connie raised her hand as a signal to quiet down, which took a few seconds. "Alright, good job everyone," she said. "Let's move out in a quiet and orderly fashion to our workstations."

For the past three days Richard, Loretta, and Tony had been manning workstation D, where they packaged the contents of unassembled ceiling fans. From Colbourne the fans were shipped to retailers around the Midwest.

Packaging the fans involved three steps, and each person handled one. Richard stood to the far left of a long and narrow table with a sheet metal top. Tony's work area took up most of the middle of the table, and Loretta was positioned to the far right. Richard took a large, flat piece of cardboard covered with cuts and creases and quickly transformed the one-dimensional sheet into a three-dimensional box. His speed and accuracy were a testament to the number of times he had performed the operation. Then he inserted a molded piece of foam plastic through the top of the box, making sure it sat firmly on the bottom. Two additional small pieces of foam were placed to the front and back of the box. Then he slid the box to his right for Tony to grab when he was ready to begin inserting the fan housing, blades and plastic bags filled with parts. When Tony's operation was complete he slid the box to Loretta, who finished the packing process by applying tape to the box seams and labels to the top and sides.

This was Richard's job from 8:15 AM to 3:15 PM five days a week. A new day might bring with it a different product to assemble or pack, but the routines were always essentially the same. It was marginally challenging for the first hour or two, after that it took little or no thought to do the work. Richard was grateful for the job, but it left his idle mind open to attack by the forces that tormented him.

"Make the box," Author said dryly, as Richard performed the first step.

"Fill the box," Melissa said, narrating the start of the second step.

"Slide the box." Richard paused instead of sliding the box.

"Slide the box," Author said, emphasizing the word *slide*.

"Shut up," Richard said quietly, but still loud enough for Tony to hear.

"I didn't say anything," Tony responded.

"I wasn't talking to you."

"Who were you talking to?"

"Never mind, I'm sorry."

This time Author's voice was firm and resolute. "Slide the box."

Richard dropped his eyes to the floor and clenched his fists.

"Slide...the... box." The pronunciation of each word was slow and tinged with anger.

"No! Stop telling me what to do!" Richard fired back, his resentment growing and his fists clenched tighter in an effort to control his desire to lash out. Suddenly he realized that he was being watched, and he turned to see Tony and Loretta looking at him with wide eyes and open mouths. They had seen Richard in episodes like this before and knew it could sometimes turn out badly.

"Are you OK Richie?" asked Loretta in a soft and measured tone.

Richard didn't respond, he just obeyed the command and slid the box to Tony.

"GOOD. NOW MAKE THE BOX. THEN FILL THE BOX. THEN SLIDE THE BOX."

Richard located Connie and waved her over as she was leaving another workstation.

"What's up Richard?" she asked.

"The voices are bothering me. Can I get my headphones and listen to some music?"

Connie paused to look at Tony and Loretta. She saw concern on their faces. "I'll allow it for this operation since there are no power tools or jigs involved. But keep it low enough to hear Tony and Loretta. OK?"

"OK," Richard said, thankful for the diversion of music.

He walked to his locker, grabbed the combination lock and looked both ways to make sure no one was watching. He tried dialing the combination, but the trembling in his hands prevented him from doing it accurately. He spun the dial and tried again. This time he talked himself through it. "23 right, 12 left, 17 right." He jerked open the lock and then the squeaky door. Rummaging through a mess on the top shelf he located his portable CD player. A CD holder containing five CD's hung on the locker door. He knew right away which one he wanted to listen to. He pulled Billie Holiday's Greatest Hits from the CD holder, slammed the door and replaced the lock.

Richard liked Billie Holiday because of her distinctive singing style, but also because he felt connected to her. Like him, she had led a troubled life. Her heroin addiction created problems in her personal and professional life, and it ultimately killed her. To add insult to injury she was arrested on her deathbed, because in 1959 narcotics addiction was a crime not an illness. Richard had been arrested many times, none of which at least in his mind, were the result of any wrongdoing on his part. He looked at the picture of Billie on the CD cover and wondered whether or not her troubles had followed her into death. He hoped not for her sake and his.

Billie overpowered Richard's tormentors as she sang, "God Bless the Child" and "I Love You Porgy". They were rendered speechless by the outpouring of her emotion in "Fine and Mellow". Richard listened until the CD player went silent, then he started it over from the beginning. Time passed and Richard got lost in the rhythm of his work and the soothing tone of Billie's voice. He silently thanked her for the few moments of tranquility knowing they would not last.

He spent his fifteen-minute break from 9:45 to 10:00 at the smoking table located outside at the far end of the building. At 11:30 a loud buzzer sounded, signaling lunch. Like cattle to a hay bale, everyone on the shop floor stopped what they were doing and headed to the break room. Richard followed his well-worn path back to the smoking table. It was a relief to sit after standing for so long at his workstation. He lit up, took a long draw from his cigarette and closed his eyes, trying hard to hear Billie over the sounds of trucks and geese and the cry of a distant train whistle. He didn't stop to think that he could turn up the volume on his CD player. Billie's voice faded away as the level of pain increased throughout his body. His face contorted and he buried his head in his hands so he had something to hold on to while he endured what felt like stings from a thousand angry bees.

Suddenly he felt the pressure of a hand on his shoulder, and he swung around to fend off another attack. The aggressor took a step back, raising his hands to show he meant no harm.

"It's OK Richie, it's just me."

Startled and still in pain, Richard locked his crazed eyes on the man as his brain slowly processed what had happened. It took a few seconds before he realized that the figure standing in front of him was his brother.

"Is it OK if I sit down?" Charles asked.

"Yeah," responded Richard, frantically rubbing his arms.

"How are you doing today little brother?"

"I'm dying."

Un-shaken by his remark Charles asked, "What do you mean you're dying?"

"I mean the glass in my veins is killing me." To Richard his comment wasn't a complaint, but a simple matter of fact.

Charles knew that misfiring neurotransmitters in Richard's brain caused the sensation of pain when there was nothing physically wrong with him. He also knew there was no point to telling Richard that he wasn't actually feeling pain, because he was. His brain sent signals to his body that caused the sensation of broken pieces of razor sharp glass coursing through his veins and ripping his insides to shreds. Richard had told Charles about the glass in his veins many times before, but Charles never got used to the cruelty of his illness.

Carl Maznik had taught Charles that the best thing he could do when Richard experienced any kind of delusion or hallucination was simply to remind him that while he was experiencing something traumatic, it would not actually do him any physical harm.

"I know how painful that is for you," Charlie said. "But remember that while it hurts like there's glass in your veins, there isn't actually any real glass in your veins, or you'd be dead. And I'm sitting here talking to you, so I know you're not dead."

Richard continued rubbing his arms, trying to relieve the pain. "Yeah, I know. But it still hurts."

"I know. I wish it didn't," Charles responded. Without letting on to his brother, he wrapped his hand around his own forearm and ratcheted his fingers in so deep that it caused him to close his eyes and grit his teeth. He wanted to feel what his brother felt. But after a few seconds he released his grip. *This doesn't even come close*, he thought.

Anhedonia. The word careened into his thoughts unexpectedly. He had first seen it years ago in an article about schizophrenia, and it made him sad every time he was reminded that his brother suffered from it. It meant the absence of joy and the inability to feel pleasure. *His illness is doubly cruel*, he silently fumed. *Not only is joy and pleasure absent from his life, more often than not he also has to deal with these damned phantom pains!*

Charles felt his anger rising and he made a conscious decision to put on a happy face for his brother's benefit. "Well, today's menu includes fresh albacore tuna fish sandwiches on whole wheat bread, sweet honey dew melon, and thinly sliced lightly seasoned potatoes also known as chips," he said, as if he was a chef describing fine cuisine to a food critic. He pulled the items from an insulated lunch bag and set them on the table. Charles preferred not to eat outside where it was cold, but he knew his brother wanted to stay away from the others and smoke as many cigarettes as possible before he went back to work.

"Did you put onion in the tuna fish?" Richard asked.

"Yup. Just the way you like it little brother."

Richard unwrapped the sandwich and started eating. Globs of tuna mixture fell to the table as he devoured the first half of the sandwich in three bites. Charles was always amazed at the aggression and singular focus Richard brought to a meal. It was as if vultures would grab whatever they could off his plate if he made the mistake of pausing. Instead of bringing the sandwich to his mouth, Richard held it in a fixed position in front of his face and lurched forward as he took each bite, like a wild animal ripping into a carcass.

Trying to take his mind off the feeding frenzy, Charles chimed in. "So, the arrangements for mom and dad's fiftieth anniversary seem to be coming together nicely. It's this Saturday you know."

"Yeah, I know. I don't think I'm gonna go," Richard said, his voice muffled by a mouth full of food.

"You have to go. They'll be heartbroken if you don't," Charles retorted, knowing that a little guilt would change his mind.

After finishing his sandwich, Richard grabbed a handful of chips and shoved them in his mouth.

"Besides, Esther will be there, and you know how much she loves you." Charles knew this would be the clincher. There was no way Richard would disappoint Esther.

"Yeah. I know."

Richard loved his little six-year-old niece. She was one of the few people he didn't mistrust. And certainly the only one who could sit on his lap and sing him songs. Hugs from Carl and Charles and the rest of his family were OK, but he simply would not accept from others the kind of physical closeness he accepted from Esther. And it wasn't because she was a child. Richard had known other children and disliked them intensely. He found them to be nosey, chatty without purpose, and most of all needy. He especially disliked the ones who cried and threw tantrums when they didn't get what they wanted. When one of those was around he simply scoffed and walked away.

"So, will you come?" Charlie asked again.

After a considerable pause Richard rubbed his arms again. "I guess so," he relented.

"Thanks Richie, everyone wants you to be there."

Charles said this knowing that not everyone really wanted him there. There were people who would attend the party that would prefer to have Richard absent rather than deal with his strange behavior. Charles understood the discomfort people often felt around his brother. But, in the end he didn't care a bit about what those people thought. He wanted his brother to be with his family, the people who loved him.

"Do you think I had a lobotomy?" Richard asked abruptly.

"No, I don't think you did. In fact I know you didn't," Charles said, pointedly. "I know it's much easier for me to say this than it is for you to believe, but if you really did have a lobotomy you wouldn't be able to function the way you do. The thing that makes you who you are would be gone. You'd have no personality."

Charles had read that somewhere, but he didn't really know if it was true. He did know that frontal lobotomies were performed on people with schizophrenia back in the mid 1940's and 50's. He recalled one article that described the barbaric procedure. Holes were drilled through the patient's skull so long thin blades could be inserted to sever the nerve connections between the frontal lobe and the rest of the brain. The procedure was not a cure for the illness. At best, it made patients less aware of their affliction. Some critics claimed that the primary goal was only to make patients more quiet, orderly and easy to control.

One doctor was known for expediting the procedure by lifting the patient's eyelid and inserting an ice pick-like instrument over the eyeball and through the bone at the back of the eye. Then the instrument would be forced side-to-side to sever brain tissue and nerves. There were some accounts of the procedure being done without the benefit of anesthesia, or even muscle relaxers.

It's no wonder the idea terrifies him, Charles thought.

"Sometimes I feel like I don't have a personality. I feel dead," Richard said, his eyes pleading with Charles to provide some kind of answer to the numbness he felt.

"Well little brother, you're not dead. You're very much alive. So let's live! What would you say about going to the cabin to do some fishing next weekend?"

Richard loved Charles' cabin. He loved sitting on the glassy lake in Charles' boat, reeling in fish, smoking cigarettes and drinking coffee. He thought it was as close to heaven as he'd get in this life.

"I'd like that Charlie," he said with a modicum of emotion in his voice.

Charles was glad that his brother found some happiness at the thought of spending time together. "So, it's a date then!" he replied.

Richard said things to Charles that he wouldn't say to others. He could tell Charles about the glass in his veins, or about how the cook at Fern's diner tried to poison him, or about Francis Tadley's plot to spread lies about him. Richard never felt judged by Charles, even though they often saw things differently.

"You know Francis Tadley?" Richard started.

"The mail man? Yeah. Why?" Charles asked, even though he knew what was coming.

"I think he's an evildoer."

Charles breathed a heavy sigh. "I know you do, but you can't go around telling people that because they won't understand what you mean. In fact some people, including Francis Tadley, might get upset."

"So what! He's the one spreading all that vile crap about me. Why do you think I'm banned from all the cafés in the area? I'll tell you why! It's because he sends letters that make people think I'm bad. I would never hurt anyone unless they hurt me first. I have to defend myself - Don't I?"

"Richie, I don't think Francis Tadley is sending nasty letters about you to anyone. You know the reason you aren't allowed in some of those places is because people get upset when they see you talking to yourself. And don't forget about the time you slapped that customer in the face at that café in Spring Grove."

"They wouldn't think that badly about me if someone wasn't telling them lies. And that someone is Francis Tadley!"

"Well, I suggest you keep that sentiment to yourself."

Richard lit another cigarette and looked away, dismissing Charles' comments.

"Hey, lunch is almost over for you and I need to get going," Charles said, switching the conversation with his brother from fantasy back to reality. He gathered up the cellophane, plastic cups and containers left over from the meal.

"OK. I'll see you later," Richard said, standing to hug his brother good bye. "I love you."

"I love you too, bro."

Charlie departed and Richard sat there until the buzzer sounded, forcing him to crush out his cigarette and return to the shop. Tony and Loretta were waiting dutifully at the workstation. Richard grabbed a piece of cardboard and picked up where he had left off before lunch.

"MAKE THE BOX... FILL THE BOX... SLIDE THE BOX..." Author's voice resumed, as if he too had just returned from a break. Richard did the only thing he could to control his frustration, he reached for his headphones.

Four

Charles Davis Buell was the son of Edmond and Agnes Buell, fourth generation German emigrants whose ancestors first came to Cutters Mill, WI in 1852. Of the five Buell children, Julia was youngest, followed by Richard, then Charles, who was only one year older than Richard. Anna and Edmond Jr. were oldest. The Buell's, like many other families in Southwestern Wisconsin, were hard working salt of the earth people who were grateful for the freedoms and opportunities offered in America. To them, Cutters Mill was more than a town. It was a homestead, a place that generations of Buell's and other families had helped to forge with their own hands. Every building, every street, park and business was brought into existence by the ingenuity and sweat of the town's people. Names like McGladry, Cutter, Tainter, Krause, Gifford and Buell were revered. They were pioneers. Without them Cutter's Mill would not exist.

Charles left work at 6:30 PM as usual. As he drove through the middle of town he came upon the old Baptist church. A new church was built in 1914 to accommodate the town's growing population. But the old building still stood as a monument to the pioneering spirit that had turned a dirt road along a river into a bustling city. Charles slowed down to look closely at the church's weathered stone walls and the bell tower that called the town's faithful to their knees each Sunday. He recalled how his grandfather, who he had always referred to as Papa, had the habit of using every day objects and events to teach life lessons. The church was the object of one such lesson. He remembered how papa's eyes flashed as he spoke.

"Charlie," he had said. "This old church is more than a building. It's much more than the stone and mortar you see. But you have to have spent precious moments here to really know that in your soul. I've seen births, deaths, marriages, baptisms and all the really important moments in life right here. Our people were called forth into the world from here. And it's from here that we'll all return home. Life's ups and downs work themselves out here, because the spirit of God and of our people lives here - always will." Then he chuckled, "Plus, a fair amount of my paycheck ends up here, so I consider myself a shareholder."

Charles missed Papa's witty humor and frontier wisdom. He knew that when Papa said, "Our people," he didn't mean only the Buell's German ancestors. To Papa, "Our people" included everyone who put their heart and soul into being a good citizen and forging a life in Cutter's Mill. It didn't matter where they came from or what language they spoke.

Charles learned many important life lessons from his grandfather, but they did not agree on everything. Papa was a Packers fan, while Charles liked the Bears. That difference of opinion had led to many spirited Sunday afternoons in front of the television. Papa thought abortion was wrong and Charles thought women should have the right to choose. Papa believed in the existence of a God who cared about people, Charles did not. He thought a God who was supposed to be all-powerful and caring would not allow the suffering and injustice that existed in the world. Papa reasoned that good and bad coexisted in the world, but in the end good would win out.

Charles loved and respected Papa and his whole family, but he could never understand why people chose to believe in a formless super being that was supposed to be in control of everything in the universe yet stood idly by while evil seemed to rule the planet. Hitting a little closer to home he wondered how anyone could worship a god that allowed mental illness. God, he thought, was brought into existence by the minds of men who were desperate to find answers to the mysteries of life and of the universe. People simply resigned themselves to the notion that God was the only one with all the answers, and that trying to know God was the best hope a person had. Charles viewed that logic as a shabby crutch that would someday break under the weight of fact-based scientific discovery.

Charles passed the church and turned right at the corner where another landmark sat. The town hall was the second public building erected in Cutters Mill, right after the church. Like the church the building was no longer used for its original purpose, but instead held the mayor's office and planning commission. The keystone in the building's foundation was engraved with a quote by author Henry David Thoreau. Alexander Cutter, the town's founder, commissioned the engraving in 1848. Charles couldn't make out the weathered inscription from his car, but it didn't matter because he knew it by heart.

"If you have built castles in the air, your work need not be lost; that is where they should be," Charles said, repeating the quote from memory. "Now put foundations under them." Even as a boy Charles knew that it meant that men should dream and aspire to great things. The words and the wisdom behind them were indelibly stamped on his mind.

Turning on the car radio, Charles tuned it into a local station playing music from the 1960's and 70's. He thought, as he had many times before, about how ironic it was that the town's namesake, a lumber baron, should have the last name of Cutter. In the early 1800's Alexander Cutter built a business on the area's abundant hardwood and softwood forests and their close proximity to the Mississippi river. Cutter & Sons harvested pine, fir, maple, walnut, and oak trees from all over the upper Mississippi River Valley, and teams of log drivers coaxed them downriver to the company's mill. There, the lumber was cut and shaped for use in the construction of hundreds of local homes and fine furnishings. The mill brought with it many employment opportunities. Some people found jobs at the mill as saw operators, others worked the drying kiln or stacked finished lumber in the warehouse. Still others used the wood produced at the mill in their jobs as carpenters or cabinetmakers. Charles' father Edmond worked the mill from the age of 19 until his retirement at the age of 65. The mill had produced lifetime employment for many of the town's residents. Like a mighty oak seeding the ground with acorns, the mill prospered and the town grew up around it.

The 1970's song "Cats in the Cradle" came through the radio, bringing Charles back to his younger days and how he had tried everything to avoid following in his father's footsteps. It wasn't that he had disliked anything about his father or his life in Cutters Mill. Quite the contrary, Charles created a life outside Cutter's Mill simply to show his father that he had had the wherewithal to do so, and that his father had done a good job raising his boy. It was important to Charles to make his father proud.

After high school Charles had joined the Army and endured almost an entire year of intense training before joining the elite 2nd Ranger Battalion under the 75th Ranger Regiment. The 2/75 was one of the toughest, most highly trained groups of commandos in the United States Army's Special Operations Forces. Charles loved being a Ranger. Although he didn't gloat about it, he knew that many men fantasized about being part of the prestigious fraternity. As a Combat Engineer his job, when he described it to friends and family, was to "build stuff and blow stuff up."

In 1984 Charles' unit was deployed to Grenada for Operation Urgent Fury, which was launched to prevent the takeover of the island by a brutal group of leftist thugs. Then First Lieutenant Buell earned a Bronze Star for defending his platoon while under fire. Charles was only a few feet away when a sniper's bullet ripped through the shoulder of one of his squad leaders. Another soldier, PFC Martin Churchill, was hit in the chest and died shortly after from internal bleeding and collapsed lungs. Charles and three others identified the sniper's location and returned fire with M-16's and a ring mounted 50-caliber machine gun that ultimately found its mark. The experience shook Charles emotionally, but it also strengthened his resolve to devote himself to defending those who could not defend themselves.

Unfortunately, things did not turn out the way he had planned. Charles's tour in Grenada lasted another eight months after the attack on his platoon. Upon returning to battalion headquarters in Fort Lewis Washington he spent another three years soldiering and training for whatever would come next. During a night reconnaissance mission in mountainous terrain, he and three other soldiers got caught in a rockslide that badly damaged Charles' right knee. The injury never fully healed and prevented him from running, climbing and doing the heavily lifting his job required. He was assigned to a number of light duty jobs, all of which were fine. But he missed being in the field and on the front line. Eventually he decided that he'd rather not be a soldier if he couldn't do the things he loved. Charles had faced up to the possibility of leaving the Army in a body bag. But in his wildest dreams he could never have imagined leaving voluntarily. But that's what he did. When it came time to reenlist he decided to call it quits.

Jaded and disappointed by the hand life had dealt him, he decided to get as far away as he could from the world he had known. One night while drinking heavily with some of his closest Army buddies, he decided to figure out where he would go next. He tacked a map of the world on the wall, and with a dart in his hand told them he would spend three months at whatever location the dart landed.

Charles was not normally one to throw caution to the wind. Every move for the past eight years as a Ranger had been calculated. His life and the lives of others had depended upon it. But in the end clear thinking and planning had not prevented things from going wrong. He drew back, closed his eyes and launched the dart towards his new temporary home. It landed on Jiangsu, China.

Charles extended his stay and wandered the country for seven months, exploring its coastal regions. He carried everything he brought with him on his back including, among other things, two changes of clothes, a sleeping bag, small tent, and Thoreau's book, Walden. He didn't stay in one place long enough to form any real connections with the people he met, and that's the way he preferred it. He kept moving. His knee injury caused him some pain, but he pushed on. His savings lasted five months. After that he worked odd jobs to earn enough money for food, and sometimes for lodging when he didn't feel like sleeping in his tent. He healed a great deal during that time. The simple, meager existence of the people he observed reminded him that life was often times unfair, but was still meant to be lived purposefully. At the end of seven months Charles knew it was time to go home.

He arrived in Miami Florida with the intention of hitchhiking northward to his final destination back in Cutters Mill. Charles wasn't prepared for what happened when he got into a car that had pulled over to pick him up on Highway 1, just outside Miami. The sight of the olive skinned beauty sitting behind the driver's seat made him stammer and stumble over his words as he tried to thank her for the ride. Up until that moment Charles had never been shaken at the sight of a woman. But he was completely flustered by her long dark hair, which dropped in ringlets down to the middle of her back, and by her teardrop shaped dark brown eyes and beautifully proportioned body. She was fresh and flawless, and it distracted him so that he failed to produce his name when she had asked for it. He still remembered the sleeveless light blue dress she wore and how it rode slightly up her thigh.

Charles' reminiscing ended when he turned into his driveway and saw Isabel and their six-year-old daughter Esther through the picture window of their home. Fourteen years had gone by since he had climbed into her car on Highway 1. Still, he couldn't help staring at the stunning beauty that was his wife.

Isabel noticed her husband sitting in the driveway and waved. Esther ran to the front door as her father got out of his car. "Daddy, daddy, daddy! Mommy is making Moros y Christianos for dinner," she yelled, knowing that her father loved the traditional Cuban dish of black beans and rice.

Charles picked her up, put his lips on her cheek and blew, which made a sound like someone sitting on a Whoopi cushion. Esther giggled and returned the gesture of greeting they had lovingly termed a Zorbit when she was three.

"How's the mill daddy?" she asked.

"Still made of wood," he said, straight faced and serious.

Esther giggled at her father's pun. "How's your job as Vice President of operations?" She asked, raising a stiffened hand to her brow and offering a crisp salute. Charles had taught his daughter to ask the question in exactly that manner two years earlier in order to surprise Isabel with news of his promotion.

"Finer than frog's hair," he replied.

"But daddy, frogs don't have any hair!"

"Yes they do, but it's so fine that you just can't see it."

Esther covered her mouth, screaming with delight. "Daddy stop! You're fooling with me!" Her mild scolding included a soft slap to his shoulder.

"I swear it. One time I came upon a frog, and his hair was so fine tha--"

"OK that's enough with the frog hair already," Isabel interjected, wrapping her arms tenderly around Charles' neck and giving him a kiss that lasted longer than most men get when they come home from work at the end of the day.

"I'm glad you're home," she said, her breathy Spanish accent perfuming the air.

"Me too Chabela," said Charles. "How was your day?"

"Oh, you know how it is with us stay-at-home moms. We get up around ten o'clock, watch TV all day and wait for our husbands to come home so we can hand off the children and go out on the town with our girlfriends," Isabel replied, looking at Charles as seriously as she could. "I'll be back by midnight," she said, pausing for effect and then flashing a bright smile, tossing back her hair and laughing.

Esther joined in the laughter. "Mommy you're being silly!" she said.

Pancake, their Jack Russell Terrier, had been waiting dutifully at their feet for acknowledgement. When Isabel looked at her she jumped up and down and began barking.

"Esther and I would be happy to spend the evening together wouldn't we?" Charles said, looking at the miniature version of his wife. "What do you say we eat the delicious TV dinner mommy made for us-- " This time the slap to his shoulder came from Isabel, and it wasn't so soft. "Ouch! And then play 'Chutes and Ladders' and read a chapter from 'The Lion, The Witch, and The Wardrobe'?"

"OK. But I want mommy to be with us too!"

"Oh," Isabel interjected. "I had no idea that you had such a lovely evening planned. I've changed my mind. I would much rather be here with you," she laughingly replied, playfully poking Esther's side and making her giggle.

Charles lowered Esther to Pancake, who happily licked and pawed at her. They both ran off as the laughter and barking faded into the living room. Isabel and Charles walked hand in hand back to the kitchen where they opened a bottle of wine, sipping and talking as they finished preparing the evening meal.

Five

Dust bunnies scampered across the wood floor as Richard tried to corral them with a well-worn straw broom. He was intent on capturing them all but he knew that for every one he managed to get into the dustpan, ten more would appear within a week. It was a frustrating task, but cleanliness was one of the things the Bureau of Mental Health auditors would be looking for during their visit the following day. Carl and some of his staff would handle the daunting paperwork requirements for the audit. Richard and some of the other residents were tasked with cleaning and organizing. Their work was subject to inspections by Carl.

The kitchen, bathrooms and Carl's office had been dusted and swept. All that remained for Richard were the hallways and public areas. Judith Krump and Josh Camden were dusting and organizing the day room when Richard walked in. The room had three small tables, each accompanied by two chairs. A big, well-worn couch faced a small television that sat in the corner. Shelves placed along one wall held a multitude of books and board games. Richard stopped under the arch separating the day room from the foyer. He watched Judith as she sprayed furniture polish onto a rag and wiped one small table from top to bottom. Ready to move to another table, she looked up and saw Richard staring at her.

She dropped her gaze away from Richard and to the floor. "Hi Richie," she said with a sad look, the corners of her mouth drooping as she spoke.

"Hi Judith," he said, baring his teeth in a nervous smile. "How are you?"

"OK. I'm cleaning."

"Me too. I need to sweep in here. You almost done?"

Without responding, Judith retrieved a small, well-worn hand-held radio from the pocket of her sweater. She placed the top edge of the radio on her right temple and looked upwards towards the ceiling. The radio didn't work. It had no batteries, and even if it did its age and condition rendered it useless. But that didn't matter, because for Judith it was a communication device. It provided a connection to another dimension and the beings that lived there. Judith often relied on them for instructions about what she was to think and do. Normally it was comforting. But sometimes they instructed her to do things that were discomforting, even disturbing. Still, she obeyed.

On one occasion she had walked from Alpha House to the downtown area of Cutters Mill. When she arrived at Benland's Paint and Hardware she stripped off all her clothes and walked up and down the sidewalks, whimpering about being punished for something she had done. Someone eventually called the police. By the time they arrived she was laying on the sidewalk curled up in the fetal position and crying uncontrollably. She told police that "the family", as she referred to them, said she needed to pay penance for having impure thoughts about one of the Alpha House residents. On another occasion she drank a cup of laundry detergent because the family told her it would prevent her from getting breast cancer, which her mother had died from years ago.

Judith stood there waiting for the family to give her instructions, while Richard pretended to sweep. He watched as she gazed at the ceiling, sliding the radio back and forth against her temple and stopping when she found the sweet spot that brought the family's message through clearly.

Judith Krump always dressed to avoid being noticed. On this particular day she wore gray pants, a white long sleeve shirt buttoned all the way up to her neck, and a baggy black sweater that was clean but well worn. The clothing hung loosely on her tiny frame. Her salt and pepper hair was wrapped in a tight bun that protruded slightly from the back of her head, and eyeglasses with big frames and thick lenses magnified her sad looking eyes. Judith's thin, pursed lips mouthed silent words as she received and then repeated her instructions.

"I'm done here. I'm going to my room now," she said, sliding the radio back into her sweater pocket. Head down, she shuffled across the floor as if she were afraid she would fall if her feet left the ground. She stopped when she reached Richard's side, lifting her gaze to look him in the eyes. Richard flashed another nervous smile and Judith quickly shuffled out of the room. Josh followed her.

Richard walked backwards and swept dirt and dust bunnies toward him as he worked his way across the room. Nearing one of the small tables he turned around to avoid running into it. Mr. Lazarus sat there, smirking. A bit startled, Richard stepped back.

"You like her, don't you?" asked Lazarus.

"What do you, what do you mean?" Richard stammered.

"I mean you—like—her," Lazarus said, emphasizing each word as if Richard didn't comprehend it the first time.

"She's nice."

"Yeah, she seems nice enough. A little fruity with the radio and all, but still nice," Lazarus said, smiling now.

Richard looked away from Lazarus, not knowing how to continue.

Lazarus' smiled disappeared. "Do you know what tomorrow is?" he asked.

"Tomorrow is Friday."

"Yes. And what happens on Friday?"

"I don't know. What happens on Friday?" Richard asked, quickly tiring of the leading questions.

"Francis Tadley delivers the mail! That's what happens!" Lazarus yelled, the weight of his shaking fist pulling him forward. "You need to find a way to intercept the letters he's been sending all over kingdom come about us!"

"I work tomorrow and somebody will get to the mailbox before I do."

Lazarus shook his head in anger and disbelief of what he had just heard. "Do you mean to tell me that you can't manage to take a little time off work for something as important as this? Are you at all concerned about what he is doing to us? Are you?" Lazarus steamed, slamming his fist on the table.

"I can do it on Saturday. He delivers on Saturday too," Richard said, apologetically.

"Richard, who are you talking to?" Mark Valjean asked as he walked into the room. Mark was one of the Alpha House orderlies and was helping with preparations for the upcoming audit.

"Nobody. I, I was just talking to myself about something I have to do."

Richard looked nervously at Lazarus, who was impatiently drumming his fingers on the table.

"How's the cleaning coming?" asked Mark.

"I'm almost done in here." Richard continued to sweep, hoping that Lazarus would go away.

"Tomorrow's the big day!" Mark said, referring to the audit.

"Yup, big day tomorrow."

"Where is Judith? She was here a while ago."

"She went to her room."

"I need to talk to her about her meds," Mark said. "But I guess that can wait until later."

Walking up to Richard, Mark put a hand on his shoulder. Richard tensed up, glaring at him like he had just grabbed his crotch.

"Whoa! Whoa! Take it easy!" Mark countered, retracting his hand. "I just wanted you to know that your brother Charles seems very concerned about you. He came by to talk with Carl while you were at work a few days ago. I'm not sure what they talked about, but he seemed worried."

Richard remained stiff and unresponsive.

"Isabel was there too." Mark chuckled and raised his hand to pat Richard on the shoulder, but caught himself mid-way through and quickly switched to scratching his head. "Your brother's a lucky guy to have a woman like that."

"You know, I had an island girl once," he continued, chuckling again. "Her name was Celiz, but everyone called her Sally. She was some Puerto Rican beauty! You know what they say about Puerto Rican girls."

Richard had no clue about who "they" were or what they said about Puerto Rican girls. Neither did Mark Valjean, so he decided it would be best to stop the charade before he said something really stupid.

Lazarus rolled his eyes and shook his head. Richard could see that he was growing impatient.

"I don't know, I should probably get back to work," he answered, starting to sweep again and hoping Mark would take the hint.

"Oh yeah. We'd better get back to it. I want to get out of here at a decent hour. Do you need anything?"

"No."

"OK, well I'll see you tomorrow then. Have a good night, OK?"

"OK," Richard said, thankful that he was leaving and that Lazarus hadn't flown off the handle.

"What a nut job," Lazarus chimed after he was gone. "I had an island girl once!" he repeated mockingly. "You know this place is filled with kooks, and most of them work here."

A bit put off by the exchange with Mark Valjean Richard blurted, "I don't like people touching me."

Lazarus didn't acknowledge his comment. "Then there's that other guy," he said. "What's his name? Valjean's buddy?"

"You mean Scott?"

"No, the other guy. The black guy."

"Oh, that's Darius. Darius Green."

"Yeah, Darius," said Lazarus. "There's one you need to look out for. He's too nice. People like that have something up their sleeve."

Richard furrowed his brow. "I like Darius. What's wrong with him?" he asked.

"For one he's from Detroit. Nothing good ever comes out of Detroit. Second, he's always writing things down. Did you ever notice that?"

"He's supposed to keep track of things."

"Well, where do you think Tadley gets his information from?" asked Lazarus. "Green is his source, don't you see? Tadley needs someone who has first hand information about us."

Richard paused for a moment. "I never thought about that," he said.

Lazarus raised his voice again. "You never thought about that? You never thought about that! What would you do if I weren't here to protect you? I can't do everything! I need you to be more aware of what's going on right in front of you."

"OK. I'll keep an eye on him," Richard replied, his right hand quivering at his side as he tried to reassure Lazarus.

"He dresses funny too. Have you ever noticed that he only wears tan cargo pants, the ones with the baggy pockets? Every day, tan cargo pants. I'm pretty sure they make them in other colors. And those baggy pockets always seem to be full of God knows what."

"I'm gonna finish sweeping now."

Lazarus closed his eyes, rubbing the bridge of his nose as if he was trying to sooth a migraine.

"Fine," he said in an exhausted tone. "Don't forget about Saturday."

"I won't. I promise."

Lazarus stood up and fixed his cold blue eyes on Richard. The weight of his stare forced Richard's eyes to the floor, and Lazarus walked out of the room without saying another word.

By 8:15 PM all the audit preparations were complete. Richard had just returned from the smoking table and was sitting alone in a corner of the day room, watching others who were there. Clarence, Josh and Tamara regularly watched TV from 8:00 to 10:00 PM on

Thursdays. The line-up featured reruns of "Bonanza", followed by "The Andy Griffith Show", then "Matlock" and finally "Golden Girls".

Whenever Richard was in a room with a television, he consciously focused his attention elsewhere. The last time he tried to watch a news program the anchor commented about how he had been responsible for a tornado that had killed 26 people in Oklahoma. Another time a stand-up comedian cracked jokes about his tendency to twitch and shake uncontrollably. The audience laughed hard at his expense, and in his embarrassment Richard threw an empty catsup bottle at the TV. It was a source of anxiety he could do without.

Richard looked around the room and saw Sam and Ben, who everyone called Booger, playing checkers at the same table where Mr. Lazarus sat earlier that day. Judith was sitting at another small table on the opposite side of the room. Head down as usual, she paged through a "Home and Garden" magazine. Feeling Richard's stare, she slowly looked up and locked eyes with him. She held her gaze for longer than Richard had ever experienced before. Then she slowly dropped her head back down to the magazine and stared. She didn't flip any pages. After a few moments she looked up again to see Richard still looking at her. Reaching into her sweater pocket she pulled out the radio and placed it on her temple.

"I'm going to my parent's 50th wedding anniversary on Saturday," Richard blurted loudly, wanting her to pay attention to him and not her radio family.

Everyone including those watching television turned to look at Richard, and then at Judith. With six pairs of eyes staring at her she lowered the radio and dropped her head in embarrassment. "That's real... that's real nice Richie," she said, without looking up.

"There's gonna be steak and shrimp and champagne and three kinds of pie."

There was silence in the room except for the television. Everyone's eyes were on Judith again as she clumsily fumbled with a page from the magazine.

Richard continued, "Maybe you could--"

"OK, I'm, I'm tired!" Judith interrupted nervously. "I should go to my room now. So, I'm going to go to my room now and maybe sleep or something. And then I won't be too tired tomorrow. So I'm going now."

Richard tried to interject. "I just wanted--"

"Richie you missed some dust bunnies," Judith interrupted again, pointing to the floor underneath one of the bookshelves. Richard turned to look and, taking full advantage of the diversion she had created, Judith scurried past him and out of the room.

Booger pointed at Richard and laughed, then he covered his mouth to prevent an unwanted response from Sam, but it was too late. Sam reached over and slapped Booger on the side of the head. "Be nice!" he screamed.

"Ouweee! I was just--"

"Be nice!" Sam screamed again, this time pointing his finger at Booger for emphasis.

Richard scratched his head, still stunned by how quickly Judith could think, talk and move.

"Women!" shouted Clarence from his seat on the couch. "You can't live with 'em!"

Tamara, who was sitting next to Clarence, reached over and pinched him hard on the arm.

"Ouch! That hurt!"

"You deserve it!" she said. "I'm a very nice person! Women are very nice people! Watch yourself bub!"

Booger laughed again and then quickly moved backwards to avoid another slap from Sam.

Richard started to laugh but it produced a series of coughs, each hack louder and more phlegmy sounding than the last. When the coughing stopped he reached for his coat.

"HE'S ALREADY SMOKED A PACK AND A HALF TODAY, AND IT'S A WORK DAY. I HONESTLY DON'T KNOW WHERE HE FINDS THE TIME OR MONEY TO SMOKE SO MUCH," Author said.

Melissa followed, "IT'LL PROBABLY BE WHAT KILLS HIM, IF HE DOESN'T GO BROKE FIRST."

The whistled theme song from "The Andy Griffith Show" bellowed from the television as Richard left the room for a cigarette. Minutes later Judith peered out her second story bedroom window in the back of the house and quietly watched as Richard puffed clouds of gray smoke into the cold night air.

Six

Warm sunlight filtered through the living room window as Richard stood at the kitchen counter in his apartment. He opened the small plastic bottle of Prolixin and dispensed seven pills into his hand. Then he transferred them to a plastic container with seven compartments, each labeled for a different day of the week. Richard had been taking Prolixin for years. Over the course of his illness his doctor had switched medications several times in an effort to arrive at a balance between controlling his anxiety, hallucinations, and delusions while producing the least number of irritating side effects. Unfortunately for Richard, the shaking in his hands and involuntary muscle contractions in his neck were side effects that afflicted many who were on a steady regimen of antipsychotic drugs. Tardive Dyskinesia, as it was called in the mental health field, was irreversible.

Richard dispensed three more medications into the container, one for blood pressure, another for cholesterol, and an aspirin that his doctor had said was good for his heart. He opened the compartment marked for Saturday and poured the pills into his hand. Then he turned on the faucet and dumped the pills down the drain, making sure that they all disappeared. Richard had been flushing his pills down the kitchen sink for the past six days. Alpha House staff tried to monitor how everyone took their medications. Those who had been caught not taking their meds were forced to swallow them in the presence of a staff person. Richard had been diligent about taking his medications and so had managed to avoid suspicion by the staff. Recently however, he began thinking that the pills were poisoning his mind, making him feel numb and causing him to make bad decisions. With Mr. Lazarus' encouragement he decided to stop taking them altogether. The pharmaceuticals intended to counteract his illness remained in his system for a while, but with each passing day there was less and less of them. Richard felt cleansed, as if his system had been purged of mold, dust and cobwebs. Author and Melissa were more vocal, and Mr. Lazarus showed up a lot more. But the *new normal*, a term he uttered only to himself, was a refreshing change from being doped and dead all the time.

A small forest of neatly manicured maple and oak trees stood on the Alpha House property. Across the street Tainter Park held twenty acres of trees and walking paths, a large playground, a veterans memorial, and a monument to Louis Tainter, one of the town's founding fathers. Mid to late October hosted a vivid display of color. But by early November the leaves in the yard and park had paled and lost hold of the branches that bore them. Only the eyes and nose of the neighbor's dachshund Dottie was exposed as she paddled her way through piles of crisp brown leaves in front of Alpha House. It was 9:45 AM and Judith, Sam and Ben were raking when Richard arrived on the front porch. Senior orderly Darius Green was sitting in a wicker chair overseeing the clean up and writing on a pad of yellow paper. The rustle of raked leaves and Dottie's playful barking prevented him from hearing Richard as he stepped out the front door and walked up behind him.

"Should I rake or bag?" Richard asked.

"Good lord! Richard, you scared me!" Darius wailed. "Don't sneak up on me like that!"

Richard's unblinking eyes locked on Darius, and he maintained his gaze for an uncomfortable amount of time before responding. "What do you want me to do?" His stare persisted.

Still wide-eyed, Darius turned his attention to the piles of leaves in the yard. "Ah, I guess you should bag."

After a long moment, Richard nodded his head in agreement. "So you want me to bag then?" he asked, seemingly uncertain of Darius' previous instruction.

"Yeah, go bag leaves," Darius' said in an edgy tone.

Richard moved forward but stopped short of the front steps. He turned back to look at Darius. "I hear voices," he said matter-of-factly. "And they tell me to do things."

Darius knew that schizophrenics were in one moment able to make lucid and accurate assessments of themselves and their illness, and in the next say and do things that were irrational. Still, hearing the statement come from Richard in the same manner someone might use to comment on the weather was chilling.

"What are they telling you to do?" he asked, the irritation in his voice replaced with a tinge of concern.

Richard looked up to the sky momentarily and then turned his attention to the leaf-strewn yard. He proceeded down the steps and onto the lawn where he picked up a rake and began to work, never responding to Darius' question.

By 12:30 PM most of the leaves had been bagged. Richard made his way to the end of the driveway carrying a large brown paper yard waste bag with the top folded over. He set it next to twenty-nine other bags he had carefully organized into three rows for the trash pickup on Monday. He reached into his shirt pocket for a smoke, not caring that he wasn't supposed to light up anywhere but the smoking table out back. He savored the sense of accomplishment he felt as he surveyed the clean yard.

Sam and Booger were standing in the middle of the yard arguing about something. Darius was pacing back and forth on the porch, looking up periodically from his note pad. Richard eyed him with suspicion, wondering if Mr. Lazarus' concerns were correct. He had never doubted Darius' intentions before. But now he was beginning to think he might be one of them. An evildoer.

Judith and Mark Valjean, the Alpha House orderly, sat on a bench under a leafless tree near the left side of the house. Although Richard couldn't hear, he could see that Mark was doing the talking while Judith stared at her lap. Richard assumed they were talking about her meds, as Mark had indicated to him earlier. He watched as Judith pulled out her radio and positioned it on her temple. Mark reached up and gently pulled it down, and Judith offered no resistance. As he continued to talk, Judith wiped tears from her cheeks. Richard sensed that she was increasingly unable to cope with whatever was being discussed. Moments later she bolted from the bench upon which she and Valjean sat, ran up the front porch steps and hurried into the darkened interior of Alpha House. Richard had seen her cry many times before, and he understood her pain. He thought he might talk with her about the benefits of purging her system of medication.

Dottie suddenly began barking and Richard turned to see mailman Francis Tadley approaching the mailbox on the front porch of the house next door. He pretended to work at organizing the bags as Tadley dropped off the neighbor's mail and then started down the sidewalk towards Alpha House. *Stinking evildoer*, Richard steamed to himself. *Your time is coming*. Richard had called Tadley an evildoer to his face many times before. The first time it happened Tadley told Carl, who promptly suggested he ignore it. Carl dutifully told Richard that he needed to keep his opinions about Tadley to himself. But Richard could not help pointing out what he knew to be true. He felt it was his right, and in fact his duty to expose the evildoers.

Today was different. Richard would not confront Tadley. He kept his eyes down and carefully adjusted the bags so that the printing on the front of each one faced the street. Tadley, who wanted nothing more than to deliver the mail without being verbally assaulted, exhaled in relief as he walked past Richard and onto the front porch. The metal lid on the mailbox squeaked as he opened it to insert the day's mail, and then made a loud clank as it slapped shut. After Tadley turned to go, Richard scanned the front porch and yard and saw that Darius and Mark were gone. He waited until Tadley was a good distance down the sidewalk before walking briskly to the porch steps. Still scanning from left to right he saw Sam and Booger happily chatting about something at the side of the house. No one else was around.

The lid of the mailbox groaned as he opened it. He winced at the sound and stopped to looked around again before opening it completely. He quickly retrieved the contents of the box and closed the lid that, to his relief, did not squeak on the way down. Unzipping his coat, he stuffed the mail inside and zipped back up again. With one hand in his coat pocket to prevent the mail from falling out he opened the front door and headed to his room.

Once inside his apartment Richard removed the rubber band from around the bundle of mail and spread it out on the kitchen counter. The contents included two magazines, three pieces of what appeared to be junk mail and four envelopes that looked official enough to contain the information he was looking for. He wrapped the magazines around the junk mail, placed the rubber band around the bundle and put it inside his coat.

He stared at the four letters sitting on the counter. He knew evildoers were deceptive. And he had no doubt that while the carefully typed addresses on the front of each envelope made them appear innocent, they contained information about him that would in some way make his life even more miserable than it already was. He smirked at the thought that he had faced the evildoer Tadley and won. "Victorious!" he crowed. "Victorious at last!"

He left the envelopes on the counter as he headed out the door of his apartment and back to the mailbox, the junk mail still tucked inside his coat. Just before reaching the front door, someone entered the hallway behind him. Not knowing who was there Richard stopped in his tracks, afraid to turn around. For a moment he stood there, frozen with fear. His hands in his coat pockets to hold the stolen mail in place, he could feel the bottle of nasal decongestant he always kept there. He could think of nothing else to do but pull it from his pocket and squirt a little up each nostril. *Not a great diversion*, he told himself as he began to withdraw his hands. *Just act casual, like you need to clear your nasal passages and have no idea that someone is about to tackle you to the ground for stealing the mail.* The mail bundle inside his coat, which his hands had held into place, began to slide out. He abruptly thrust his hands back into his pockets, barely catching the bundle that was now partially exposed below his waistline. Shimmying the mail back into position inside his coat, he froze when the person behind him spoke.

"You OK?" Carl asked.

Richard whipped around to face him. "Uh, yeah. I'm OK. I'm good," he said trying to avoid eye contact and praying that Carl was not on his way to retrieve the mail.

"Watcha doin?" Carl continued, reaching for the knob on the hallway bathroom door.

"Um, I was just going outside to um, to have a cigarette."

"Smoking table's that way," Carl said, pointing to the back of the house.

"Yup. I just thought I'd go the long way and get a little exercise." Richard closed his eyes in disbelief of what had come from his mouth.

Carl smirked and opened the bathroom door. "Oh, well by all means go get some exercise before you um, before you smoke."

As soon as Carl was inside the bathroom Richard rushed to the porch to place the bundle back into the mailbox. He wasn't aware of the loud squeak as he opened the metal box or the clatter as the lid slapped shut, and he didn't look to see if anyone else was around. He just wanted it to be over. Only moments after completing his task he was sitting at the smoking table out back, deeply inhaling the only drug besides caffeine he would allow into his system.

Later, back in his apartment, Richard nudged the letters on the kitchen counter. He considered opening them but thought Mr. Lazarus would appreciate being the first to see his prize, so he left them be. He felt strong and vengeful, like a soldier who had gone to battle and came out victorious and unscathed. He was a warrior. He had fought and won. And he looked forward to the battles that were yet to come.

Seven

Esther picked at her food and squirmed in her seat as she waited for the celebration of her grandparent's 50th wedding anniversary to begin. "Daddy, are you going to say your words?" she asked, tugging on Charles' jacket sleeve.

"In just a few minutes Chipmunk. People are still eating."

Porter's restaurant was one of the only places in town that could handle large groups. It was often used for weddings, graduations, birthdays and the like. The large room held seventeen round tables, like white islands floating on a sea of dark blue carpet. Seventy-two people had already filed through a well-stocked buffet set against a long windowed wall, and some had gone back for seconds. A steady hum of indiscernible conversation was accented by the clanking of glasses and dinnerware.

Esther grabbed a red crayon from a dainty yellow purse she kept at her side. She put the finishing touches on a drawing she had been working on for a while. "Can I give this to Uncle Richie?" she asked, holding up the creation for her father to see.

Charles eyed the drawing of two people holding hands under a large tree in the middle of an open field. Brightly colored butterflies and birds were drawn in mid flight. Esther's name was scrawled on the bottom in red, squiggly, mismatched letters.

"Is that you and Uncle Richard?"

"Yes," she said. "We're taking a rest before Uncle Richie goes back."

"Back where?" Charles asked.

"Back home silly!" Esther giggled.

"Well, of course! I don't know why I didn't see that before," Charles said, playing along. "Uncle Richard loves your drawings. He puts them on his refrigerator you know."

Esther smiled and neatly folded the drawing until it was the size of a pack of baseball cards. She slid out of her chair and walked two tables over to where Richard sat with his mother, father, brother Edmond and sister Julia.

Richard turned with a jerk as Esther tapped him on the shoulder.

"I made this for you Uncle Richie."

As usual, Richard's defenses came down as soon as he saw his little niece and heard her tiny voice. "Oh, thank you," he said.

Esther extended her arms and Richard leaned over to receive a hug and a peck on the cheek. Charles watched in amazement, wondering how his daughter had managed to wrap the reclusive and antisocial man so tightly around her little finger. Richard started to straighten up after the hug and kiss, but Esther drew him back in by extending the little finger of her right hand and wiggling it back and forth as if to say *Come back to me, I'm not through with you yet*.

"It's about a resting place," she whispered in his ear. "You can open it later if you want." She looked him in the eyes, smiled and turned to go.

"OK, I'll open it later." Richard looked at the still folded gift for a moment before putting it in the pocket of his coat.

"That's so sweet," said Agnes. "Isn't that sweet?"

Richard nodded his head in agreement, watching Esther sit back down next to her father.

"So, how's work been going?" Richard's mother continued.

"Fine ma."

"How many hours are you putting in now?"

"I don't know, about 30 I guess."

"Sounds like they've cut back a bit," Edmond Jr. chimed in.

"Yeah, I guess. Do we have to talk about work now?" Richard said, telling more than asking everyone to change the subject.

Richard's father didn't think about the response he was likely to get before asking the next question. "What would you like to talk about?" he said.

After a moment Richard's face tightened. "I'd like to talk about why that SOB Harlan Foster can get away with banning me from Fern's Café."

"OK, we're not going to do this now," his father retorted. "Talk about something nice or keep quiet."

"Richard! You don't use that kind of language!" Agnes scolded. "Your father is right, we can't discuss that here. We'll talk about it later."

"We will talk about it later. It's not fair to me!" Richard fired back, gobbling the last remaining piece of beef from his plate and then belching loud enough to cause people at other tables to turn and look. Agnes glared at Richard the way mothers do when their children misbehave.

"Excuse me," he said sheepishly.

Just then Charles stood up and asked for everyone's attention. "On behalf of my family I'd like to thank you all for coming here today to help us celebrate fifty years of wedded bliss between mom and dad."

Agnes and Edmond chuckled at the wedded bliss comment and then leaned towards each other and kissed. Applause and whistles filled the room.

"Doing anything for 50 years takes patience and dedication. Now my mother will be the first to admit that he can be difficult to live with," Charles said, glancing at Agnes. "Isn't that right Ma?"

"We have an understanding," she responded. "Edmond doesn't talk to me at any point before my second cup of coffee, and I don't speak at any point before my second cup of coffee."

The crowd laughed and applauded again.

"Now my dad is a pretty even-tempered guy," Charles continued. "But don't let the Brill Cream and crisp white shirts fool you. He has his moments."

"I once asked my mother if she had ever considered divorce. She looked at me seriously and said, 'Divorce? Heavens, No! I have, however, considered murder on several occasions!'"

The crowd's laughter escalated to an all out roar. Agnes covered her head in embarrassment and Edmond pretended to look shocked.

Charles waited for the laughter to die down before he continued. "Seriously, you two are an inspiration to all of us who have pledged lifelong commitments to our spouses. Life's not always easy. Sometimes it seems hard enough to care for yourself, let alone a spouse and five misbehaving children to boot. Thanks mom and dad for showing us what dedication looks like. Thanks for teaching us about selflessness and real love. May you have many more happy years together."

Charles raised his glass, as did everyone else in the room. "Here's to Edmond and Agnes Buell and the life they created together," Charles said, looking proudly at his parents.

The crowd sipped their champagne and smiled. Someone in the back of the room tapped a knife against the side of a glass, prompting several others to do the same. At once the room was alive with clatter that signaled it was again time for Edmond and Agnes to kiss. Warm coos came from some of the women, while the men simply smiled. After the kiss, Agnes and Edmond waved from their seats and thanked everyone.

Richard took the opportunity presented by the lull after Charles' speech to grab his coat from the back of his chair and head outside for a cigarette. As Richard whisked by Charles' table, Charles leaned over to Isabel and whispered in her ear. "Chabela, I've noticed some of the men looking at you. What should I do about that?"

"Maybe they're taken by the beautiful dress you bought me," she said, smiling shyly.

"I don't think so," Charles retorted.

"Maybe they're jealous because they're not related to the happy couple."

"Probably not."

"Maybe they're in awe of the beautiful love we share."

"Yeah, I don't think so."

"OK, well then maybe they're just horny!" Isabel chimed, grabbing Charles' arm with one hand and covering her mouth with the other to suppress her laughter.

Charles grabbed his chest as if someone had just stuck a fork in his heart. "Ouch, that hurts! That really hurts!" he said. "Am I to stand idly by while my wife is ogled by other men? Should I not defend your honor, and even more importantly, my pride?" he continued in his best, serious tone.

"That's OK," Isabel said, continuing her charade. "Tell them they can look but they can't touch, 'cause I already got me a boy toy."

Moving in close, Charles' touched his nose to Isabel's.

"Is that what I am? Your boy toy?"

She paused for a moment, and then the playfulness left her face. "No," she said. You're my man. My big, strong, handsome, loving man."

Tugging gently on his right ear, Isabel pulled him in for a kiss. But before their lips met, Esther yanked at Charles' jacket sleeve again.

"Daddy, what are you and mommy talking about?"

Charles turned and held Esther's chubby little face in his hands. "We're talking about growing old together, just like Papa and Grams," he said, kissing her forehead.

Charles turned back to Isabel, wrapped his hand around the back of her neck and pulled her towards him. Her breath was sweetly scented by champagne.

"I love you," she said.

"I love you too."

They kissed and then moved apart far enough to look into each other's eyes. Feeling the weight of other people's stares, they broke eye contact and looked around the room. Charles' single cousin Eric was watching, as were several others at his table. Eric raised his glass with one hand and gave a thumbs-up with the other. Charles nodded back.

"I have to use the restroom," he said to Isabel and Esther. Standing up, he secured the top button on his dress jacket and headed towards the banquet room door.

The hallway to the right led to the front of the restaurant and the hallway to the left led to the bathrooms, kitchen and waiter's station. As Charles began turning left he noticed some commotion. Several people hovered over a waiter who was lying on the floor. Silverware was scattered about and a waitress knelt beside him. Charles' stomach tightened as he approached.

"Jenny, what happened?" he asked.

"Richard hit Lance. He just hauled off and hit him for no reason," she said, patting blood from the waiter's nose.

Charles had been in this place many times, but it still sickened him. He knew better than to ask why it had happened. He knew there was no logical explanation for Richard's aggression. He also knew his victim was dazed as much by the senselessness of the attack as he was by the attack itself.

"Where's Richie?" Charles asked.

"I don't know. He took off right after he hit Lance. All I know is that he ran out the door."

Charles looked at the bloodied waiter. "Are you OK?"

"Yeah. I'll be OK," he said in a muffled voice, staring at the ceiling and holding a napkin to his nose.

"I'm really sorry about this. I can't imagine what came over him." Charles was lying. He knew very well that the slightest, most innocent of gestures could be misinterpreted by Richard as aggression. Perhaps Lance had smiled at him at the same time the voices were telling each other how Richard shouldn't tolerate being mocked. Perhaps he had made the mistake of saying hello when all Richard heard was *Asshole!* Any number of possibilities existed and it was useless for Charles to try and figure out why Richard had once again lashed out at a person who was almost certainly innocent of any wrong doing.

Charles opened the front door to the banquet hall and looked around to see if Richard was nearby. He saw only light car traffic and two people walking on the other side of the street. He paused for a moment to consider whether or not he should go after Richard. He quickly decided that he was not going to ruin his parent's party by doing anything to disrupt the celebration. If at all possible, he wouldn't even tell anyone but Isabel about what had happened until the party was over. Charles went back inside and walked up to Lance, who was now on his feet. He apologized again and asked if there was anything he could do. The bleeding from his nose had stopped and there was no visible damage to his face.

Bill Nance, the restaurant manager, walked up with a scowl on his face. "Hey Charles."

"Bill, I'm really sorry about this. Sometimes he just flies off the handle."

"Yeah, I know. It doesn't look like he did too much damage. It's just so senseless."

"Listen Charles," continued Bill. "I can't allow your brother in here for a while. Whether or not Lance will press charges is up to him. But I have to protect my employees and my customers. Who knows what he might do next time. I'm sorry, but I have no choice."

"I completely understand," Charles quickly agreed. "I'll make sure he stays away from here. Thanks everyone for being so understanding."

Returning to his table in the banquet hall Isabel asked, "What took you so long?"

"Richie got into trouble again," Charles replied in a low voice. "I don't want to talk about it now. I'll fill you in later."

He grabbed a spoon and scooped up cake and ice cream from his dessert plate.

"It'll be OK," Isabel said, reaching to hold his hand and reassure him.

Charles didn't utter a word, but shook his head in disagreement and continued eating his dessert.

Eight

"This will probably be the last time we get out this year. It's cold, but the fishing should be good," Charles said as he lowered the anchor off the side of the small aluminum boat and into the coffee colored water of Atkins Lake. Early morning sunlight glittered off the gently undulating surface, like thousands of finely faceted jewels displaying their brilliance in flashes of blue, white, and yellow. Water softly slapped the boat's hull with a metronome-like rhythm.

Richard removed his gloves and reached down to retrieve his fishing pole and the small container of night crawlers they had purchased at Slippery's Bar, Grill and Bait Shop on the way to the cabin the night before. The gentle sway of the boat, the lullaby of the water and the soft whisper of the wind through the trees on the nearby shore were soothing. He didn't want the distraction of voices, not his or Charlie's or the ones inside his head.

"Uh Huh. Maybe we should keep quiet so we don't scare the fish," Richard said, baiting his hook and hoping his brother would take the hint.

He did. Once Charles had lowered his line into the water he poured coffee from a thermos into two foam cups and handed one to Richard without a word.

He's happy, Charles thought. *I wish he could have this kind of peace anytime he needed it. But it's too late for that now. It's too damned late*. Charles took in a deep breath and exhaled as if trying to expel the black soot of anger and guilt that filled his insides every time he thought about his brother's illness. He raised his head to look at the sunlit water stretching to the shore on the other side of the small lake. It was beautiful and he knew he should be thankful, thankful to have this place, thankful for his family, his job and all the other things that were a part of his life. But he felt only bitterness, bitterness about his brother's illness and bitterness towards the people who treated his brother as if he were an animal that needed to be fettered and caged. His mind was rancid with disgust, and that disgust was beginning to feed off his self-pity.

The plans he had made for a career in service to his country were discarded like worthless scraps of garbage. His opportunity for a life of honor and bravery that few people could attain was replaced with a droll existence in a mediocre job, in an insignificant midwestern town. He loved Isabel and Esther very much, but he had always dreamed there would be more. Charles huffed and shook his head, disappointed in the reality of his life. He looked to the sky, which was bright blue and cloudless except for a long trail of wispy white cutting across its expanse. *If there is a god*, he thought, *it must live up there, because it certainly does not live down here.*

Bringing his eyes back down to earth he glanced at his brother, who was happily sipping his coffee and jiggling his fishing pole up and down. The sight of him instantly replaced the bitterness and disgust he felt with anguish for what he had done. When they were kids, before Richard was diagnosed, he did not see his brother's illness. What he saw was a kid who lacked the ability to keep up with him physically and intellectually. Back then his brother was painfully uncoordinated, a problem that stayed with him into adulthood. The game of baseball, which Charles had loved, seemed always to include his little brother dropping balls at the most critical moments, or getting tangled in his own feet and hurling to the ground before the ball was caught. Charles always left Richard in the dust during bike races, and while he relished the victories he felt angry that winning required so little effort. He felt the same about Checkers, Go Fish, Hide and Seek and many other games. Charles had gotten bored with his brother, and over time he began playing more and more with other kids in the neighborhood who came closer to matching his abilities. That's when the scolding began. His reasoning was simple but heartless; his brother was not being the person he wanted him to be, so verbal corrections were necessary.

Don't be such a retard! Charles winced at the memory of the words that had once come from his mouth. Now they stabbed at his heart.

Are you stupid? Go sit down so we can get someone who knows how to catch a ball!

The echo of those words was followed by the image of his little brother dropping his head and shoulders in defeat without uttering a word in self-defense, as if to say *You're right, I don't deserve to be here playing with you.* Charles wished more than anything that he could go back in time to punish that cruel child; to reissue those same cutting and deeply painful words and put the shame on himself where it belonged. But that was not possible. Charles knew he did not cause his brother's sickness, but that fact did not lighten the enormous weight of guilt he felt for having caused him pain. He would live the rest of his days knowing that his mentally ill brother had suffered unspeakable shame at the hands of the one person who should have protected him. Charles couldn't bear to think about it any longer.

"Having fun?" he asked, pushing past the lump in his throat and the knot in his stomach.

Richard didn't answer. Instead he quickly jerked his pole upwards, setting the hook in the mouth of the fish that had just swallowed his bait. The pole began arching downwards in great jerks.

"I got him! I got him! He's a big one!" The usual dull tone in Richard's voice was gone and a vibrant, child-like excitement emerged. His brother's eyes were wide and beaming, and the deeply etched lines of his face disappeared against the pull of his smile.

He's smiling, Charles thought to himself. *He's smiling!* Tears welled in his eyes but he quickly wiped them away. "Yeah! He's a big one alright!" Charles' responded, managing to choke out the words and slap Richard on the back. "Looks like a walleye by the way he's fighting." He swallowed hard. "Give him some line... Take your time... Don't force it."

"Should I give him some line?" Richard asked frantically, unaware that Charles had said anything.

"Yeah! Give him line! You're doing great! We'll be having fish for dinner tonight!"

"Yeah, we're havin' fish for dinner Charlie!" Richard howled, looking at his brother with smiling eyes and waiting for his nod of approval before turning his attention back to his catch.

***

Just an hour before Richard saw the sleeping trees, the field of gently swaying autumn grass, and the snow dusted rolling hills. Those images had slowly been consumed by the darkness that followed the setting sun. Looking out from the porch the blackened space was like a movie screen, and on it played the moments of his day. He saw his brother wake him from a deep and peaceful sleep and whisper "Good morning little brother. Let's go fishing." He recalled the glorious smell of freshly brewed coffee tinged with the scent of wood smoke and sizzling bacon. There was the slap of water on the hull of the gently rocking boat, and the first exciting moment his line tightened after setting the hook. He recalled how sure he was that his line would break from the force of the five-pound fish trying to escape, and the sense of mastery he felt for having landed it. He saw the wire mesh fish basket hanging over the side of the boat, brimming with bass and walleye. Best of all he saw the look of bliss on Charlie's face as they sat across from each other at the dinner table, picking small bones from the buttery goodness that filled their mouths. The voices had been quiet for hours and Richard was at peace. "Thank you God for this very good day. And thank you for my brother Charlie," he said, closing his eyes as he prayed the simple prayer.

"YOU ARE MY CHILD AND I LOVE YOU." The reply startled Richard and his eyes flew open. For the briefest moment his defensive instincts began to rise and he started to mentally prepare himself to silence the intruding voice. Then he realized that it came from neither Author nor Melissa. It came from a place other than his head, someplace deeper inside him. As quickly as it rose his urge to lash out was washed away, and a sense of peace and warmth overtook him. He laid a hand on his chest, over the spot where the voice seemed to come from. The warmth grew inside him like a slowly building fire. It gathered strength, emanating from his center and gradually spreading to the furthest parts of his body.

"Charlie! Charlie! Come here!" he yelled.

The sound of a metal pot clanking as it hit the sink was followed by a flurry of footsteps to the cabin door. "What? What's wrong?"

"Did you hear that?"

"Hear what?"

"That voice! That voice just now!"

Charles relaxed his tensed body. "No Richie, I didn't hear anything. Are you OK?"

"Yeah. I'm OK," Richard said, rubbing his chest. "I thought I was having a heart attack or something, but it wasn't a heart attack. It felt strange and good. It felt like--"

"Are you sure you're OK? " Charles questioned as he rushed over and knelt beside his brother, stroking his hair and searching for signs of incongruence in his face. He saw only calmness and serenity.

Richard smiled. "I feel good. I think I'm OK. Thanks Charlie."

"Whew! Don't scare me like that. What did the voice--" Charles began to ask the question but decided to stop because he didn't want anything to shatter the sense of peace his brother had found. He quickly changed to a subject he thought might also add joy to the moment. "Do you want some coffee?" he asked.

"No - I'm good," Richard said, convinced that nothing would make him feel any better than he already felt.

Charles stood and walked back to the cabin door. He paused to look at his bother again, unable to recall a time when Richard had turned down coffee. *Something is either very wrong or very right*, he thought. *And I'm not sure which one it is.*

The dinner dishes had been cleaned and the kitchen put back in order. Richard sat in a deep, well-worn leather chair facing the fireplace, his arms splayed out at his sides and his eyes relaxed and heavy. Flames licked and danced about the small heap of bur oak, which crackled and spat tiny red embers onto the stone hearth. Charles' feet rested lazily on a coffee table made from a wagon wheel, which sat in front the couch on which he was lounging. Both were in a blissful trance that only full stomachs and a good fire can produce.

Charles knew they had to talk about it, but he didn't want to shatter the fragile cocoon of tranquility that had been formed over the past two days. Tomorrow morning they would return to Cutters Mill to once again shoulder the responsibilities and burdens they had left behind. And, like it or not, it was his job to help his brother cope with the real world.

"Hey Richie," Charles said, breaking the silence. "I know you probably don't want to, but we need to talk about what happened at mom and dad's anniversary party."

Richard looked away and jostled in his seat, trying to distance himself from the discomfort growing inside him.

"Tell me what happened."

"HE SHOULD TELL HIM WHAT HAPPENED. *RICHIE* SHOULD TELL," Melissa said, stating his name like it was something to be despised. "HE SHOULD TELL HIM HOW THAT SON-OF-A-BITCH OF A WAITER WANTED HIM DEAD."

Richard turned towards Charles with a look of desperation.

"Do we have to talk about this now? I don't want to talk about it now, OK?" he pleaded, covering his head with his hands and rubbing his skull to ease the mounting pressure.

"FILTHY EVILDOER!" Author's faceless voice echoed in his head.

"I hate this just like you do," Charles responded. "But we have to try and get this problem under control."

"IT WAS SELF DEFENSE!" Melissa growled.

"What problem?" Richard screamed. "I was defending myself! Do you really expect me to just stand there and let people attack me?" Richard's voice had a force behind it that had appeared suddenly, his body was now upright and rigid.

Taken back by the change in his demeanor, Charles' instinctively matched his brother's posture. "What made you think he was attacking you? He doesn't even know you! Why would he want to harm you?"

"RICHIE KNEW WHAT HE WAS UP TO!" Author and Melissa yelled in unison.

"I could read his thoughts! I knew what he was up to!" Richard said, clutching his head.

The fire issued a loud pop as Charles stretched his hand toward Richard to make his next point. "Richie, look at me."

Richard shook his head violently.

"Richie, look at me!"

Richard turned toward Charles with a frenzied look in his eyes.

Say the right thing. Say the thing he needs to hear, Charles screamed to himself. He opened his mouth to speak, still not knowing what would come out. "I love you," he said. "I just want you to know that I love you."

The words were as unexpected for Charles as they were for his brother. They softened Richard's countenance, like receiving a hug when he expected a punch. He paused and then flopped his head against the chair. "I love you too. I just... I just don't know what to do."

"There's a lot I don't know too," Charles responded. "But there is one thing I do know. I know that your fears feel like they are real, but most of them are just illusions. For some sick reason--" Charles stopped when he realized that the bitterness tainting his words would only make matters worse. "For some reason that neither of us understands, your mind plays tricks on you. Tricks that cause you to believe there are problems when there really are no problems. We have to find a way for you to recognize when this is happening, when your mind is playing tricks on you."

"How do I do that? I don't know how to do that," Richard said, the desperation returning to his voice.

"I think we should treat it like a test."

"What do you mean a test?"

"I mean that when a problem comes up, when the voices are telling you things or when you hear someone else's thoughts, you should test them to see if they're true."

"You just said that my mind plays tricks on me! How do I know what's true if my mind plays tricks on me?" Richard's agitation swelled and he raised his hands and clenched his fists.

"I know, I know," Charles reacted, also raising his hands with palms outward in a consoling gesture. "It's OK Richie, were just talking." He waited for his brother to calm down before continuing. "I think we have to have some sort of standard to measure things by."

Richard held his head in his hands again.

Charles paused to think about how he should say what was on his mind. "Do you trust me? Do you trust that I will always love you and never again... I mean never do anything to hurt you?"

Richard nodded his aching head in affirmation. "Yes Charlie, I trust you but--"

"Do you trust that I would never allow anyone else to do anything to hurt you?"

"Yes, I do. But you can't know what everyone's thinking and what's in everyone's heart."

"No, I can't know. I'm human just like you, and I'm not perfect. None of us are perfect. We're all flawed. So let's not have perfection be our goal. Nobody can be perfect, so it would be foolish to have perfection as our goal."

"Yeah, things will never be perfect," Richard sighed, dropping his hands from his head. "I know that. But I want to feel good. I just want things to be better."

Charles snapped his fingers as if a previously dead circuit in his brain had just been electrified. "That's it Richie!" he said. "What if our goal is simply to be *better* than we are now? To start moving in the right direction, towards a place where at the least we don't suffer as much and at best we are much happier?" He was encouraged by his own words, and he realized that he had used the words *we* and *our* instead of *you* and *yours* when he spoke. Somehow it seemed appropriate.

"I'd like to be happy." Richard raised his head, looking at Charles like a helpless child. "Do you think I could be happy?"

Charles had asked himself that question a thousand times, and the uncertainty of the answer was as painful as the question. "I hope for that more than anything little brother." He straightened up in an effort to tell himself and his brother that it was possible. "Now let's go back to the test we talked about, and the standard we could use to determine if things are true or not. I think the most challenging thing about this is that it will require you to change the way you think about some things," he said and then hesitated. "But I think it will work."

Richard nodded his head dully, encouraging his brother to continue.

"As screwed up as this world can be, I believe that for the most part people want to do what's right, and they don't want to hurt others. Sure there are people who are really messed up like murderers and child molesters and the like. But, there are far fewer of them than there are good folks. I believe you are surrounded by people who love and care for you - our family and friends, everyone at Alpha House. Carl!" Charles said enthusiastically. "Carl would give his right arm for you, and you've seen Carl's arms so you know what a sacrifice that would be."

Richard smirked.

The tiny bit of levity was encouraging, but Charles knew that what he was about to say had been said before - maybe not in the same way, but for the same reasons. He knew that asking his brother to rely upon his mind to discern truth was like expecting a car to run on peanut butter. He chose his words carefully. "Richie, I think you need to believe in your heart that people are generally good. You have to choose that thought over all the other thoughts and over all the voices," Charles said, emphasizing the word *choose*. "I think that's the standard you should use to measure whether things are true or not." He paused to let the words sink in.

"You said you trust me. I'm asking you to believe that what I'm telling you is true. People are not scheming against you, and they're not out to hurt you. When you start to think someone is planning to hurt you, you need to ask yourself a few questions to test whether or not it's true. Why would this person, who I know is good, do something bad to me? Is this person really a threat, or is my mind telling me to be threatened? Nine times out of ten I think you'll see that it's your mind playing tricks on you." Charles reached over and set his hand on Richard's shoulder. "You can choose to treat them like a friend instead of an enemy. The point is you get to decide if they pass the test or fail. You get to be the one in control of whether or not you feel threatened."

The words felt inadequate as they left his mouth, like sincere but desperate encouragement given to someone dying of cancer. Charles hopes hung on the idea that conducting a test with controllable outcomes might appeal to his brother, but the irony of it was like a slap to his face and he summoned all his energy to hide his doubt. *There are no rational solutions to his problems*, he told himself. *And in the end reason will not prevail.*

"Sometimes I feel like I can win the fight," Richard said. "But most times...most times I know that the evildoers are too strong for me."

He tried to subdue it, but Charles' frustration with his own doubt and his brother's willingness to cede defeat surfaced in the dry and exhausted tone of his voice. "What makes you think everyone is against you?"

"Everyone isn't against me, just the ones who have been sent to torment me! I know because of the things they say about me, the way they look at me and the things they think about me!"

Charles flopped back against the couch not knowing what to say, but the ache he felt for his brother pushed him to play along. "Who sends the evildoers to torment you?"

Richard stared blankly into the flickering red and yellow flames. "Satan," he replied flatly.

Charles eyes grew wide in terror. He gasped and then his breath left him. His stomach heaved in great spasms, and he could feel bile rising up his esophagus. Bolting from the couch, he raced to the kitchen sink and reached for a glass sitting next to the coffee maker. But the contents of his stomach had already reached his mouth and he was unable to hold it back. He vomited and the glass fell from his hand and shattered in the bottom of the sink.

All things considered, Charles was more likely to believe that evil was real than he was to believe that God and his goodness ruled the earth. But that's not what caused the physical reaction that racked his body. Instead, it was brought on by the realization that his brother thought that the most malevolent force in the universe was after him. Satan himself wanted him to suffer. Charles stomach churned again as he reached for another glass. Richard sat motionless while Charles filled the glass with water and guzzled it. He hung his head over the sink again, expecting to vomit. When he didn't, Charles closed his eyes and took deep breaths. When he opened his eyes he saw Richard's pillbox sitting on the counter, the compartments marked Saturday and Sunday were empty.

"At least Mr. Lazarus is on my side," Richard said, as a matter of fact. For him the statement was nothing more than a benign admission. But for Charles it was the slow, creaky opening of another door behind which lay the unknowable horror of his brother's mind.

"Did you say Lazarus? Who's Lazarus?" Charles choked out the words.

"A man who helps me to see what's going on so I can undo the plots of the evildoers." While uttered in his usual monotone, Richard's statement was loud and certain.

Charles was stunned into silence. *Could he be imagining a person? I can't believe this*, his mind raged. *I can't believe he has what he thinks to be a person prodding him toward his delusions. How do I compete with that? Damn it! Damn it to hell!*

Charles turned and walked abruptly back to the living room and stood directly in front of his brother. "Richie, do you actually see this Lazarus?"

"Yes. Sometimes we meet at different places, and sometimes he just shows up," Richard said, looking up from the fire to see Charles' reaction. Charles' face was pale and his jaw was clenched. "Don't worry, he's my friend," Richard added.

Charles was far from comforted. "Has anyone else ever talked to this Lazarus?" he asked.

"No, he's only here to help me."

Charles was horrified at how quickly his brother slipped from relative normalcy and into full-on dementia. He pushed through confusion and anger to try and find anything that might prevent his brother from suffering at the hands of yet another phantom.

"Is he here now?"

Richard turned towards the fire. "No, he's not here." He wouldn't admit it, but he wished Lazarus were there. *Charlie means well*, he said to himself, *but he doesn't see things the way we do.* The dying fire issued a pop.

"Listen Richie. You need to stay away from him. I'm not asking you - I'm telling you! Stay away from this Lazarus!"

Richard sighed and looked painfully at his brother. "Do you think God wants me to be well?"

The abrupt change of subject from one imaginary apparition to another threw Charles off momentarily. When the question finally landed Charles exploded. "God? Richie, if there is a god I don't think he cares for anything but himself! Why do you ask me about God? Do you plan to wait around for some sort of miracle to occur? Are you hoping that things will be better if you pray? Don't waste your time! It's a joke Richie. It's all a god damned joke and our pathetic lives are the punch line!"

Richard stared back at Charles like he was holding a knifepoint over his heart. "Charlie, you...you don't believe that God will help me?"

Charles couldn't bear to look into his brother's eyes, so he turned away. He had never come right out and told Richard that there was no god to care for him, or fix things in this life or the next. Now, as if he hadn't suffered enough, he had just told his brother that he didn't even have that hope to hang on to.

Heartless, cruel bastard! Charles silently yelled to himself. *You haven't changed at all! You're still the same mean spirited kid! You claim to look out for your brother but look at you now, standing in front of him and denying the existence of the only savior he thinks he has! Lie dammit! Lie!*

Charles wilted to his knees before his brother. "Look, I'm sorry I said that. This whole thing makes me crazy. I...I don't claim to know what God wants for any of us. But I know what I want. I want you to be well, and I will do whatever is possible to make that happen. But we need to work together. Are you willing to do that?"

Richard silently turned his eyes to the fireplace. The flame had gone out.

Nine

The clock on Carl Maznik's office wall read 2:17 PM. His eyes grew heavy as he leaned over the pile of receipts he was processing as part of the monthly budget report. He told himself he would shut his eyes for fifteen minutes and laid his head on the desk with his arm for a pillow.

Charles showed up at 3:00 PM for the meeting he had scheduled with Carl the day before. Isabel and Esther bundled up warmly and went across the street to Tainter Park to whirl on the merry-go-round and make snow angels in the two inches of powder that had fallen the night before. Charles stood at Carl's office door, not knowing if he should wake the sleeping giant. Seeing him spread out over his desk, he was amazed at the girth of his torso. He had seen Thanksgiving turkeys smaller than the muscles surrounding his shoulders. He thought about calling his name, but instead softly rapped the doorframe three times. He got no response, not even a budge. He knocked louder and still got no response. "Carl" he said, rapping three more times. "Carl!"

"Huh?" Carl responded hazily as he lifted his head from the desk. A line of drool extended from his lower lip to a small pool that had gathered on a pile of papers. He had the imprint of his wristwatch emblazoned on the left side of his reddened forehead, and he let out a deep belch when he sat upright. His eyes swollen from sleep, he slowly focused on the figure standing at the door. "Oh wow. I'm so sorry about that. I must have dozed off," Carl said, feeling wetness on his chin and wiping it. He flashed a big grin and the redness of his face deepened. "How embarrassing, I'm so sorry."

Charles was a jumble of emotions. Given the purpose of his visit he was somber, but the sight of Carl's red, drool laden and wristwatch imprinted face made him look so comical that he couldn't help smirking. Inside he was laughing uncontrollably. "No, no, no, don't be sorry," he said, letting go of a few well-controlled chuckles. "We all take a little nap now and then." It didn't seem appropriate to walk in without an invitation, so he stood at the door smiling and rocking from side to side to dissipate the energy of what felt like a tightly wound spring ready to snap inside him.

"Hey Charles, what can I do for you," Carl asked, still half unconscious.

Charles glanced at the clock on Carl's office wall, partly to draw Carl's attention to the time, and partly because he knew he would lose control if he continued to look at Carl. "Well, ah, I think we had an appointment to talk about my brother."

Carl's eyes widened as he recalled the meeting and realized he had slept for almost forty-five minutes. "Oh Yes! Of course! I can't believe I was out that long. Please come in."

The wooden chair opposite Carl's desk creaked as Charles sat. "Long day?" Charles asked with a look of restrained amusement.

"I guess so. I was doing the budget which is always a sleeper," Carl said, pointing to the paperwork on his desk. When he saw the pool of saliva floating on top of the electric bill he looked back up at Charles and burst out laughing. With that Charles let go and they both howled like hyenas during mating season. Carl's signature snort came through like trumpet blasts as he inhaled between laughs and Charles, now gasping for air, had a white knuckled grip on the arms of his chair. His body heaved back and forth uncontrollably as the tightly coiled spring inside him released its energy.

"You have the outline of your wristwatch on your forehead!" Charles yelped, barely able to get the words out for lack of breath.

Carl reached up and felt the indentation. "Oh no! What's next? Did I wet myself?" he howled, looking between his legs for signs of a stain.

Tears streamed down their cheeks, and eventually the gut busting laughs turned to delightful whimpers.

"Weh-heh-hell, I guess we should get down to business. Oh, God that was good," Carl said as he reached up to wipe his eyes, and then down to wipe his paperwork.

"Yeah, I have a feeling we'll enjoy recalling this scene many more times," Charles chuckled one last time. He exhaled long and slow and the smile disappeared from his face. "Carl," he said soberly. "Did Richie ever mention a Mr. Lazarus to you?"

Seeing the change in Charles's countenance, Carl steadied himself and thought for a moment. "I don't believe so. Who is he?"

"As far as I can tell he's an imaginary person - a delusion or hallucination, I don't know. Richie says he helps him figure out who the evildoers are."

"What?" Carl's astonishment was evident. "Are you sure? Schizophrenia doesn't often result in vivid visual hallucinations."

"I'm pretty sure. He talked about him in the same way he talks about the voices, but he seems to think of him as a friend."

"A friend? Did he say anything else?"

"Not really. I was kind of upset when we were talking about it and I just told Richie to stay away from him."

"Hmmm...well, he has had some mild visual hallucinations, and vivid ones do occur in some cases. But I'll have to look into it to see what's going on. Give me a few days to talk with him. I'll review his dosages and work up an assessment," Carl said, pausing to scratch his head. "I'll contact you again when I know more about what's going on."

Charles nodded in agreement. "Carl, there's something else I need to tell you. Richie hit a waiter over at that banquet place on Vine."

"Oh, no! What happened?"

"Well, we were at mom and dad's 50th anniversary party on Saturday and I guess Richie thought the guy said or did something and it set him off. I'm not sure exactly what happened. I got distracted with all that stuff about Mr. Lazarus and I didn't really ask. I'm sure it's the same kind of thing that's happened before."

"Yeah, the last time he got physical was about nine months ago if I remember correctly."

"That's about right. It was that lady - that lady at Fern's diner earlier this year."

The levity they had shared just a few moments earlier was now gone, and Carl could see by the look on Charles' face that he was heartbroken about what was happening to his brother. "It's so hard watching someone you love live in such pain, isn't it?" The image of Carl's autistic sister flashed in his mind. "It's like they're trapped in a glass box that surrounds them wherever they go, and their illness and all its nastiness is in there with them. They can see the outside world, they just can't get to it."

Carl continued, staring into the distance as Charles listened. "When Angie and I were kids," he said, referring to his sister, "I used to get upset with her. It was tough dealing with her illness. A few times it even made me mad. I just wanted to shake her and say 'Snap out of it!'" He paused and felt an old but familiar shame surfacing. "I actually said that once, and I'll never forget what she did. She looked at me for the longest time, searching my face, reading me. She knew. She knew that I was unhappy, and she knew that she was the cause of it." Carl swallowed hard and spread his fingers over his eyes. "Then she reached up with the tips of her fingers and gently closed my eyes," he said, pausing to relive the moment and the pain that went with it. "It was as if she was saying 'maybe it would be best if you don't look at me any more'. She wasn't being hateful; she was being empathetic." Carl shook his head in disbelief. "She was thinking about me. It was like she was telling me, 'I know this is hard for you, and maybe it would be best if you just turned away and got on with your life.'" Carl's trembling fingers stroked an eyelid. "At least that's the way it felt to me at the time."

Slipping his hand under the desk, he felt the brass key in his pocket. It was all he could do to resist slipping it into the locked drawer and retrieving the little white pills that would ease his mounting pain. "That's when I realized that Angie had no choice in the matter," he continued. "And, I realized that while her illness was a big part of who she was, it didn't completely define her. She was aware of things in a way that most people never understood. She had her own little quirks and a really unique personality," he chuckled softly. "She used to save little scraps of soap that were too small for anyone to use. When she had enough, she'd smash the scraps together with her hands to make a new bar. And she'd use that bar until it was small enough to be added to other scraps she had saved, and she'd make another new bar." The corners of his mouth curled up in a soft smile. "I don't ever recall her washing her hands or bathing with anything but her homemade soap bars."

The memories warmed Carl and he leaned back in his chair and placed his hands behind his head. "Eventually I started to appreciate her for who she was. I learned what it took to trip the triggers that would make her laugh. She would get angry and sad and needy, just like anyone else. And she could tell what I was feeling. When I got to feeling badly about some stupid thing she would sit at my feet and grab one of my ankles and hold on tight," Carl said, holding an imaginary ankle at chest level and gritting his teeth to demonstrate her grip. "'Smile!' she'd say. Charlie, she would not let go until I smiled at her. And she could tell fake smiles from real ones!" He paused again to soak in the memory of her. "We had each other for nineteen years, and then she died."

Carl's sleep swollen eyes met Charles'. "I miss her a lot. I wanted so many things for her. What do you want for your brother?"

The question took Charles by surprise, and his immediate reaction was to dismiss it. "It doesn't matter what I want for him, because he'll never have it."

"It does matter. Richard is not the only one who suffers from his illness. You suffer too, and so does your family. Not expressing your hopes and desires for him is like pretending you don't have any," Carl said, smiling tenderly. "And I don't think that's true."

Charles felt his temperature rise and his jaw tighten. "Richie does not have a normal mind and he can't just choose to be well, so why bother uttering meaningless hopes and dreams." As soon as the words escaped his mouth Charles realized that just two nights earlier he had told his brother that he could, in fact, choose to be well.

"I'm not talking about Richie, I'm talking about you," Carl replied, looking directly into Charles' eyes. "There's no harm in expressing your hopes and desires for him to someone like me. You have to find ways to talk about these things or you'll become bitter. Trust me, I know."

"I'm already bitter! And that bitterness comes from knowing he'll never have the things I want for him, the things every human being should have!"

Carl reached across the desk and placed his hand on Charles' forearm. "Maybe. Maybe not. We can't know. But, would he have any less of the things you want for him if you talked about it?"

Charles glared at Carl and opened his mouth, intending to fire back a terse response. Instead, he closed his mouth and turned his head away. Then he flopped back against the chair and pressed his hands to his eyes. Anguish-filled moments passed, and all that could be heard was the ticking of the second hand on the wall clock.

"I want him to have joy," he finally let go, his words spilling out in a whimper. "I want him to be at peace. For God's sake, I want…I want him to have romance! The love of a good woman, and the unconditional love of a child! I want him to have what I have!"

Carl placed his hand over his mouth to prevent the pain he felt from escaping his lips. He had always sensed a subtle bitterness in Charles, and now for the first time he realized why; Charles couldn't fully enjoy the blessings in his life because he felt his brother would never have those same blessings.

"Damn the sickness! And damn the sadistic god that caused it!" Charles screamed, his anger piercing the air like thunder. Both waited while the echoes subsided.

"I cursed God once after Angie died," Carl said, closing his eyes as he spoke and quietly asking God for forgiveness. "I told him that I hated him. I told him I didn't need him anymore." He opened his eyes and cleared his throat "But I've changed my mind about that…and I hope that someday you do too."

"I don't see that happening," Charles countered coldly.

Carl shook his head in empathy. "I understand. Thank you for telling me about what you want for your brother."

"Do you think he'll ever get better?" Charles asked.

"I don't know. I hope so. Some people slip in and out of schizophrenia; some come out of it and never suffer from it again; and some people never escape it."

Charles began to open his mouth to ask how many people escaped it, but he decided he didn't want to hear the answer. Instead, he just nodded his head in acknowledgement. "Brief moments of peace and lucidity overshadowed by the longest, most terrifying dreams you could possibly imagine," Charles added. "That's what Richie goes through every day."

Carl nodded, knowing that Charles was right. "Richie is welcome here for as long as he wants," he said.

Charles knew it was Carl's way of saying that his brother might never get better.

"He's lucky to have you for a brother."

"Please don't say that."

"Why not? It's true."

"Nothing I've done has helped him."

"How do you know that?"

"How many years has it been? Twenty-nine? Thirty? I've lost count. Whatever it is, we're still sitting here talking about how screwed up his life is. Not only have things not gotten better, they've actually gotten worse. Now he's got some sort of spooky imaginary friend and I..."

"You what Charlie?"

"I don't know if I can deal with it."

"Do you mean to say that you don't know *how* to deal with it?"

"No," Charles said, hesitating. "I mean to say that I don't know if I am *capable* of dealing with it."

"You're not capable?" Carl's countenance changed and he sat forward, looking sternly at Charles. "Think about what you just said. You just told me about what a nightmare his life is. He's the one living that nightmare, not you. You can't deal with it? I'm going to be blunt," he said pointedly, his outstretched finger aimed at Charles. "You need to man up! He needs you! Do not check out on him!

Carl was as surprised by his angry response as Charlie was, and for a few moments neither said anything. "Look," Carl finally said, "that didn't come out the way--"

"It's fine," Charles interrupted. "And you're right. I'm just frustrated and I'm not thinking clearly. I'm not checking out," he said, looking directly at Carl. "I will not check out on my brother."

Ten

Richard was staring blankly at some distant place when she grabbed his hand. She knew it would take a moment for him to respond, so she waited patiently while he eyed her. When he smiled, she knew it was OK to proceed. "Come on Uncle Richie, dinner is ready," Esther urged, grabbing as many of his fingers as she could fit into her tiny hand and tugging to propel him out of his chair. He stood upright after her third tug and dutifully followed her into the dining room like a puppy dog trailing after its master. The room was filled with people and abuzz with conversation. She led Richard by the hand to one of two empty seats nearest her grandfather, who sat at the head of the table. When Richard and Esther were seated the conversation quickly died out and everyone turned to Edmond Senior.

"Papa, are you going to say your words now?" Esther's prompt caused everyone to laugh.

Edmond smiled and stroked his granddaughter's cheek. "Yes I am little one, and thank you for the smart introduction."

Edmond Aaron Buell was small in stature, but he had an immense presence. Years of working timber at the mill had given him a lean physique, and he was stoic and perpetually clean-cut in an understated sort of way. His granite colored hair was neatly parted on the left, and he wore one of the ten finely pressed white linen shirts hanging in his bedroom closet. Edmond rarely attracted even the slightest bit of attention in a crowd of strangers; even with his family he was quiet and unpretentious. But his soft countenance was not caused by disinterest or shyness. He was simply a man of few words, and when he spoke his words were thoughtful and measured.

"Well, this truly is a blessed gathering. We don't often have all of us together in one room. I'm grateful to God for his many blessings, and most importantly for all of you. Let's give thanks together before we partake of this wonderful Thanksgiving feast."

Edmond prayed. The deep, even tone of his voice compelled his family to take in every word. Even those around the table who were not in the habit of praying kept their heads bowed and eyes closed, feeling certain that the simple and powerful statement of thanks for life's blessings was a good thing.

After the prayer, a moment of quiet slowly gave way to the tinkling of porcelain, silverware and glass as the family began their meal. Coming home had always been a comfort to the Buell children who didn't live in Cutter's Mill. Julia had moved to Columbus Ohio to pursue a career in IT at a large financial firm. Edmond junior thought about moving back to Cutter's Mill from Boca Raton after his divorce, but decided to stay and pursue a new relationship.

It was good to be back in the old house again. It had changed very little since they were children. The living room and dining room furniture were the same as they had always been, well crafted, gently worn but cared for, and sitting exactly where they had been placed decades ago. There were no store bought decorations on the walls, only photographs capturing family members, happy graduates and newborn babies. The mantle above the fireplace held pieces of handmade artwork from every child in the family including Esther. The church bell like chime of the grandfather clock announced each hour from its place in the living room. And, an assortment of exquisite scents filled the room: homemade apple pie, cranberry-walnut stuffing, evergreen scented candles, and freshly carved turkey.

"Everything's great mom," Edmond junior said with a mouth full of food. "How do you get the turkey to be so moist?"

"I could tell you, but then I'd have to kill you. Are you willing to die to find out?" Agnes asked with a smirk.

"Well, if I'm dead I guess that means I can't enjoy your turkey anymore, so after careful consideration I'd have to say no."

Agnes chuckled. She was a kitchen sage and she knew it. "The secret is to place pads of butter under the skin and bake it at 450 degrees for twenty minutes," she said, always eager to pass her wisdom along to others. "Then you turn the oven down to 325 and let it go until it's done, no basting."

"Huh, who would have figured it was that simple," said Edmond Junior. "Speaking of turkeys, how are things with you Charlie?"

Esther laughed and turned to her father. "Daddy, Uncle Edmond just called you a turkey!"

"Yes he did, but we must consider that Uncle Edmond's brain has softened from spending so much time in the Florida sun. He's not really aware of the nonsense that comes out of his mouth. We should feel sorry for him, I know I do." Charles picked up a pea, flinging it across the table at his older brother. It bounced off his forehead and landed in his water glass. Edmond raised an eyebrow as everyone but Agnes laughed. "It's on!" he playfully growled, picking up a glob of mashed potatoes with his spoon and raising it.

"Boys! Boys! Stop this nonsense!" Agnes intervened.

"He started it!" Edmond yelled back, lowering his spoon.

"Charles, apologize to your brother."

"I'm sorry *Eddie*," Charles said, grinning ear-to-ear and reveling in the knowledge that his brother despised the nick name Eddie.

"Apology not accepted."

"So, how are things in Florida?" Charles asked seriously. "How's work? Are you dating anyone?"

"Work is good. We've been planning a merger that's proved to be a lot more challenging than any of us thought it would be. We're supposed to have things wrapped up by the end of January, but it's looking like it may take a little longer."

"Uh huh. Are you dating anyone?" Charles asked, moving to the question he really wanted answered.

"Ma, can you pass the peas," Edmond said, fishing the little round vegetable from the bottom of his glass. "Ah, you know I've had a few dates here and there, but nothing serious."

"We're all wondering when you're going to come home with the next Mrs. Buell," Isabel added, only half joking.

Edmond forced a subtle smile, eyeing his plate and pushing his food around. "I don't think that will be happening any time soon."

Edmond's discomfort was obvious, and his sister Julia took it upon herself to change the subject. "Well I have some news," she interjected.

Everyone turned their attention to Julia as she began to speak, but her words never reached Edmond's ears. He replayed the question that had just been asked of him, but in his mind he answered in a stunningly different way than what he has just offered to his family.

I do have someone that I care for very much, he thought. *But I can't bring them home because you'd never accept them...or me.* Edmond knew his family, especially his mother and father, to be kind and tolerant. But he was sure they'd be shocked and even hurt when they discovered that the person he'd fallen in love with was a man.

It's not that he wasn't attracted to women; after all he'd been married once and had kids. He also had had several serious relationships with other women before getting married. It took him almost a year after his divorce to begin dating, but each time he was left feeling that the relationships would ultimately end as his marriage did, and for the same reasons. He concluded that he would never understand women, and they would never understand him. He needed someone he could relate to, and he had found that in Steven. He wasn't seeking a homosexual relationship, it just happened. The first several dates weren't even dates in his mind, at least not at that time; they were simply get-togethers for coffee, or dinner, or a movie. It felt a little awkward at first, but he really liked Steven and he saw no reason to stop. He was lonely and Steven filled his need for companionship.

When the relationship became sexual he felt some guilt, but not enough to call it off. The anonymity provided by living so far away from his family enabled him to continue enjoying his new companion, and with time guilt visited him less and less. Eventually he came to terms with the relationship, which had grown deeper and fed needs he had ignored for so long. Steven was the one he wanted to be with. Just a month ago Steven had brought up the idea of moving in together. Edmond relished the thought of being with him all the time, but he knew it would make it much tougher to keep their relationship a secret. He shared his concerns with Steven, who empathized with him but also suggested that maybe it was time to be honest with everyone about their love for each other. A voice in Edmond's head told him that this moment, with his family at Thanksgiving, was not the right time. Having convinced himself, he drifted back into the conversation at the table.

"Well that sounds wonderful Julia! What's the young man's name?" Agnes asked, pressing for details about her daughter's new love interest.

"His name is Fareed Mustafa."

"Fareed, Fareed," Isabel said, repeating the name in hopes that it would help her identify its origin. "I've never heard that name before, but it sounds so exotic. Where does he come from?" she asked excitedly.

"He's from the Middle East, from Egypt" Julia replied, looking at Isabel and then at her father. "But don't worry, he's not a terrorist or anything. He's in IT like me."

"Julia," her father responded. "You like him so I'm sure he's a wonderful person."

"How can you be so sure?" Charles asked jokingly. "Does he happen to have a pilot's license?"

Julia raised a spoon full of mashed potatoes ready to launch them. "Don't push me bro! I won't be as kind as Edmond!"

"Doesn't he think you're too thin?" Richard cut in, as if it was obvious that her weight should be a problem.

"Ah, no Richie he doesn't think I'm too thin," she answered tersely, quickly dismissing her brother's bluntness. *Too thin*, she thought. *You must be kidding me.*

"Richard that's rude! Now apologize to your sister!" Agnes scolded. But she and Edmond Sr. had also noticed Julia's weight loss. She had always been thin and delicate, but it seemed she had lost more than ten pounds since they last saw her.

"I'm sorry - it's just that she's so thin," Richard said, filling his mouth with food and turning to his sister. "I'm sorry, you look fine."

Julia acknowledged the insincere apology with a half-hearted shake of her head. *I understand*, she thought to herself. *You have no filter between your brain and your mouth and I just want you to stop talking now.*

"That's lovely dear. We look forward to meeting him sometime soon," Agnes added, wanting to encourage her relationally challenged daughter.

Julia took a second helping of mashed potatoes, turkey, green beans, and bread. She ate ravenously while the conversation turned to the economy, the bankruptcy of a farmer the Buell's had known for decades and other news about life in Cutter's Mill. When she had eaten her fill she excused herself from the table and went to the bathroom.

She stood in front of the bathroom mirror, and what she saw repulsed her. She pinched the skin on her cheek, which to her had the consistency of a marshmallow. She stepped back, turning to the left and right to evaluate her profile. "Bulges," she said. "I bulge everywhere." She jerked one side of her skirt down and lifted her blouse, which revealed a jutting hipbone and ribs that protruded under her skin. She placed her hand on a large black and blue colored welt over her rib cage and winced as she tenderly pressed it. *He didn't mean to do it*, she told herself. *He's a passionate man and sometimes he loses control. But he loves me; Allah be praised he loves me. I just need to be more careful about what I say to him in the presence of his friends.*

Julia pulled up her skirt and knelt at the toilet. She opened her mouth and stuck two fingers down her throat until she gagged. It took a few seconds for her to vomit, and once she did the contents of her stomach emptied into the cold porcelain bowl. When she was satisfied that she had expelled everything she flushed the toilet and rinsed her mouth with water from the sink. Standing in front of the mirror again she preened her wavy brown hair and put on lipstick and three kinds of makeup. Her hands relaxed at her sides, she stood with supreme posture and flashed a convincing smile. She imagined herself standing among her admiring friends, in her beautiful home, with her adoring husband and the three perfect children they would have. She looked so happy, so content.

You can do this, she told herself. *Fareed likes things a certain way. He likes me to look a certain way, and he's right. I owe him that. Things will be better once I've completed this transformation. Just a few more pounds – maybe two more gym workouts per week and everything will be as it should.*

"Allahu Akbar," she said smiling at the image still glowing in her head. "Allahu Akbar – God is great."

Beginnings lead to endings

And endings start anew

The flesh he wears in this life

Is just an anteroom

———————————————

In silken shroud he wraps himself

To make his earthly tomb

But grave it's not

For providence makes

A warm and restful womb

Eleven

The wall clock read 7:45 PM when Richard turned on the satellite radio that was perpetually tuned in to receive "The News of the World," a program broadcast in English by a station out of Brussels Belgium. He had tried other stations, but this was the only one he had found where the newscasters didn't make derogatory comments about him. He wasn't sure why. Maybe they were too far away to know he existed. Maybe it had something to do with the expanse of land and the mysterious waters off the eastern coast of the U.S. that separated them and kept him safe. Maybe God had blessed him with some radio friends who wanted only to keep him company. It didn't matter, they talked about things other than him and he was free to think and do as he pleased without the disruption of yet another taunting voice. Sometimes he listened intently to their reports, but tonight he wanted them only so he didn't feel alone. He turned down the volume and their muffled voices brought him comfort, much like what he felt at Thanksgiving when his family happily talked in one room while he sat by himself in another. He was close enough to hear the buzz of conversation, but far away enough to not be involved.

Richard looked at the drab, off-white walls of his apartment. They lacked any sort of ornamentation – no pictures or decorations of any sort. Only a small wall clock hung over the couch. The refrigerator, which held a number of Esther's drawings, was the apartment's epicenter of color and art.

"Pictures don't give me any joy," he said aloud, responding to his own observation about the sparseness of his home. Not only did decorations not bring him joy, more often than not they were bothersome. At one point he had set a pair of ceramic cat figurines his mother had purchased for him on the coffee table. But he didn't like the way they looked at him, so he moved them to the kitchen counter. But their presence there made breakfast uncomfortable, and after two weeks he gave them back to her and said he couldn't have them in the house.

Richard's home contained only the things he felt he truly needed: a couch and coffee table, a bed and dresser, a small kitchen table with one chair, and the most frequently used appliance, a coffee maker.

A gallon jug sat on the coffee table in front of the couch where he sat. Less than an hour ago it was filled with cold water. Now, after topping off his ice-filled glass for the ninth time, the jug was almost empty. Some time ago Author had suggested to Melissa that ice-cold water would detoxify Richard's body and prevent disease. The one Richard thought the evildoers were trying to send his way was prostate cancer. So, he made a point of emptying the gallon jug of it's icy contents each and every day between the hours of 6:30 and 7:30 PM to make sure he didn't succumb to it. He knew there was a chance he would die from lung cancer, but cigarettes were one of the few comforts he had and he was not about to give them up. If he died at least he would do it knowing he was in control and not those who sent the diseases.

"HERE HE GOES AGAIN WITH THE ICE WATER. WHAT A LOSER," Melissa said, criticizing as one does when the target of their comment is out of earshot. Richard heard every word and he knew she didn't care.

"HE'LL GET CANCER ANYWAY. HIS FATHER HAD IT, AND HE WILL TOO," Author added.

Richard couldn't make sense of why Author and Melissa now taunted him for drinking ice water. After all, detoxifying his body was their idea. His body shook violently as if the ice in his glass had somehow made its way into his veins. "No I won't get it! The cancer they sent won't survive as long as I make my body a miserable place to live!" he shouted. He waited for a response, but to his satisfaction the voices were quiet. The corners of his mouth turned up in a twitching smile and his body quivered, his satisfaction drawn from the knowledge that his counterattack had once again frustrated the malicious plans of the evildoers. In less than an hour Richard had ingested nearly a gallon of water that was only a few degrees above freezing.

His trembling hand reached for a book on the coffee table. "The Big Book of Bugs" was emblazoned on the cover in large green letters along with a close up of the head of an ant. He had taken the book from the Alpha House day room earlier that week. He flipped to the beginning of a chapter titled "The Metamorphosis of a Moth." He had read the chapter several times already, and what captivated him most was a sequence of time lapsed photographs that recorded the process of change from ordinary caterpillar to breathtakingly beautiful moth.

He read aloud slowly and deliberately in order to soak up every word. "The caterpillar's life is spent eating, growing and molting its skin a total of five times before finally spinning a cocoon from which it makes its final transformation. The stunning creature that emerges from the cocoon is the Polyphemus Moth. So big it completely covers a man's hand. Its tan colored wings consist of four sections, two large ones nearest its head, and two smaller ones nearest its tail. The center of its tail wings boast eyespots, round pools of brilliant color like wide open eyes of the deepest purple and brightest yellow." Richard drew the book closer and marveled at the stunning creature.

"You're amazing. So beautiful, and so perfect," he said, finding it hard to look away. The eyes staring back at him seemed as if they were the eyes of God. They entranced him, and after several minutes of taking in their beauty he turned his attention to the beginning of the photo series. The first photograph showed a caterpillar, a green and dirty yellow colored worm with stumpy legs and bristly hair.

I know you, he thought. *I understand you. You're sluggish and unattractive and hunted by predators. You live with the hope that you will someday become something lovely, and yet you feel hopeless because fate always seems to find a way to squash you under foot and then scrape you from the sole of its shoe.* Richard set the book down, still opened to the picture of the caterpillar and the moth. He was numbed by the weight of the words he had just formed in his mind, and amazed at how keenly those words captured how he felt about his own life. He looked back to the moth. "I want to be made into something beautiful," he said.

He emptied the remains of the gallon jug of ice water into his glass, took another large gulp and set the glass down. His body twitched and trembled as he leaned back against the couch and covered himself with a small blanket his mother had made. Closing his eyes he could feel his body begin to settle into the cold, and he convulsed less and less. Sleep, he knew, was only moments away.

Soon the darkness behind his eyelids began to give way to a faint light, which slowly revealed several members of his family - his mom and dad, Charles, Isabel and Esther. They stood over him, waiving their hands as if bidding him farewell. Their smiles were comforting and he paused to enjoy them. Then their appearance began to fade. Strand by comforting strand, a blanket of fine silken thread was spun. Like the cocoon of the glorious moth, it cradled his body. Each additional layer brought with it increasing warmth and an ever-deepening sense of peace. Soon his entire body was encased and the hazy silhouette of his family melted away.

Their image was replaced by a brilliant sunset of flaming amber and yellow, undulating against a horizon. The setting sun, he knew, would bring peace and rest. He knew with equal certainty that the sunrise and the coming day would bring with it epic transformation, the likes of which he had never known.

***

The mellow sounds of acoustic guitar and violin floated from the radio. Richard's eyes opened slowly, and he blinked a few times before realizing he was still sitting on the couch. He glanced at the wall clock, which read 9:37 PM. He had been asleep for more than two hours. Closing his eyes again, he clung to the incredible feelings left by his dream. In it he had been transformed. He had become a new creature. One that was beautiful. One that was free of the bad things.

"Don't shut your eyes again, we need to talk."

The voice startled Richard, but he knew before he spun around who was behind him. Mr. Lazarus sat at the kitchen table holding an envelope. Still dazed from sleep, Richard's mouth hung open but no words came out.

"Why are you looking at me like I just farted during Sunday prayer?" Lazarus sneered. "Did you not hear what I said? We need to talk! Get your ass up here!"

Richard stood, straightened his wrinkled shirt and combed his hair with his fingers as if he was back in school and had just been summoned to the principal's office. His reaction was immediate and unconscious, and in the moments it took him to preen himself he realized that he was once again absentmindedly following Lazarus' orders. Richard's countenance quickly shifted.

"Get out! I've had enough of you! Get out!" Richard bellowed, sternly pointing a finger at the door.

"Oh, what's this?" Lazarus chimed. "He does have a backbone. Well that's just really impressive Richard. But the question I have is why you are directing your anger at me when you should be directing it at the people who are trying to get you committed?"

"Committed? Committed to where? Nobody's trying to get me committed!"

"That's not what this letter says," Lazarus countered, waving the envelope back and forth like fish bait on a shiny metal hook.

"Is that one of Tadley's letters? The ones I took from the mail box?"

"Yes it is."

You shouldn't have opened it. It's wrong! I never should have taken it in the first place. Give it back!"

"Give it back? Give it back? What do you intend to do? Are you going to tape it closed, put it back in the mail box and hope that they don't come to get you?"

Richard opened his mouth to continue the verbal joust, but the instant he did he recalled his brother's plea – 'Stay away from Lazarus!'

He walked over and ripped the letter from Lazarus' hand. "I'll show you what I'm going to do with it!" Pulling a cigarette lighter from his pocket, he lit one end of the envelope and tilted it until flames consumed it. He took a few more steps and dumped the burning envelope into the kitchen sink.

"What the hell are you doing?" Lazarus bellowed, running to the sink and grabbing what little remained of the charred paper. He blew on it trying to extinguish the flames, but it only made them burn brighter.

"Dammit!" he screamed, throwing the blackened mess back into the sink. Lazarus turned to Richard with his fists clenched and raised. "You've really done it this time boy! That's it! You're on your own! I am through coddling you! Hell's comin' and you couldn't care less! I'll tell you what boy –"

"Don't call me boy! I'm a man and I--"

"You're a man are you? OK man I'll tell you what; you don't deserve to know who is after you! You can figure that out on your own! From now on you can handle things without me!" Lazarus turned and walked towards the apartment door. Before reaching for the doorknob he stopped and turned back toward Richard, his perverse smile cocked to one side. "Be careful of those you work with," he said in a whisper. "They are not who they seem to be." He winked and then paused long enough to see Richard's mouth drop open. Satisfied that he had produced a sufficient level of panic, he turned and walked out the door.

Twelve

Sunlight filtered through the curtains covering the bedroom window and cast a bright yellow swath across the foot of the bed. As if coming out of anesthesia, Richard's slowly emerged from a night of deep sleep. He felt warm and rested and, at this moment, nothing cluttered his mind. Still wrapped in blankets he stared at the ceiling, marveling at its texture and how the dappled patterns of the stucco finish formed shapes like clouds in a summer sky. Directly overhead he saw a turtle, and to the right there was a silhouette of an old woman. He searched the ceiling for other figures but found none. He lay there for several minutes, existing only in the moment, no past, only the present. Then a beckoning from the future overtook his desire to remain in bed. *Coffee, coffee, coffee*, he thought. *I need coffee.*

Saturday mornings were Richard's favorite. He didn't have to go to work and his schedule was usually free and easy. Unless Carl or one of the orderlies needed him for something he could do what he wanted. He removed the plastic lid from the coffee can, stuck his nose inside and inhaled deeply. The richly nutty aroma was almost like a first sip, but not quite. With masterful skill and efficiency he brought together coffee maker, coffee grounds and tap water in less time than it takes a Starbucks patron to decide which fancy flavoring or topping he should add to his soy latte.

Unlike other nights he got up only twice to pee, so he went to the bathroom to expel the last few remaining cups of water from his bladder. The fractured reflection of his face in the broken bathroom mirror reminded him how difficult his life could sometimes be. The events of the prior evening were brought back to mind, the caterpillar and the moth, Mr. Lazarus and the letter. He thought about how good it felt to have taken control with Lazarus. Snatching the letter from his hands and burning it was a good move. But Lazarus' comment about evildoers at his workplace stayed with him.

Yearning for his morning fix, Richard threw on a sweatshirt and sweat pants, filled a large mug to the brim with steaming coffee and headed for the smoking table.

Judith Krump stood in front of the kitchen cupboard, the doors of which were spread wide open. Her hands rested in the pockets of her tattered sweater and she peered over the top of oversized glasses, gazing intently at long rows of cups of different shapes and colors. Richard noticed her when he passed by on his way to the smoking table. He fantasized about her while he smoked, the two of them walking hand-in-hand along some sunlit forest path. It was a scene he had replayed many times over the past few weeks.

Judith was in the same spot when he returned. He stopped, thinking she might turn around. She didn't. She kept staring at the cups as if she was waiting for one of them to speak.

"Ahem," Richard cleared his throat to attract her attention. He got nothing.

He looked around to see if there was another way of pulling her out of her trance. Maybe he could drop something, or bang some pots and pans together like he was preparing to make breakfast. He decided to try a more subtle approach first.

He cleared his throat again. "Ahem!" Judith was unmoved. "Good morning Judith," he said. Still he got nothing.

"Judith!" he said louder this time. Her head twitched, but she didn't turn around.

"Gooood moooorning!" he said slowly and loudly one last time. Finally, she turned to face him but immediately dropped her eyes to the floor.

"Good morning Richie," she finally replied in her quiet, sad voice.

Richard paused for an awkward moment, not quite knowing how to say what had just now jumped into his mind. Finally, he got up the nerve to speak.

"Um, I was planning to go to Tainter Park in a little while. Do you want to come with me?"

Oh, that was smooth, he thought. *You should have eased your way into it! How are you doing? Have you eaten breakfast? That's a lovely sweater! You should have talked about the weather for God's sake! Why doesn't she answer?*

"OK. I'd like that," she said, her eyes still cast downward.

"You would? I mean of course you would. It's a pretty park, and there's not too much snow on the ground or anything."

You just get smoother by the minute, he thought. *Here's where she changes her mind and says she has to finish her knitting or something.*

"What time should we go?" Judith asked, lifting her eyes to meet Richard's.

"Ah, well, I have to get dressed and wash the dishes and--"

"How about 10 minutes," she interrupted.

"Um, OK. Yeah, 10 minutes is good. I'll come by your room in 10 minutes then." Richard stood for a moment trying to come up with something witty. He got nothing so he forced a smile, turned and ran headfirst into the thickly painted doorjamb separating the kitchen from the hallway. He turned again to Judith, smiling in embarrassment. "When did they put that there?" he asked rubbing his forehead.

Richard Buell had never dated a woman. In forty-four years he had not so much as touched a female in an intimate way. He thought about it and fantasized about it, but he had never had a romantic relationship. He'd never even had the innocent pleasure of holding a woman's hand. His social ineptness, the constant battle with his voices, the paranoia and fault finding with everyone he met had, up until now, prevented him from even asking someone to join him for coffee. Somehow Judith was different, and asking her to go with him to Tainter Park was like discovering that he could turn charcoal into diamonds. He didn't even know if she really liked him - for all he knew she was just bored and had nothing better to do. She was, after all, staring at coffee cups when he approached her. None of that mattered. He felt euphoric. His stomach was knotted and his head hurt from banging it against the massive doorjamb, but he couldn't keep from smiling. He anxiously paced his apartment for exactly 9 minutes and 45 seconds before leaving his room and walking down the hall to Judith's door.

Moments after his knock Judith appeared at the door dressed in an oversized brown wool coat and a fake fur hat that was pulled down to a point where it almost covered her eyes. As usual, she clutched her large purse in both hands like a mini partition between her and what ever was in front of her. Without uttering a word she walked past Richard and headed to the front door.

"Judith wait," Richard pleaded as he followed her. She stopped and turned toward Richard, who walked past her, opened the front door and held it while she passed through.

"Thank you," she said with an embarrassed smile.

They crossed the street in front of Alpha House, walked past the Tainter Park veteran's memorial and picked up a gravel path that circled the park. They strolled past a playground, band shell, and outdoor pavilion, but no words were spoken. Judith reached into her purse, pulled out her radio and began to raise it to her forehead. Richard laid his hand on her arm.

"Don't touch me!" she yelled, halting and stiffening her entire body. "Don't you touch me!"

"I'm sorry!" Richard yelled back, drawing his arm away. "I was just hoping you would talk with me instead of...instead of..."

"The family," she said, completing his sentence.

"Yeah, the family."

Judith raised the radio to her forehead. "No," she said. "I mean...I mean not yet."

Richard lit a cigarette and walked a few paces ahead of her partly because he felt rejected, and partly because he figured she wanted some privacy. He heard mumbling but couldn't make out her words. *It's OK*, he told himself. *She hears voices. I hear voices. I hope they help her.*

His cigarette was half gone when Judith caught up with him. "We're having chicken for dinner tonight," she said pleasantly.

"What?"

"Chicken. Tonight. For dinner. That's the meal – chicken." Her manner and tone suggested he should have gotten it the first time.

Richard was caught off guard by the comment and didn't know how to respond, so he said nothing.

"My mother is coming to visit tomorrow. It's been so long since we talked. I think we'll play checkers," she said playfully.

Judith's mother had been dead for almost twenty years, and Richard knew it.

"That sounds like fun. Maybe we could all play cards together too," he added, wanting to give her something to lift her spirits when she realized her mother wouldn't be coming.

They walked in silence a while longer before Richard spoke. "Judith, do you ever hope for something better?"

"No, I like chicken. I also like roast bee--"

"No, I mean from life. Do you ever hope that your life will get better?"

Judith walked along side Richard, silent again. No one had ever asked her that question before, but she had wondered about it privately many times. The thought of verbalizing a response made her feel anxious, but she decided that she wanted Richard to know how she felt.

"I feel sad a lot," she said, her voice quivering softly. "I feel scared a lot too. Sometimes I don't know..." She stopped walking and dropped her head. "Sometimes I don't know what's real. And it scares me. Sometimes I think the family isn't real, because people tell me that. But they are real; I know that. And sometimes, when I'm with certain people...like you Richie, I know you're real too."

They walked again for a while before Richard responded. "I know how you feel," he said. "Evildoers exist, even though people tell me they don't. I know that. Sometimes they're just not who I think they are."

Ironically, even though he had just mentioned them, the evildoers were not foremost in his mind. Instead, Richard realized for the first time that he had someone in his life that didn't have answers. The thought was oddly comforting. Judith would not try to heal him, because she had no idea about how to heal herself. It was a strange feeling that put him in an unfamiliar position. Maybe he could offer help instead of always being the one to receive it from others. Maybe he could confide in Judith and she could confide in him.

Taking advantage of the opportunity to suppress Richard's optimism, Author's voice lurched into his consciousness. "MELISSA, PLEASE TELL ME THAT I HEARD HIM INCORRECTLY. PLEASE TELL ME THAT RICHARD DOES NOT ACTUALLY BELIEVE THAT HE CAN HELP THIS PERSON."

"ITS RIDICULOUS," Melissa responded dryly. "HE WILL DO MORE HARM THAN GOOD. NOTHING BUT MORE PAIN AND CONFUSION WILL COME OF THIS."

Pushing past the uncertainty placed in his mind by the two tormentors living there, Richard spoke. "I think maybe we could help each other," he said, fiddling with the zipper on his coat. Then he stopped walking, knowing that he should speak but unsure about what he would say. "Judith," he said, pausing abruptly to gather his thoughts.

"Yes?" she prompted him.

"Judith, do you know that I would never hurt you?" The words seemed to come out on their own and he wasn't sure why he had spoken them.

She raised her head and stared with wide glistening eyes for what seemed to Richard to be an almost unbearable amount of time. "That means a lot Richie," she finally relented. "Thank you for saying that."

Richard looked down and fumbled with his zipper again. "Judith." He liked saying her name, so he said it again. "Judith, I think I heard the voice of God."

She walked forward and stopped in front of him, her eyes never leaving his. She smiled and gasped, covering her mouth with her hand. "What did he say?" she asked, trembling with anticipation.

"He said that I was his child," Richard's voice cracked. "And, he said that he loves me."

Judith jumped up and down and clapped her hands. "Oh, I knew it! I knew it!"

"You knew what?" Richard asked, confused but laughing along with Judith.

"I knew I wasn't the only one!" she exclaimed, continuing excitedly but in a measured fashion as if she wanted to get her story exactly right. "One time this past summer I heard a voice that was very different. I was in my room, and I was just sitting there thinking about my aunt Sylvia and her dog Otis. Otis is her bulldog and he's very cute, but they had to neuter him and he slept for a week. Anyway, I was just sitting there and all at once I heard a voice say, 'You mean everything to me.'" Judith paused to allow the words to sink in; her eyes brightening in a way Richard had never seen before. "I know it wasn't anyone from the family because my radio was…well it doesn't matter. I jumped up and looked around the room, and as I was looking I heard it again. 'You mean everything to me.'" Hearing the words come from her mouth made her gasp again. She had never shared the experience with anyone. "Richie," she continued, "I started to get this warm feeling and I thought I was going to faint, so I sat down. But the warmth felt so good. It was like the time my mother took me to Bertrand's Bakery for hot cocoa and apple strudel when I was seven…" her voice trailed off as if something more pressing had come to mind. "I miss my mother. I hope she can come tomorrow," she added, pressing a hand to her eyes.

Richard wrapped his arms around her and she buried her head in his chest. "If I mean everything to him, then why? Why am I living like this?"

Richard wanted more than anything to answer her question in a way that would give her hope, but he didn't know how. "I don't know why things turn out the way they do", he said. "I've spent years being mad about it. I'm still mad about it. Life just happens, you know? How we handle it is what matters most though. It's up to us. Maybe God is just trying to tell us that we don't have to do it alone."

Richard released his embrace and led Judith to a park bench alongside the gravel path. He sat first, and Judith sat next to him. Her body slumped forward and she folded her hands in her lap. She tried hard to suppress her crying, but soft sobs escaped her lips.

"Are you OK?" Richard asked.

"No. I feel scared and alone," she said, dabbing at the corners of here eyes.

"You're not alone."

Judith reached for Richard's hand and rested her head on his shoulder.

He cast a panicked stare at the top of her head, unsure of what he should do next. *She laid her head on my shoulder*, he said to himself, stunned and thrilled at the same time. *Her head is on my shoulder, and I am comforting her*. Reaching up, he rubbed the throbbing walnut sized lump on his forehead. Then the corners of his mouth turned slightly upward and he placed his other hand on her shoulder, squeezing it gently.

Thirteen

Breakfast consisted, as it always had, of a large bowl of plain oatmeal, a mound of cooked spinach smothered in butter, and a tall glass of orange juice. He would completely consume the oatmeal before moving on to the spinach. It's the way he had always done it. Richard sat at the kitchen table gobbling the bland tasting goo in large spoonfuls and washing it down with a swig of OJ after each bite. The sun that had lit his weekend was gone, and the ashy Monday morning sky released tiny white flakes that angled past the living room window. The sweeping motion of the snow entranced Richard and he stared out the window as he ate the morning's porridge.

He had decided upon his daily menu long ago. The criteria driving his choices, he had told himself, were disease-fighting nutrition and ease of preparation. "You are what you eat," his mother used to say. And he believed it. With the right foods he was certain his body would fend off disease like Iron Man deflects bullets. And preparing meals would take no more than a few simple steps.

A nutritionist assigned to assess his diet had once told him that he needed more variety in the foods he ate. But Richard dismissed the advice, believing he had made his choices thoughtfully and deliberately. In reality the comfort he felt with the foods he had selected had nothing to do with tastes he enjoyed. Pleasure was irrelevant. Avoiding pain was not. Like two food critics living inside his head, Author and Melissa had tormented him until he ate what he was told to. So, like breakfast, lunch and dinner were always the same. Lunch included a bologna or tuna fish sandwich, potato chips and a soda. Dinner was pizza or canned salmon - eaten right out of the can – and some sort of frozen vegetable. He was allowed milk during mealtimes, and every now and then he could have egg rolls. No matter what he ate it was always coated in a heavy layer of salt, the only thing that seemed to awaken his smoke damaged taste buds.

Richard brought his dishes to the kitchen sink and washed them. Then he picked up the pill container sitting next to the coffee pot, opened the lid marked Monday and dumped all five pills down the drain.

***

"Is the guy going to press charges?" Connie Trapoli asked as she held the phone to her ear.

"No, apparently he has someone in his family with a mental illness," Carl said, referring to the waiter Richard had assaulted at his parent's anniversary party. "I guess he's seen enough of it to know how hard it can be," he added and then paused momentarily. "Connie, there's something else. Charlie came by the other day and told me that Richard may be imagining a person; someone he calls Mr. Lazarus. Do you know anything about that?"

"You mean a person - like an actual being?"

"Yeah, I was surprised as well. He says that he helps him figure out who the evildoers are."

"Wow. Ah, no, that's a new one to me. I have not seen or heard anything that would indicate that Richard imagines an actual person. I must say that concerns me."

"It concerns me too. I wanted to talk with you about it before I speak to him."

"Well, I'd like to know what I should do," Connie said with concern in her voice. "Is it safe to have him working here around other people?"

"It's hard to know for sure, but I am inclined to say we should probably play it safe. The incident with the waiter is the first one in about six months, and I did speak with him about it. He says he's sorry about what happened, but this Lazarus thing has me a little concerned. I need to talk with him, maybe reassess his meds."

Connie twisted a lock of her hair, as she had the habit of doing when she was thinking. "He's at his workstation now. How about if I tell him that you requested he go back to Alpha House right away?"

"That's fine, but don't say anything about this Lazarus. It might upset him," Carl said, knowing that Connie was a professional and would no doubt handle the situation with tact and empathy. "I'll be here when he arrives. Thanks for helping out."

"No problem Carl. Richard is a sweet guy and I want to help in any way I can."

Connie hung up the phone and peered over the top of her cube wall. She looked through a throng of swiftly moving employees and piles of boxes and caught a glimpse of Richard's unkempt sandy colored hair and his headphones, which he had not asked permission to wear. She waded through the sea of activity to Richard's workstation and motioned to him to remove his headphones. "Good morning Richard," she said cheerfully, deciding not to mention the headphones.

Richard stared blankly at her as if her greeting had not yet registered. "Hi," he finally responded, his voice as flat and unenthusiastic as a New Jersey tollbooth operator.

"Can we talk for a moment," she asked, motioning towards her office.

Again Richard stared and took his time before responding. "Yeah. What about?"

"Well let's not start here, come on back and we'll talk about it."

"SHE'S ON TO HIM," Melissa said, whispering as if Connie could hear.

Richard blinked and shook his head as if trying to rid himself of an annoying fly, repeatedly flitting about and then landing on his scalp.

"MR. LAZARUS WAS RIGHT. SHE'S AN EVILDOER," Author whispered back.

Richard shook his head again and swatted at the air.

Connie took a half step back, circling Richard with her eyes but finding no insect. "Are you OK?" she asked. "You seem a bit distracted."

Richard pawed at his face and then looked at Connie. "My brain is burnt," he said flatly. The creases etched into his face grew deeper and darker as he spoke. "You know? My brain. It's burnt."

Connie placed her hand on Richard's forearm, which stiffened as soon as she touched it. "Let's go back to my desk," she said, looking into his eyes and trying to discern his mental state. "Come on, let's talk."

Richard nodded and began to follow her. He had taken only a few steps when things began to change. A comforting numbness moved in, as if he had taken a strong sedative. Movement in the shop slowed down considerably and his field of vision curved inward at the edges, as if he was looking through a parabolic lens. The sounds of the shop floor melded together into a low, resonant hum. He moved effortlessly as if he was floating forward with his feet inches from the ground. Then the movement stopped.

"Would you like to take your coat off?" Connie asked as she sat behind her desk.

Richard did not respond. A fluorescent light flickered overhead, but he paid no attention to it. Instead, he stared straight forward, unblinking.

"You can go ahead and sit if you like," she said, motioning to an old wood and leather chair sitting in front of Richard.

Moments went by before he responded. "I'd rather stand," he said.

"Richard it's OK, were just talking. Please sit."

Several seconds passed again and he issued a slow shake of his head, indicating that he understood. Still he remained standing.

Connie let out a sigh. "OK, you want to stand. No problem. Richard, Carl and I were talking and he--"

Suddenly, a surge like electricity jolted Richard's body and he gasped, his mouth and eyes opening wide. Connie froze, unsure of what was happening. The haze he was in had vanished, and his senses were suddenly revived like he had received a shot of adrenaline. There were pronounced contrasts between light and shadow, foreground and background. All the colors in Connie's cubicle including the black of her desk blotter jumped out at him. His sense of hearing and smell peaked dramatically, as if he was instantaneously relieved of a severe head cold. He could feel with exquisite sensitivity the fabric of his shirt and pants as they pressed against his skin. Richard's lips curled into a self-indulgent smile, unaware that Connie was eyeing him.

"Richard, have you been taking your medications?" she asked as she reached for the desk phone.

He didn't answer. Instead, he opened the flap of his coat, reached inside and retrieved a 12-inch steel crescent wrench. He didn't recall picking it up on the way to Connie's cube. He only knew that it was there, waiting to be used.

Connie's eyes widened at the sight of the thick hunk of gleaming metal. She retracted her hand from the phone and inched back in her seat. "What are you doing with that wrench?" she asked anxiously.

Richard looked at her with a fierceness she had not seen before - like the look a ravenous lion gives to a gazelle just before he wraps his jaws around her neck. "Connie," he spoke calmly, "I'm going to ask you a question, and I need you to be honest with me." He moved the wrench from his left hand to his right hand. "Are you planning to have me committed?"

"Richard, you're scaring me," Connie said, placing her hands on the desk and shifting her weight forward as if she was about to rise from her chair.

"Never mind," he said coldly. "I think I know the answer."

Richard stepped to the side of her desk, raised the wrench above his head and swung hard. Connie instinctively raised her hands to guard herself but the weight of the wrench and the force of his swing broke through. The blow landed with a hollow thud as it made contact with the top of her skull. She fell off her chair and landed on the floor to the right of her desk. Richard knelt next to her body and raised the wrench again. "Be careful of the people you work with. They are not what they seem," he said, before striking her again. This time the blow landed on the left side of her face, just above her jaw.

He stood up and stared wide eyed at her lifeless body. His right hand began to shake violently and the wrench dropped from his hand, clanking against the concrete floor. He looked around frantically to see if anyone had noticed, but no one was in sight. He looked back down to her body. Blood ran down her face and pooled on the floor. She was not moving.

Richard began to hyperventilate. Again, he knelt beside her body. But this time he began going through the pockets of her blue jeans. He found nothing. Standing up, he began scanning her desk and credenza. There were piles of paper, packaging materials, and small parts strewn about. His eyes landed on a small ceramic dish. Walking quickly to it, he reached in and plucked out a set of keys and stuck them in his coat pocket. Hurriedly, he walked out of the cube with his head down to avoid eye contact with anyone he might meet on his way out of the building. He passed the bathrooms and some storage shelves before reaching the break room. "Thomas! Anyone but Thomas!" he mumbled to himself as he approached the area where his coworker sat.

"Hey Richard, I pinched my thumb so they--"

"Not now Thomas!" Richard interrupted. "I have to go!"

He whisked past Thomas, past the time clock and water fountain and out the shop door.

Snow dusted gravel crunched under his feet as he quickly made his way to the end of the lot where the staff parked their cars.

"Green Toyota! Green Toyota! Green Toyota!" he said aloud, nervously scanning the lot for Connie's car.

"Where is it? Where is it?" he blurted, darting from car to car and hoping that either Author or Melissa would assist in his escape. Still he saw no green Toyota.

Suddenly, Richard remembered the keys he had taken and pressed the little horn icon on the remote. Three loud honks pulsed through the air before he was able to press the button again to silence the horn. He followed the sound and found her car hidden behind a large white Chevy Suburban near the end of the parking lot. His hands were shaking hard. He fumbled with the remote control on the key ring as he tried to unlock the doors. The key ring fell to the ground and Richard's eyes darted around the lot as he reached down to retrieve it and try again. This time a clunking sound indicated the doors had unlocked.

It had been a year and a half since Richard had driven a car. But he wasn't concerned about that, he was thinking only about leaving. He stuck the key in the ignition, started the car and put it in reverse. Easing out from behind the huge Suburban, he noticed that the door leading to the shop was open. He hoped that he had left it open and not someone who had already discovered his crime and would at any moment jump in front of Connie's car to stop him from leaving. If that happened, he decided, he would not hesitate to drive over them. He put the car in drive, trying hard not to accelerate too quickly as he drove past the shop door and onto the drive that connected with the main road in front of the building.

Once he left gravel and hit tar he floored it. The tires squealed as he roared through the small industrial park. He blew through two stop signs before deciding it would be best to slow down a bit. He approached the intersection at Route 17. A turn to the left would lead to downtown Cutters Mill. A turn to the right would take him northward, and away from his hometown. Richard turned right. He was hyper sensitive about his speed and position on the road. He needed to escape and foolish mistakes would attract attention. Nervously he eyed the rear view mirror. Sweat glistened on his forehead and upper lip. He reached inside his coat pocket for a cigarette and lit it. Oddly colored smoke plumed upward, and his lungs locked up as he inhaled the first puff. Coughing violently, he pulled the cigarette from his lips and saw that he had lit the filter end instead of the tobacco. He rolled down the window, threw the cigarette out and quickly replaced it with another that was properly lit.

The nicotine did not calm him. Soon, Richard began rocking back and forth in exaggerated movements, trying to expel the devastating realization of what he had done. "Oh no!" he cried, his face twisted in terror. "I killed Connie! I killed her! I killed Connie!"

He gripped the steering wheel hard and his lower lip began to quiver. "Ahhhhhhh!" he screamed with all the force his lungs could produce.

"Oh no! Please God noooo!" he screamed again, his body shaking and convulsing as he cried out.

Slamming on the brakes, the car skidded to a stop in the middle of the road. Richard lunged forward, slamming his head against the steering wheel. "Get out! Get out of my head and leave me alone!"

Again he slammed his head against the steering wheel, this time with enough force to cut a gash in his forehead. Then, he reached up and frantically clawed his face with his fingernails, tearing his skin and drawing more blood.

"What the hell are you doing?"

In the back of his mind, Richard knew that Lazarus would show up. He always had. The old man was always there when he messed up. He was dependable in that way. But in this moment Lazarus was the last person he wanted to see.

Richard swung hard at the passenger seat with his right hand. It traveled through Lazarus' body, hit the headrest and bounced back. He swung again, this time aiming for his chest. Again, his hand passed through Lazarus and hit the seat as if he was nothing but vapor.

"What's this? Now you're taking a swing at me? You want to hit me now?"

"You're not real! You're not real! Get away from me! I don't want you near me! Look what you did!" Blood ran down Richard's forehead and cheeks. "Look what you did!"

"Look what I did?" Lazarus returned fire. "What did I do? My whole god damned existence revolves around you! I look out for you! I protect you! And this is the thanks I get!"

"You lied to me!" Richard's entire body heaved the words with such force that spit flew from his mouth as he spoke.

"I lied to you?" Lazarus screamed with equal force. "You stupid son-of-a-bitch! I lied to you? You live in an upside down world Richard!"

Lazarus thrust his anger-contorted face close to Richard's, the rancid, rotting-flesh smell of his breath assaulting his nostrils. "You lied to you!" Lazarus screamed. "There isn't a thing you do or say that isn't of your own making! Your own choice! You are your own enemy!"

Turning forward, Lazarus slammed his fists into the dash. Richard's raspy labored breaths were all that broke the frenzied silence that followed. Each moment that passed brought him closer to the truth about what he had done, and who he had become. Slowly his breathing calmed, and he rested his body against the seat back.

"I did it," he stated matter-of-factly. "I did this terrible thing, and now I have to pay for it."

Lazarus stared out the windshield, his mind calculating, his knotted hands still pressed hard against the dash. "Drive boy," he said, still looking straight ahead.

"What?"

"Drive, damn it! Drive the car!"

Richard grabbed the steering wheel, put the car in gear and floored it.

"Where are we going?" he asked, looking frantically about.

"You know damn well where we're going! Just drive!"

Fourteen

Agnes Buell stood over the kitchen sink and stared helplessly out the window as the coffee maker gurgled and hissed beside her. She and Edmond had received the news of Richard's attack less than an hour earlier. Gripping the counter, she allowed herself to cry for a brief period and then composed herself enough to speak. "Father, our boy is lost again," she said, her voice strangled by the tightness in her throat. "He's lost and we need to find him. Please be with him now. Hold him until we can hold him again. Please forgive him for what he's done. My sweet boy would never hurt anyone. There's something inside him that makes him do these terrible things! It's not him!" she blurted in a hushed but forceful tone, biting her lip to allow her mounting anger to recede. "But my boy is inside there somewhere, and I want him back."

She raised her head and wiped hot tears from her wrinkled cheeks. "I also need to ask for your forgiveness. I've tried to understand, but I can't. I can't understand why he has to suffer so much. I know life is unfair; it's unfair for everyone. But Richard's illness is unbearably cruel! It's a living hell! Why? What good can come of it? I want him to be well. I want him to have peace. Won't you do tha--" Her impassioned prayer stopped abruptly when she felt a hand come to rest on her shoulder.

"Are you alright dear?" Edmond asked, having walked in from behind her.

"No," she said indignantly. "I'm not alright. I'm scared - I'm scared for our boy." She paused and wrung her apron into a knot. "And I'm mad at God!"

Wrapping his hands around her waist, Edmond pulled her in tight. "I'm scared too. But we need to be strong and do what we can to help Richard. Sheriff Langford is here. We should go and talk with him."

Still in Edmond's embrace, Agnes turned around to face him. She laid her head on his chest and breathed deeply for a few moments. The smell of his cologne steadied her. She stood upright, straightened her rumpled apron and nodded towards the kitchen door. "I'll bring out the coffee," she said.

"Can I help?"

"No, I'll be out in a moment."

"OK love. It's gonna be OK," Edmond responded before kissing her on the cheek and walking out to join the others.

Bending slightly, she wiped her moist eyes with the checkered cloth of her apron. She gathered cups, saucers, sugar, cream and spoons and placed them on a large wooden tray along with a carafe of coffee. She took another deep breath. "Please help us find Richard," she asked resolutely.

Charles, Edmond, Carl Maznik, Sheriff Langford and Deputy Steinmitz were sitting in the living room when Agnes entered.

Everyone stood as she approached. She set the tray on the coffee table and walked up to Sheriff Langford. His policeman's cap was tucked under his arm. His graying hair, which was swept to one side, reminded her of how long he had been a friend of the family. She reached up and laid her hand on his chest, which was covered by a deep blue, finely pressed shirt and an unzipped black leather jacket. Light glinted off the two gold sheriff's insignia attached to each side of his collar.

The sheriff bent down to kiss her cheek. "How are you?" he asked.

"I've been better Jimmy."

He shook his head, "I know you're hurting right now. What happened is terrible. We're all very concerned, and we are going to do everything we can to find Richard and get him the help he needs."

"You're right about that. But first things first," she added soberly. "How is Connie doing?"

The sheriff raised his head and drew a breath. "She's hurt pretty badly. Her left cheekbone is shattered, and her skull is fractured. There is some swelling and she has a serious concussion."

Agnes gasped and covered her mouth.

"But the doctor says she's gonna pull through - she should pull through," the Sheriff added, his voice trailing off and punctuating the uncertainty and gravity of her condition. "Her family is understandably upset. I expect they'll be pressing charges."

Everyone stood in silence, agonizing over the fate of Connie and Richard.

Feeling the urgency of the situation, deputy Steinmitz blurted a question. "Do you know where Richard is at?"

The sheriff quickly threw him a look, and he knew instantly that the question had come across as abrupt and disrespectful. "Sorry," he muttered.

"There is no need for apologies Pete," Edmond jumped in. "Let's get on with it. Time is wasting."

Everyone nodded in agreement.

"OK, let's get started," the sheriff said. "All we know is that Richard took Connie's car. But nobody at Colbourne seems to have a clue about where he went. Does anyone have any ideas?"

"Sometimes he rides his bike up to Peek's Hill when he wants to be alone," Carl said, looking to Edmond and Agnes for their agreement.

"OK, we'll check that out."

"Ah, not too long ago he talked about wanting to go to Saint Louis to see the arch," Edmond added. "But, he talks about a lot of things like that and never does them. Besides, I doubt he's thinking about vacationing now."

"It's slim, but we'll contact the Saint Louis PD," Sheriff Langford replied, nodding to the deputy who began taking notes.

"Charlie, what about you? Where would Richard go if he was scared or troubled?"

"That's the problem Jim. When he's scared he tends to separate himself from everyone. He goes where there are no people. That could be just about anywhere," Charles added, knowing that he wasn't being completely honest.

"Does he have a cell phone? Could we try calling him?"

"No. No cell phone," Agnes interjected as she picked up the carafe and began pouring coffee for the deputy.

Blowing away the rising steam, he sipped. "Who saw him last?" he asked.

"I guess that would be us," said Agnes. "He came over to do laundry and have dinner two days ago. Today's Thursday--"

"Tuesday," Edmond finished his wife's sentence. "We had dinner on Tuesday. He likes his mom's enchiladas."

"Did he act any differently? Did he say anything at all that might help us to understand where he might have gone?"

"The usual stuff," Edmond said, stroking his upper lip as he thought. "He complained about the voices, but that's not uncommon. He talked about how he wanted to do something other than fold boxes at work. He ate, smoked a few cigarettes outside, grabbed his laundry and left. That's all I remember."

Agnes directed her attention to her son. "Charles, are you sure he didn't try to contact you? Sometimes he goes to you when he's got a problem."

"No Ma, I already called Isabel and she said he hasn't called or come to the house."

"Have you contacted other police departments?" Charles asked, directing his gaze at the sheriff.

"Yup, we already alerted all the PD's in the surrounding counties. Many of them already know Richard from previous incidents," the sheriff's words trailed off as he realized they would only add to the Buell's suffering. "Sorry," he said, looking first at Edmond and Agnes and then at Deputy Steinmitz.

"It's OK Jimmy!" Agnes said firmly. "I want you all to stop walking on eggshells around us! You're right. A lot of Police know Richard. Maybe that sad fact will prove useful to us now."

"OK. We'll get started on what we have," the sheriff said, thankful for the mental and emotional toughness Agnes and Edmond had always displayed regarding their son's illness. "If any of you hear anything at all please contact me or Pete right away."

Sheriff Langford and Deputy Steinmitz shook hands with everyone and began to leave. The sheriff stopped short of the front door and turned around. "I won't mince words here," he said soberly. "Richard is in serious trouble. The sooner we find him the better it will be for him and everyone else. Let's all pull together." Everyone nodded in agreement and the two officers left.

As the deputy backed the police cruiser out of the driveway, the sheriff turned to him. "Pete, since you're working this case with me there are some things you should know. The Buell's are good folk, and I would do just about anything for them. Charlie and I have been close friends since elementary school."

"Yeah, I know you guys are pretty tight."

"We are, and Charlie's a great guy. But sometimes," the sheriff added, shifting in his seat, "sometimes he has a temper. Especially when it comes to his brother."

"How so?"

"Well he's sensitive about others hassling him. And he really doesn't like it when he thinks Richard is being threatened."

"Who's threatening him? Isn't he the threat here?"

The sheriff glanced at Pete and paused for a moment, knowing he had very little history with the Buell family. "One time," he continued, "when we were still in high school, tenth grade I think, Charlie, Richard and I were walking back from Marshall's drive-in on a Saturday evening. We ended up running into Zach Wolf and a couple of his buddies. Now Zach has mellowed out a lot, but back then he was an asshole. He was loud and obnoxious, and sometimes he could be just plain mean. He was one of those guys that liked to pick on the weakest or shyest person in a crowd - a real jerk. So he started picking on Richard. We all tried to ignore it and walk away. But then he made a mistake that I am sure he regrets to this day."

"What happened?"

"He called Richard a retard," the sheriff said, shaking his head in disbelief as he recalled the memory. "Man, did he pay for that. It all happened so quickly I barely even saw it. Charlie turned around, walked up to Zach and threw a kick that hyper-extended his knee."

"He hyper-extended his knee? Like, bent it in the wrong direction?" Pete asked, wincing at the thought.

"Ninety degrees in the wrong direction. I heard it snap," the sheriff added, rubbing his own knee as if he could feel the ligaments and cartilage ripping away from the bone.

"Ouch!" Pete cried, also grabbing his knee to ease the pain he imagined.

"Yeah, and he was just getting started. When Zach hit the ground Charlie jumped on top of him and just beat the living hell out of his face. From beginning to end the whole thing only lasted seven or eight seconds. But when he was done, Zach had lost three teeth and his nose and jaw were both broken. Zach's buddies and I were barely able to get Charlie off of Zach. We had him for a moment, but he managed to get away from us and he jumped Zach again. I thought he was gonna continue the beating, but instead he pulled Zach off the ground by grabbing his shirt and the hair on the back of his head. I don't know how he did it because Zach's leg was completely broken, and Zach's a big guy. But he held him up in front of Richard and told him to apologize. Zach was spitting blood and teeth and he knew what was coming if he didn't apologize. So he did. Then Charlie just let him drop to the ground and he walked away."

"No way! Charlie doesn't seem like the kind of guy who would do that."

"Like I said, I've known him most of my life and he's not normally a violent guy. But when it comes to his brother it's different. He's hyper-protective."

Tiny, wet snowflakes flecked the windshield and the Sheriff gazed into the sky as he continued. "Word got out around school about the beating he gave to Zach. After that nobody who new Charlie ever bothered Richard again. Over the years there have been a few other incidents with people who weren't aware of

Charlie's, how can I say this, um… pit-bull like intolerance of Richard bashing. Fortunately, I don't think anyone else paid as high a price as Zach Wolf."

"Wow! What triggers that kind of aggression?" asked Pete.

"I don't know, he would never tell me. But whatever it is it runs deep inside him."

"Why are you telling me this?"

"I'm telling you because although Richard brought this on himself, he is in a threatening situation. And now you know how Charlie Buell reacts when his brother is being threatened."

"Are you saying that we need to be careful of Charlie?"

"It's hard to say," the sheriff paused. "This situation is going to be tense. Richard is going to be arrested and it could go to trial. If it does, people are going to say bad things about him." The sheriff looked into the Deputy's eyes. "Charlie Buell will do just about anything to protect his brother. We just need to keep that in mind."

***

Charles hit the speed dial button on his cell phone and put it to his ear.

"Hi Chabela, it's me."

"Where are you?" Isabel asked with concern in her voice.

"I just left mom and dad's house. But I'm going to the cabin."

"The cabin? Why are you going to the cabin?"

"There's a chance that Richie may have gone there in Connie's car."

"Is Jim with you?"

"No Chabela. I'm going on my own," Charles said, pausing. "I didn't tell Jim about the cabin."

"Charlie! Jim is your friend and he's the sheriff. He's involved in this now. Why didn't you tell--"

"You don't understand," Charles interrupted. "Jim has good intentions, but I know Richie and he's scared out of his wits right now. He knows he's in trouble and he won't do well with the police, even if it is Jim. I need to calm him down first and then I'll bring him in."

"Charlie, are you sure--"

"Isabel, I said I'd bring him in!" he responded forcefully. "I'll bring him to the police department myself."

"It worries me, but OK. I'll be praying for you and Richie. How's Connie?"

"Jim says she has a broken cheek bone and a skull fracture. But he thinks she'll pull through OK."

"I'll pray for her too," Isabel said, choking back tears. "You be careful. I love you."

"I love you too. Tell Esther I'll be home soon."

Charles turned onto Route 17 and accelerated to eighty miles per hour. The speed limit was fifty-five.

Fifteen

Richard pulled Connie's car onto the long leaf covered gravel driveway leading to the cabin. He crushed out his cigarette in the ashtray, which was piled high with butts he had put there during the three and a half hour drive. A leafless tree branch hung low over the driveway and scraped against the car as he eased forward, making a sound like fingernails raking against a chalkboard. Four pairs of spooky red dots floated and bobbed in the driveway ahead of the car, the headlights of which stretched outward to reveal a family of raccoons as they scampered away from the swath of light and into the trees.

Coming to a clearing near the end of the driveway, the car's headlights illuminated a sturdy rustic looking log cabin with a wraparound porch and corrugated steel roof. Richard stopped the car on a small gravel parking area next to the cabin. When he turned off the engine and lights the world outside went black. Knowing he would need light to get inside the cabin, he turned the car on again and backed out until the headlights illuminated the front door.

He stepped out of the smoke-choked car and into the crisp night air. The sweet scent of apples and decaying leaves enlivened his senses and he raised his nostrils to inhale the autumn perfume. Even though he couldn't see it he knew that there was fruit lying at the base of the apple tree growing alongside the cabin. He thought about the white tail deer he had often seen from the kitchen window, devouring the last remaining remnants of summer food to fatten themselves before the sparseness of winter set in. He zipped his coat and put on his raggedy stocking cap. Then he knelt down to pick up one of the fist-sized rocks lining the gravel path leading to the porch steps. Approaching the door, he turned the knob to make sure it wasn't open. Then he placed the rock next to the glass window on the top half of the door. He took three practice swings without making contact with the glass. On the forth swing the rock shattered the lower right corner of the window. Richard threw the rock off the porch and pulled out the few shards of glass that would prevent his arm from fitting through the jagged opening. Reaching inside, he unlocked the door handle and deadbolt. The light above the kitchen table flickered after he hit the switch on the wall just inside the door. He waited as the bulb came to life, his right hand lazily twitching back and forth at his side.

Raking at his face, he drew a deep breath and sighed. "I'm sorry Charlie," he said imagining his brother's disappointment. "I'm sorry I broke your door."

Richard went back outside to turn off the car's lights. When he returned, Lazarus was sitting at the kitchen table. Richard tried to pretend he wasn't there, and Lazarus didn't say a word but watched as Richard turned on the heat and rummaged through the cupboard to find coffee. Peering disdainfully at Lazarus out of the corner of his eye, Richard poured grounds into the coffee maker and filled it with water. Then he went outside to the porch, closing the door and leaving Lazarus inside.

He sucked down a cigarette, periodically glancing through the window to see Lazarus sitting motionless at the table, his hands splayed out on the tabletop and his eyes staring straight ahead. Dreading the thought of going inside again, Richard lit up a second cigarette and took his time smoking it.

The rich, nutty smell of freshly brewed coffee wafted through the broken window on the front door. It was more than Richard could bear, so he went inside, walked past Lazarus without acknowledging his presence and poured himself a cup. The hot brown liquid simultaneously burned and soothed as he stood at the counter, gulping it down. Accepting the inevitable he filled his cup again, walked over to the table and sat directly across from Lazarus. He drank in silence, periodically eyeing Lazarus and trying not to convey his desperation.

Eventually it was Lazarus who broke the silence. "Now what?" he asked, his cold blue eyes staring at the tabletop.

Richard didn't have an answer to Lazarus' question. He turned his gaze to the large picture window next to the table. It revealed nothing but the black of night. But Richard knew that within the darkness were thousands of trees; trees that stood defiantly even though they were ravaged by cold and dehydration. *A season of death is upon them*, he thought to himself. *Yet they refuse to lie down and die*. He remembered the beautifully colored Indigo Buntings and noble looking Cedar Waxwings that inhabited the woods around the cabin in summertime. And he wondered if they were huddled against some tree, expending their last bit of life energy in a desperate attempt to fend off death. Richard felt that death was also closing in on him, but he decided he was not yet willing to give up trying to live. Unsettling as it was, turning to Lazarus for help was his only option. Richard had come to hate him, but he felt he had no choice in the matter.

He reached inside his coat pocket, pulled out three white envelopes and set them on the table.

"What's this?" Lazarus asked with feigned indifference.

"Some of the letters I intercepted from Tadley on Saturday," Richard replied, sipping his coffee. He was unsure that providing the letters would do anything to help, but he hoped that perhaps they contained something that would help him to stay a step ahead of the evildoers.

"I thought you burned those?" Lazarus mocked, his tone of indifference turning to one of resentment and his liver colored lips curling up in a sneer.

"Just the one you found," Richard said.

Lazarus snatched an envelope from the table. He opened it, spent a few seconds scanning it and threw it aside. "Nothing," he said as he picked up and opened another envelope.

Again he scanned the letter. "Useless," he said with some irritation.

Lazarus sighed as he picked up the third and last envelope. He looked Richard in the eyes as he opened it. Richard watched intently as Lazarus dropped his gaze to read the letter. Moments went by, and then Lazarus' brow rose slightly. Something had peaked his interest.

"This is it," he said, smirking.

"What does it say?" Richard asked.

Lazarus waved the letter back and forth in a teasing manner, as if to say *I know something you don't know, and you'd better ask nicely or I won't tell you.*

"Come on!" Richard cried, trying to grab the letter but missing as Lazarus pulled it away.

"What's the magic word?" Lazarus taunted, his mischievous smile exposing granite colored teeth.

"Please! Please tell me what it says!"

"It says your going to eternally burn in the hell that is Broward Mental Hospital. They're going to send you back to the psych ward – forever!" he laughed, the glee in his voice mirroring the flicker in his eyes. "After all, you did kill Ms. Trapoli. I don't think you'll be forgiven for that."

"Let me see!" Richard yelled as he snatched the letter away from Lazarus. Quickly scanning the words he interpreted the meaning that Lazarus had suggested was there.

"I can't go back there," he said desperately. "I won't go back there again."

Richard's head fell into his hands and the room went silent. He pictured himself being led into the psych ward in handcuffs. He saw the lobotomy room, with its sharpened stainless steel instruments and electrodes. When he raised his head to ask for help, Lazarus was gone.

"Lazarus!" he yelled. "Lazarus! Don't leave me here alone!"

Richard flew up and his chair toppled over, rattling as it crashed to the wooden floor. "I don't know what to do! I don't know what to do!" he cried. Looking frantically around the cabin, Richard felt the walls closing in on him. Getting closer and closer, making it harder and harder to breath. He felt his legs weaken and he rushed forward, letting his body fall onto a small couch sitting opposite the kitchen. A pillow he pressed to his face muffled his cries for help.

"HE SAYS HE DOESN'T KNOW WHAT TO DO," Author said. "BUT HE DOES KNOW WHAT TO DO. HE HAS A PLAN."

"YES HE DOES HAVE A PLAN," Melissa responded. "BUT HE'S WONDERING IF IT'S THE RIGHT THING."

"WHAT ARE HIS OPTIONS? HE JUST KILLED CONNIE TRAPOLI. THE COPS ARE AFTER HIM. AND HIS FAMILY WILL NEVER FORGIVE HIM FOR WHAT HE'S DONE."

"IT DOES SEEM TO BE A HOPELESS SITUATION - THE POOR DEAR!"

Richard lay sprawled on the couch. His body was rigid with fear, and the musty smell of the pillow pressed to his face made him feel like he was drowning, drawing in water with each desperate breath. But he knew it wasn't really his last breath. He knew that as soon as he removed the smothering pillow his miserable life would go on, and the nightmare would continue. Resolved to produce a different outcome he threw the pillow to the floor, bolted upward and rushed to the kitchen. He reached behind the refrigerator, feeling for the small, magnetized metal box he had seen Charlie place there some time ago. Opening the box, he took out a tiny silver key and walked to a tall black enameled steel safe sitting on the floor to the right of the fireplace. His right hand shook violently as he tried placing the key in the lock on the front of the safe door. He steadied his right hand with his left, the key clanking against the lock as he struggled to insert it. Finally it went in, and with a twist the door opened.

Two Winchester shotguns and a 30-30 Savage rifle lay upright inside the metal box. Richard reached in and grabbed the biggest one. He turned the gun on its side and saw *12-Gauge* inscribed on the barrel. With his free hand he slid open a small drawer at the bottom of the safe and found a box of 12-gauge shotgun shells. He removed one and placed it in his coat pocket.

He stepped back from the safe and looked upwards, as if peering through the cabin roof and into the night sky. "I can't do this anymore," he said in a whimper. "I don't know what else to do. I don't know." Hot tears streamed from the corners of his eyes. "I'm scared! I did an awful thing! I killed Connie! The evildoers and the voices, they're taking over! I'm afraid! I'm afraid I'll disappear!" he yelled desperately, his voice trailing off and leaving behind an irrepressible silence. He waited, hoping someone would speak or something would happen to change his mind. Moments of silence passed before he moved back to the couch, sat down and placed the shotgun on his lap.

"Please tell me what to do," he muttered, stretching his hands towards heaven. "Tell me!" Again he waited, but no answer came. He dropped his hands and gripped the shotgun. "Give me one good reason why I shouldn't do this!"

Even the voices in Richard's head were silent, but he knew they were watching and waiting. He looked downward at the bluish steel of the gun's barrel and the richly colored wood of the stock. It was a beautifully simple tool that was designed for only one thing - to put an end to other things.

Richard ran his fingers down the barrel to the hammer, and then down to the trigger. He picked up the weapon and pressed down on a small lever, opening the barrel and exposing the chamber where the shotgun shell would be placed.

"Just one good reason," he pleaded one last time.

When the clock above the fireplace read 6:00 PM he reached into his coat pocket and retrieved the shotgun shell.

***

Charles saw the kitchen light as soon as he rounded the corner of the driveway leading to the cabin. He felt both relief and anger - relief because he had found his brother, anger because he knew that getting into the cabin probably required him to break something. His suspicions were confirmed when he stepped onto the porch and noticed the broken windowpane on the front door.

"Richie?" he called out, half expecting his brother to rush out and begin apologizing.

"Richie, where are you?"

The cabin was quiet when he stepped inside. He saw an empty coffee cup sitting on the kitchen table, and as he moved forward he saw the toppled kitchen chair. At first glance the living room seemed empty. Then he saw the top of Richard's head, a tuft of his hair visible over the back of the couch.

"I knew you'd be here," he said, walking over to where his brother lay.

Rounding the corner of the couch he saw Richard's face, covered in blood, his eyes closed and facing the ceiling. The shotgun lay at his side.

"Richie! Richie!" Charles screamed, falling to his knees beside his bother.

Startled out of his slumber, Richard's body jerked and his eyes flew open. "Charlie? Charlie? What are you doing here?"

Relieved beyond measure, Charles grabbed his brother and wrapped his arms around him. "I came to get you!" he screamed and then pulled away to look Richard in the face. "What happened? Why is your face all bloody? What are you doing with the shotgun?"

Richard wiped his face and looked at the crust of dried blood on his fingers. "I scratched my face on the way over here," he said, quickly diverting his attention away from his bloodied fingers and the memory of what had happened with Lazarus in the car. He looked squarely at his bother. "I was gonna do it Charlie!" he exclaimed excitedly. "I was gonna kill myself!"

Charles' eyes glistened with tears of anger and fear. "No! Don't you do it! Don't you do it little brother!" he cried, wrapping his hands around Richard's neck and pulling him in until their foreheads touched. "You can't go. What would I do if you were gone? Please don't go."

"I won't! I wont go! God sent Esther to save me!"

Charles pulled back to see his brother's face. "What? What do you--"

"When I reached into my pocket to get the shotgun shell," he interrupted, "a piece of paper fell out. I asked God to give me a reason to live, and this is what he showed me."

He held up the wrinkled drawing for Charles to see. "It's the resting place," he said, choking out the words and recalling what Esther had whispered into his ear when she handed him the picture at his parent's anniversary party. He gripped the paper with both hands and pushed it closer to Charles' face. "It's the resting place," he repeated.

Charles grabbed the paper, looking closely at it as he thought back. "She showed it to me before she gave it to you on Saturday," he said. "She said the two of you were resting and that you were getting ready to go home. I didn't really understand what she meant, but I played along. Do you know what it means?"

"No, not really," Richard said, his voice echoing his uncertainty. "All I know is God gave me Esther, and Esther gave me this. And now I want to live." Pressing the picture to his face, Richard closed his eyes and imagined his little niece extending her hand to offer him the gift she had made. Then he pulled it away and cast his eyes upon Charles. "Its a sign – Isn't it Charlie? Its a sign that things will be OK?"

"Listen to me!" Charles said forcefully. "Everything *is* going to be OK. We'll get through this! We'll get through this together!"

Richard paused for a moment and the realization of what he had done came flooding back to him, sweeping away the momentary relief he had felt. "But I killed Connie!" he yelled, his face contorted in pain. "I killed a beautiful person!"

"Connie's not dead!" Charles blurted. "She's hurt badly, but she's not dead!"

"She's not dead? Connie Trapoli is not dead?" Richard's hands flew up to grab his spinning head. "I'm alive! Connie is alive!"

"Yes!" Charles responded, his excitement about the fortunate outcome matching his brother's for a moment. Then his countenance darkened. "But Richie, you are in a lot of trouble!"

"I don't care! She's alive and I'll spend the rest of my life being thankful for that!" In the moments it took him to speak, the reality of being committed to Broward Mental Hospital began to set in. "They're gonna put me away again, aren't they?" he asked, the lightness in his voice tempered by memories of the place.

Charles did not answer. He squeezed his eyes shut, trying hard to blot out the image of the ominous looking three-story sanitarium where his brother had been imprisoned on several occasions in the past.

"Huh!" Richard said, shaking his head in disbelief. "Lazarus was right, I will end up at Broward again."

Sixteen

Steam from Charles' coffee cup rose into the still November air. He looked out over the porch railing to the meadow, which in late spring and summer was brilliantly painted with wildflowers. Now, the gracefully rolling landscape was covered in a thin blanket of snow. The long tree lined driveway meandered up the gently sloped valley, winding its way to the cabin. Sunlight crested a densely wooded hill to his left, illuminating trees on the opposite side of the meadow and adding warmth to the cool, dry winter air. The lyrical chirping of a songbird and the distant gobble of a wild turkey made the otherwise sleepy place come alive. Charles loved the cabin. The sights and sounds of the fifty-acre retreat had always calmed his soul and eased his mind.

The Adirondack chair on which he sat was one of three chairs on the porch. Another, which was identical to his, was Isabel's. The third was a small red rocking chair belonging to Esther. Charles glanced at the empty chairs and thought about how his girls loved sitting with him during the summer months when the breeze was warm and the days held the promise of fun and adventure. He pulled up the collar on his wool coat and covered his legs with a small patchwork quilt Isabel had made. Charles' surroundings were tranquil, but his mind was not. The events of the previous day weighed heavy on him.

Cupping his hands around his warm coffee mug, he thought back to a time before the troubles set in. He recalled the things he and Richard did together as kids, during the summer months. Since they were only one year apart in age they spent most of their time together. Back then life seemed to be one big carefree adventure.

There was bike riding, sand boxes, Match Box cars, GI Joe, baseball, fort building, and a hundred other things that filled their days and gave them pleasure. Being boys they had no aversion to dirt, muddy water, cow manure, worms, spiders, or anything else that crawled or slithered. At the end of a typical day they were normally covered with dirt from head to toe. Charles grinned at the memory of his mother spraying them with a garden hose in the back of the house to wash off the big chunks of grime before they were allowed to go inside for a proper bath. They had fun together. But whatever they did, Richard always followed his big brother's lead.

The lighthearted memories faded as Charles recalled the things he had said and done to taint the innocence of their childhood years. Charles was agile, energetic and quick to speak, while Richard was often uncoordinated and slow to move and talk. Richard wasn't always able to keep up with Charles, which was a constant source of irritation to the immature and selfish boy. Charles dropped his head and squeezed his eyes shut, trying hard to suppress the shame he felt for treating his brother poorly when he wasn't being the playmate that he wanted. The word *retard* echoed in his head. And for what seemed to be the millionth time he was forced to confront the ugly truth that Zach Wolf was not the first person to wound his brother with mean spirited and deep cutting words. He was. What hurt Charles even more was that his brother never attempted to defend himself. Most times he would simply drop his head in shame. Sometimes he would wander off crying. Those hurtful words and the snotty sense of entitlement and superiority Charles felt back then had made his brother feel stupid and worthless.

As an adult Charles knew that while the onset of schizophrenia was largely unexplainable, its source was connected to some sort of biochemical imbalance. Still, he could not help but feel that he had somehow contributed to his brother's illness, or at least added to his suffering. The thought of it ate away at him. How could he have been so cruel to his own brother, his own flesh and blood? Charles knew that the desire he eventually developed to protect his brother was driven by guilt and the need to make amends for his sins. He had asked God to forgive him back when he was a young man, and still believed that there was a god who forgave sins. But he had never asked Richard for forgiveness, and that fact ravaged his conscience like a cancerous tumor. Back then he had come to the simple conclusion that actions were stronger than words, and he resolved to never hurt his brother again or let anyone else hurt him the way he had. In the end, however, protectiveness and good intentions were not enough. His brother was hurting, and he would continue to hurt. In fact, his suffering seemed only to grow. The years of trying to protect his brother now seemed worthless. Words seemed to be all he had left, but he didn't know what to say to make things better.

The clanking of porcelain cups in the cabin's kitchen brought Charles back to the present. Soon, Richard appeared with a cup of coffee in his hand. He stopped to look at the duct tape Charles had placed over the broken glass on the front door. "I'll pay to have that fixed," he said.

"Thanks, we can talk about that later," Charles responded, not caring one bit about the broken glass.

Richard sat next to Charles in Isabel's chair and took two gulps of coffee before lighting a cigarette.

"How'd you sleep?" asked Charles.

"OK I guess. I don't remember anything. I like it when I don't remember anything."

"Looks like it's gonna be sunny today," Charles added, trying to focus on something positive.

Richard nodded his head but said nothing. Charles decided to give his brother some time to wake up before they talked. They sat in silence sipping their coffee and looking out over the meadow. A hundred yards out, a wild turkey stepped warily out of the underbrush and into the open. After a moment he fanned his tail feathers in a brilliant display, signaling to the rest of his troop to gather around. Soon five hens wandered out, looking nervously to the left and right. Charles and Richard watched as they made their way across the meadow. Then Richard began coughing, which sent them into a full out run into the tree line and they disappeared into the underbrush.

"I need to quit smoking," he said, grabbing his chest as he heaved.

Charles knew that his brother would probably never quit and that death by lung cancer was a very real possibility. He waited for Richard to stop hacking. "Yeah, those things will kill ya," he said.

Again they sat in silence while Charles thought about what to say next. "Richie," he said finally. "You know we need to go back today."

"Yeah, I know," he sighed. "But can we wait a while?" Richard rubbed his face hard trying to dispel the numbness setting in. The thought of facing what awaited him back home began to deaden his senses. He was not yet ready to let go of the joy of being at the cabin with his brother. He held tightly to the terrible, wonderful, dizzyingly euphoric feelings of the night before. And he began to realize he might never have that sort of joy again.

"Yeah, I figure we'll have breakfast and clean up and then hit the road," Charles said.

Richard took a long draw off his cigarette and exhaled slowly. "What do you think they're going to do to me?" he asked, his thoughts floating to the uncertain future that lay ahead.

"I don't know for sure, but I would guess they'll want to do some sort of evaluation. You've been through that before so you know what I'm talking about, right?"

"Yeah, their gonna take my blood and ask me a lot of questions. They'll probably give me more pills."

"That's about right. But Richie I think you need to be prepared for what might come next. Connie and her family are probably going to demand that you be punished for what you did. You'll probably have to go to the hospital for a while, and there's the possibility that you may go to jail."

"Do you think I should go to jail?"

Charles took a deep breath, exhaling slowly as he considered what to say. "Richie, I don't know what was going on inside you that made you attack Connie. Honestly, at this point I don't want to know. But the fact remains that no matter what you're thinking or feeling you can't just attack people like that. You need to learn to control yourself or they're gonna keep putting you in places where you can't hurt people. That's the way it is. It's the law. And, yes I agree with it. Do you understand that?"

"She was plotting against me," Richard replied. "How would you like it if people were sent to do you harm?"

Once again Charles was amazed at how quickly his brother's illness took over. Just last night he seemed genuinely sorry for what had happened; now he seemed to be defending his behavior. "I'm not asking you to like it - I'm saying you can't get violent when it happens," he added.

"How should I defend myself? What am I supposed to do?"

Charles was tempted to ignore the question, knowing that his brother would eventually dismiss any suggestions he made. Then he remembered what Carl had so passionately expressed to him during their meeting in Carl's office. *Don't check out*, he said to himself. *You can't check out.*

"Richie, when I was in Officer's Candidate School and Ranger school," Charles continued, "the TAC officers verbally assaulted us and pushed us physically to try and cut us down and mess with our minds. They did it to see if we would break, if we would either give up or lose control and lash out. They needed to make sure we had what it took to face a hostile enemy who would also mess with our minds and bodies if we were ever captured. We knew we were being tested. So, we made it into a game. Instead of getting mad or giving up when they'd do something to punish us, we would respond by saying, 'Thank you sir! May I have another?' So, if they said drop and knock me out fifty, we'd do our pushups, stand up and say, 'Thank you sir! May I have another?' Of course the TAC's were always more than happy to give another round of fifty, and so we'd do pushups until our bodies gave out. The point is that we didn't let them get to us. We didn't lose control."

Charles took a sip of coffee and tucked the blanket around his legs. "As I see it, there are two problems you're faced with. One problem, and it's a big one, is that you feel like you're being tormented and punished by evildoers and by the voices. The other problem is that you sometimes react to that stress poorly, and you end up hurting other people. I don't know what to do to stop you from being tormented. But, I think you could do a better job of controlling how you react to it."

Once again Charles felt that asking his brother to apply logic and reason to situations lacked practicality. How could his illogical and, in fact, delusional mind rely upon logic to fix itself? Not only that, why should his brother accept and even embrace such a paradox when he himself was unwilling to accept it. His reasoning was shabby, but Charles hoped that Richard would at least admit that he could do better. Even if the only reason he did it was because his big brother told him it was the right thing to do.

"Does that make any sense?" he asked, glancing at Richard and hoping for a positive reaction.

Richard's face grimaced, and he began rubbing his arms.

"Glass in your veins?" Charles sighed.

"Big pieces of broken glass," Richard said, rocking back and forth, his face contorted in pain.

"It's OK Richie, just breathe. Breathe deep."

Following Charlie's instructions Richard took long, deep breaths like a pregnant woman trying to overcome labor pains. After a few minutes he stopped rocking and his face relaxed.

"I need to call the Sheriff to let him know we're coming in," Charles said.

He stood without looking at Richard, pulled the cell phone from his pocket and began dialing. He stepped off the porch and down the gravel path towards the cars as he waited for the sheriff to pick up.

"The voices are bothering me," Richard said, as if Charles could hear him. "My brain is burnt."

Seventeen

The holding cell was sparse. A small cot-like bed sat in the corner, and above that hung a single bar-covered window set deeply into the thick outer wall. The window served only to provide light as it was set too high for the cell's inhabitant to see anything but a small sliver of sky, which on this particular day was colored an ashen gray. The concrete block walls matched the sky in color, thickly painted to cover the blurred remnants of names, dates and foul expressions etched into its surface by decades of offenders awaiting their punishment. A gleaming stainless steel sink and toilet stuck out in the otherwise drab little room, which was separated from the outside world by a dented metal door with a small, reinforced glass window. The smell of pine scented cleaner was overpowering when Richard first arrived, but once he had adjusted to it he began to pick up other odors that the cleaning solution had failed to mask. He couldn't name them, but they were foul.

He was trying hard to think about good things like Judith, and moths, and fresh coffee when the bolt on the cell door issued a hollow thud. A uniformed officer opened the door and stepped aside and Charlie walked in with a man Richard had never seen before. Richard stood and hugged his brother.

"Mom and dad wanted to be here," Charles began. "But they only allow a lawyer and one family member, so we thought it should be me." Charles stepped back so his brother could see the man he had brought with him. "Richie, this is Doyle Brennan. We hired him to represent you."

Brennan extended his hand. "Hello Richard, how are you doing in here?"

Richard stared unblinking at Brennan, who began to pull his hand back when Richard finally extended his. "OK I guess. But I don't like it here. Can you get me out?"

Brennan guessed his newest client knew a little something about the sort of criminal proceedings they were about to discuss, but he also knew Richard had never been brought up on such serious charges. "Well, I'm going to do whatever I can to make sure things go smoothly, but there is a process we have to follow. I'd like to talk about that now if we could." Richard said nothing, and in the silence Brennan decided to continue. "Can we sit?"

"You two take the bed and I'll sit on the floor," Charles said, motioning towards the bed as he crouched down and sat cross-legged, facing them with his back against the cell wall.

"The first thing that will happen is called a preliminary arraignment," Brennan began. "That's where charges are filed and a preliminary hearing is set."

"What will they charge me with?"

"Aggravated assault and battery," Brennan said, his tone sounding more like he was ordering lunch than delivering bad news. Brennan's 23 years of experience representing clients who had committed crimes of the physical nature had toughened him, and his outward appearance and manner gave the impression that he was cold and indifferent and very successful, which he was. His success, however, had been paid for with two failed marriages and a drinking problem that he suspected would ultimately cost him his liver. He wasn't particularly handsome, but his attire and precise grooming made it evident that he was a serious, measured and calculating sort of person. A finely pressed blue pinstriped suit hung smartly over his body and was accented by a yellow silk tie set against a heavily starched white dress shirt. The crisp crease in his slacks trailed down to blue argyle socks fit neatly into ostrich capped Crockett and Jones oxfords. A full head of well-trimmed and freshly dyed brown hair topped the pockmarked skin of his round and unemotional face. His eyes were closely set and small, so small they hid their color.

"Aggravated assault and battery," Richard said, as if he was reading the words from a dictionary. "That sounds bad. Is that bad?" Brennan knew by the way Richard asked the question that his naivety was genuine.

"It's a serious crime that can carry heavy consequences," he said. "But I'll do everything I can to ensure you are treated fairly. Now the next step is the preliminary hearing. That's used to determine if there is sufficient evidence to go to trial, and I believe there is enough--"

"Please don't say anymore!" Richard erupted. He stood suddenly and walked to the sink with his back facing the two men. The abrupt change in his disposition caught Brennan and Charles off guard. "I just want to get this over with," he said. "I hurt Connie and I deserve to be punished. I just want to get on with it."

"Richie, Doyle needs you to--"

"Richard, you need to work with me if you want me to help you," Brennan cut in. "You could be put away for a long time. Is that what you want?" Brennan raised an open palm to Charles, indicating that he should keep quiet and let the question sink in.

Richard's head hung over the polished steel sink; he saw a distorted, funhouse mirror like image of his face reflected back. The sight of it sickened him, but he felt it was an accurate portrait of who he'd become. His life had gotten so screwed up.

"HE'S HERE BECAUSE HE KILLED CONNIE TRAPOLI! SHE GOT WHAT SHE HAD COMING, AND NOW HE WILL TOO!" Melissa's scolding tone cut in.

"I didn't kill Connie! I didn't kill her!" Richard said, whimpering and grabbing his head.

Charles rushed to his feet and grabbed Richard's shoulders from behind. "It's OK. We're just talking," he said, leading his brother back to the edge of the bed. "You need to answer Doyle's question."

Still standing, Richard stuck his hands in his pockets and heaved a sigh. "No. I don't want to be in jail any longer than I have to."

"Then let's talk about what happened with Connie," Brennan said, careful not to insinuate that it was Richard who had attacked her.

Sitting next to Brennan once again, Richard proceeded to answer question after pointed question about his actions and frame of mind before, during, and after the attack. He answered truthfully and held back nothing. He even admitted that he had stopped taking his medications. Richard had been questioned many times for strange things he had done, people he had bothered, and a few he had even assaulted. But one and a half hours was the longest stretch of questioning he had ever endured. He was exhausted when Brennan finally scratched his last note on the yellow legal pad inside his leather portfolio. "That about does it for now," he said. "I'll be back in a few days to--"

"They're going to put me in Broward aren't they?" Richard interrupted.

Brennan paused and then looked at Richard. "Yes, I believe they will. And you could be there for a long time if we get the wrong judge. With good behavior you might be allowed to go back to Alpha House, but you'd be on house arrest, and after that probably on parole." Richard's hand trembled as he stared blankly and silently at the wall above Charles' head.

"What about prison?" Charles asked.

"I don't think that will happen. We can prove that his mental state requires him to receive treatment in a hospital."

"You won't be alone Richie, I'll visit you as often as I can and everyone else will too. It'll be OK," he said, wishing more than anything that he believed his own words.

Someone in an adjacent cell began yelling in drunken slurs as Charles and Brennan got up to leave. "I'll come by tomorrow to see how you're doing," Charles said, hugging his brother goodbye. Richard remained standing as they left. They walked through a well-lit corridor and down a flight of stairs to a small sitting area next to a guard station. A gray haired, saggy skinned officer peered at them over his glasses as they entered the room and sat.

"Well, the good news is that they won't put him in prison," Brennan said. "If he was sane he could get six years or more in a penitentiary."

"What's the bad news?"

"This is not his first offense. Over the years there have been three other instances where he assaulted another person. No judge will ignore that, even if the episodes didn't result in serious physical injury. He's also had several other run-ins with the law over small stuff like public urination, disturbing the peace and that incident when he ran from the police."

"He was scared; he thought they were going to take him to Broward," Charles retorted. "He didn't even--"

"Charles," Brennan interrupted, brushing a wrinkle from his slacks and straightened his tie. "Your brother is a sick man. You know I will do everything I can to help out here, but at the end of the day things have happened that none of us can go back in time to change. One more blow and he could have killed that woman. I suggest you be thankful for that."

Charles knew that the light scolding he had just received was well deserved. His brother was not a killer, but he didn't belong in public where he might hurt other people. He knew he needed to stop making excuses for him. *Brennan's right*, he thought. *One more*

blow and Connie could be dead, and Richie could be locked up for
the rest of his life. I wish I could be thankful for that, but I can't.
Damn the world, I just can't.

Charles extended his hand to Brennan. "I appreciate your help, " he said.

"I'll do what I can. Send my regards to your mother and father. I imagine they're pretty torn up about this."

Eighteen

Deputy Steinmitz reached down to secure Richard's handcuffs to a chain that was bolted to the floor in the back seat of the police cruiser. "I'm sorry but we have to do this, its procedure," he said apologetically.

"It's OK, it doesn't hurt," Richard said, relieved to be free of the trauma of the last 13 days. Several large red welts protruded from his forehead, and the skin around his eyes was swollen and bruised. His two-day stay in the holding cell at the Sheriff's station ended when he was handcuffed and led to a temporary detention center at county police headquarters. He needed to vacate the holding cell to make room for other incoming offenders. But his stay in solitary confinement at the detention center was the decision of Judge Vincent Shirley. Counselor Brennan respectfully requested house arrest until the trial, but Judge Shirley saw things differently. "I don't want him near others until we are able to assess his mental state and determine a suitable course of action," were his exact words.

Richard's preference for solitude made him think that solitary confinement would be something he could handle. But reality proved him wrong. Being alone was fine. Even the lousy food, the dankness of his cell, and the fact that he would be allowed to take only two full body showers a week was tolerable. The unbroken and absolute silence was not. No visitors were allowed. The only time anyone came near him was to deliver meals. Even then his food and medications were passed through a small opening in the cell door. After a short greeting the delivering officer sat silently in a folding chair reading magazines outside his cell for exactly ten minutes before collecting whatever remnants were left over from the meal. Richard said "Thank you", and in return received a relatively spirited "You're welcome" for the first three days of his stay. On days four and five Richard passed the tray back without any gesture of gratitude. By the sixth day the courtesies Richard had previously extended were discarded and replaced with desperate cries for help that started as soon as he heard the soft slapping of the officer's footsteps against the concrete stairs and into the dimly lit hallway outside his cell.

In the silence, the voices had taken over. "WORTHLESS SCRAP OF GARBAGE! HE DOESN'T DESERVE TO BE SET FREE!"

Richard had tried singing to drown them out, but they yelled louder. "HE'LL NEVER MAKE IT! HE'S TOO WEAK!"

He had repeated the Pledge of Allegiance over and over until his voice was raw. He had even recited verses from the Bible, the only book in his cell. Pacing from one end of the cramped space to the other, he read:

> "...In all these things we are more than conquerors through him who loved us. For I am convinced that neither death nor life, neither angels nor demons, neither the present nor the future, nor any powers, neither height nor depth, nor anything else in all creation, will be able to separate us from the love of God that is in Christ Jesus our Lord."

Again and again he had repeated the words, but was unable to commit them to memory because nothing could overpower the viscous, stabbing hostility of the voices. His body, mind, and spirit were held prisoner, and it had pushed him to the edge.

At three o'clock in the morning on day eight, he leapt from bed and began beating his sweat-soaked head against the concrete wall nearest the door. It took three and a half minutes of continual self-pummeling before he collapsed. The young officer dutifully delivered breakfast at seven o'clock and immediately took notice of the unusual silence during his walk to Richard's cell. The tray was placed in the opening on the door but was not taken. "Breakfast!" he yelled. Hearing no response he peered through the opening and saw Richard's feet, sprawled and still.

From that point on Richard was restrained. A special bed was brought in that held straps made of sturdy nylon webbing with Velcro closures for his arms, legs, torso and head. He spent the next four days and nights tightly bound, unable to see anything except what his eyes could take in by shifting them to the left or right, up or down. He was unbound for meals and two bathroom breaks each day, all of which were closely supervised by the young officer and two other men wearing white uniforms. On two occasions he was provided with a washbasin full of soapy water, fresh clothing and sheets because he was unable to hold back his bulging bladder and urinated while he was shackled to the bed.

The ride away from the detention center in deputy Steinmitz' parole car was refreshing, and it lifted his spirits. There was squint worthy sunlight, color and movement. The hum of the squad car's engine and the sound of barking dogs and train crossing bells were pleasing to his ears. Buildings and people whisked by as they turned down one street and then another. Even the showroom fresh smells of the shiny parole car made him feel alive again. Better yet were the hugs and kisses he got from his family, who were waiting to greet him when he was escorted out of the detention center building and into the waiting police car. Deputy Steinmitz was kind enough to allow them a few moments together before chaining him to the back seat.

"You doin' OK back there Richard?" deputy Steinmitz asked. Peering into the rear view mirror he saw Richard's swollen eyes drinking in the scenery.

"Richard, you OK?"

"Huh? Oh, yeah. My head hurts, but I'll be OK."

"We'll be there in about 20 minutes. We're going to hand you off to Broward's admissions department. They'll ask you a bunch of questions, draw your blood and issue you some clothes, OK?"

"Can I have my brother bring me some things from home?" he asked, the moth book flashing in his mind.

"You'll have to ask them about that," the deputy responded. "I'm not sure what they'll allow you to bring in."

In the 15 days since his arrest, charges of aggravated assault and battery had been filed and Doyle Brennan had pleaded guilty on Richard's behalf. He told the judge that Richard was ill and could not appear in court. When asked what sort of illness he was suffering from Brennan responded, "Hallucinations brought on by exhaustion your honor. The grief he feels over the events of December 3rd kept him awake for more than a week in solitary." Knowing Brennan's tendency to vigorously defend clients, sometimes to the point of exaggeration, the judge considered requiring a physician's assessment but decided to let it go. "We need to move forward for the sake of the victim and the accused," he had said. A non-jury trial date was set for February of the coming year. Until then, a period of almost three months, Richard would be confined to what many referred to as the Crazy Wing at Broward Mental Hospital. He faced the possibility of spending years there once the trial was over.

The sight of the building was familiar to Richard and a small part of him was relieved to see it, especially after his experience in solitary. He'd been there four other times over the years, but never for the period of time he now faced, and never for aggravated assault and battery. A place like Broward was repulsive to the uninitiated. Sickness of the cruelest and most unfathomable kind was concentrated in the four-story structure like bubbling bacteria in a Petri dish. Richard didn't like living there, but not because he was treated poorly or because the conditions were bad. Quite the opposite; the staff he'd been in contact with were good people who seemed to genuinely care about his well-being. All he had to do to enjoy the comforts of the place was abide by the rules. The thing that bothered him though, the thing that seemed always to be present was the unsettling reminder that he was sick enough to live among people who seemed like they were from another planet. Not everyone was like that. Some seemed normal enough, at least in terms of how they looked and acted. But then there were the ones who were painful to watch. Their sickness showed itself in ways that puts a lump in the average person's throat. They walked trance like through the halls, half naked and unaware of anything more than twelve inches from their face; they were chained to benches for the safety of others; they were wrestled to the ground and taken away kicking and screaming; they stood in corners and stared unceasingly at walls. As the police car pulled up to the admissions door Richard rested his welted forehead against the window and felt a twinge of pain. *I'm one of them*, he thought. *I belong here with these people. None of us belong anywhere else.*

His room, it was referred to as a room, not a cell, was sparsely equipped and much like the temporary holding cell and the detention center cell with one exception; the front wall, including the door, was made of reinforced Plexiglas from floor to ceiling. The door had a circle shaped series of holes drilled at head level for speaking through. Nurses and Techs, as they were called, manned the nurses' station, a large chest high enclosure in the center of the expansive floor. Each of the 23 rooms inside the Crazy Wing encircled the nurses' station and were visible from there. Techs routinely roamed past each room to check on patients and look for evidence of foul play. One Tech opened the door to Richard's room and stepped in.

"Mr. Buell, my name is Malcolm and I'm one of the technicians on this floor. You're one of our newest residents here, and I just wanted to make sure you're OK. Have you been to Broward before?" Malcolm knew that he had, but wanted to see how Richard would respond.

Richard didn't speak; he just nodded his head and looked away from Malcolm's face, which was very dark skinned and hard creased, but smiling and friendly.

"I'll be coming by now and then to check in on ya. Is there anythin' you need right now?"

"I'd like to see my family. I'd like to see my brother Charlie. When can I see him?"

"Well, visitors are not allowed for the first week. We wanna give you time to adjust before family comes. After that it depends on how well ya behave. We'll go over our standards tomorrow, OK?"

"When can I have a cigarette?" Richard asked, already knowing the answer.

"Oh, that's a tough one Mr. Buell."

"You can call me Richard."

"OK. That's a tough one Richard. We don't allow no tobacco or matches or lighters on this wing."

He knew it was coming, but still his mind reeled. He had managed to sneak in a quick smoke while he was with his family at the detention center, just before his trip to Broward. Before that he hadn't had one in 13 days. Now he was faced with enduring years without his cigarettes, and the thought of it made his head throb.

"I know it's gonna be difficult," Malcolm added. "But we'll help you through it, OK?"

Richard sighed and nodded his head. "OK," he said, extending his hand towards Malcolm, who gave it a hearty shake. "It was nice to meet ya," Malcolm replied and then excused himself.

Richard lay on his bed draped in a knee length gown and rubber bottomed cotton booties. He grasped the fabric just below his neck and raised it close enough to see that it had some sort of webbing woven into it. During his previous stay a Tech, who was unaware his conversation with another Tech was overheard by Richard, referred to it as a suicide gown. The cloth could not be torn and, as a result, was difficult to fashion into a noose or other device intended to end the suffering of its wearer. He tugged hard to see if it was true, and it was.

Richard didn't know what it was that called forth the voices. It wasn't the absence of medication. They had regularly assaulted him when he was taking everything he was supposed to take. The thing medication did do was make him care less that the voices were there. But he didn't like how it made him feel. He didn't like being numb. Tonight, however, he had 600 milligrams of Clozapine, an antipsychotic drug, and 30 milligrams of a hearty muscle relaxer called Diazepam inside him. After his experience in solitary confinement he was happy to feel nothing but relief from the torture he had endured. For the first time in what seemed like years, Richard slept through the night.

***

"Rise and shine everyone!" The brightly spoken but harshly received words assaulted Richard's ears and he tightly squeezed his already closed eyes. "Its 6:30 AM and time to start our day." He lifted his head, which felt like a rock, and groggily turned it towards the sickeningly cheery voice emanating from the Plexiglas encased speaker hanging in the corner above the door. He closed his eyes again and pulled the pillow over his head. *I just fell asleep*, he moaned to himself.

"Mr. Buell. Mr. Buell. Richard!" Unaware that almost ten minutes had gone by since the wakeup call, Richard lifted his head again to see Malcolm standing in the hall outside his door.

"I'm sleeping," he moaned aloud this time.

"It's time to get up. You need to get ready for your morning meds and breakfast."

Richard sighed, slowly forcing his limp body into a sitting position. His eyes remained closed. Seconds later his feet hit the floor.

"Good. I'll be back around in a bit to see how you're comin' along," Malcolm said before walking down the hall to see if any of Richard's neighbors needed rousing.

Routines. Life at Broward revolved around routines. Richard knew it but he had placed it in a part of his brain, which if properly labeled would read - *Things I'd rather forget*. It wasn't that he didn't like routine; after all there was a certain level of comfort provided by knowing what was coming. But there just seemed to be so many routines at Broward. There would be appointed times for group therapy sessions, individual therapy sessions, life skills workshops, recreational therapy, goal setting sessions, and breakfast and lunch and dinner and blah, blah, blah! *It's enough to drive a person crazy*, he thought.

Richard stared into the distance as nurses and techs fluttered about in the hallway and at the nurses' station outside his room. Serious conversations could be overheard, as could laughter. Clipboards, stacks of linen, and plastic totes containing who knows what were carried on missions to different rooms. The thing that got his attention was the odd, sickening smell of burnt rubber that seemed suddenly to have penetrated the door. Curious about its origin, Richard sniffed the air and ambled forward like an old hound on a scent trail. Eyeing the hallway to the left and right he saw nothing that seemed out of place; no smoke or fire, or people screaming about smoke or fire. Then Malcolm appeared with a tray of food in hand.

"Good morning, Richard. Looks like you're ready for some breakfast."

"Uh huh, I'm hungry. But why are you bringing me food? Can't I go to the cafeteria with everyone else?"

"Unfortunately, I just learned that we have to keep ya in your room 'til one of the psychologists is able to do an assessment. That's supposed to happen later this mornin'. I guess the judge on your case requested the assessment to see if it's OK for you to be with the general population." Malcolm was careful to watch Richard's reaction to the news. "Are you OK with that?" he added.

"Yeah," Richard said, reaching back to scratch his behind.

"Is it OK if I come in with your food?" asked Malcolm, his eyes still trained on Richard.

"Sure. I smell burnt rubber. Do you smell that?"

Malcolm sniffed as he unlocked and opened the door to Richard's room. "Nope, don't smell nothin' but eggs, pancakes and bacon," he chuckled. Time on the ward had taught Malcolm that people with schizophrenia sometimes experienced olfactory hallucinations, and the smell of burnt rubber was not uncommon. He set the tray down and removed a plastic cover from the plate. "Actually looks pretty good. I'll be back in about 15 minutes to pick up the tray. Need anything else?"

"No." Richard wanted to express his need for nicotine but decided that saying the word "cigarette" would only make him feel worse. A tickle in his throat produced a series of coughs, forcing mucous from his lungs and into his esophagus. Nauseated, Malcolm wrinkled his nose as he opened the door to leave. Richard cleared his throat, swallowed hard and ravenously attacked the eggs on his breakfast tray.

The next few hours were spent pacing his room, paging through a short stack of papers with "Resident Rules and Guidelines" printed on the top page and, when he had had his fill of those mundane activities, laying on the bed and staring at the ceiling. Unlike the bedroom ceiling in his apartment at Alpha House, he found no quizzical images hidden in its smooth and uninteresting texture.

When the large digital clock sitting on the counter of the nurses' station read 10:47 AM, a well-dressed and youthful looking man with a slight build appeared at Richard's door. He was holding a pad of paper and a manila folder. Standing beside him was a large, serious looking woman in a white nurse's uniform. She carried two plastic folding chairs. The man stepped aside and allowed the nurse to unlock the door so both could enter the room.

"Hello Richard, I'm Aatmaj Dorjee," the man said cheerfully.

The confused look on Richard's face prompted a grin from Mr. Dorjee that was born of a thousand similar reactions. "But you can call me Atty," he chuckled. Turning toward the woman in white he said, "This is nurse Fenstermaker."

Nurse Fenstermaker nodded her head and extended her hand, which Richard shook. She was taller than Atty by six inches.

Atty continued, "I think Malcolm told you we'd be coming to talk with you about how you're feeling so we can make some decisions about how to help you."

Richard knew that this was a nice way of saying they were going to evaluate whether or not he should be allowed the freedom to go outside his room and interact with other patients. He nodded his head.

"May we sit?" Atty asked, turning to see nurse Fenstermaker already seated on one of the two folding chairs she brought with her. "Yes, well let's join nurse Fenstermaker then," he added playfully. Atty's accent seemed to Richard to be incongruent with his name. It sounded as if he had spent his entire life in the Midwest, but he didn't look midwestern.

Richard sat on the bed and eyed nurse Fenstermaker as Atty began paging through his manila folder. Her middle aged round face was like a billboard on which the main advertisements were a bulbous, bright red nose and equally reddened cheeks. Her hair was pulled tight and tucked up under the only nurse's cap he'd seen at Broward. She and Atty looked like mismatched bookends sitting next to each other; one dark and ornately featured, the other like a whitewashed fence post. *She looks like trouble*, he thought.

"Mr. Buell," nurse Fenstermaker began, "Do you know why you're here?"

Richard was caught off guard by the tiny, high-pitched, munchkin-like voice emanating from her amply sized body, and he burst out laughing. She often received surprised looks when she first spoke, but she was not accustomed to being laughed at. She was agitated and it was obvious.

"I'm sorry," Richard began. "I just wasn't expecting--"

"It's quite alright Mr. Buell," she squeaked. "Now could you tell us--"

Richard chuckled again. He covered his mouth to stop more laughter from escaping his lips, but it didn't work. Nurse Fenstermaker glared at Richard and then abruptly turned towards Atty. "Perhaps you should start," she said, her cheeks turning a deeper shade of red.

Richard knew he had hurt nurse Fenstermaker's feelings, and he felt badly about it. "I'm so sorry. I don't know why I'm laughing; I guess it just sounds funny," he apologized and straightened himself. "I'll be good."

Atty tried to mask his smirk by talking. "Why don't I begin," he said.

Atty was cordial and altogether pleasant as he went through a series of questions aimed at revealing Richard's frame of mind, his connection with reality and his aggressive tendencies. Nurse Fenstermaker remained stoic and eventually worked up the nerve to ask a few questions. Richard clamped down on his tongue and tightly clutched the bed pillow sitting in his lap each time she opened her mouth.

It could have been his willingness to apologize to nurse Fenstermaker; it could also have been his inability to stop himself from laughing at her. He wasn't sure what it was, but he got the sense that Atty liked him, and he liked Atty back. Atty smiled a lot, and each time he did it revealed a mouthful of crooked and overlapping teeth. Richard liked that Atty smiled a lot and that he seemed unconcerned that his teeth were flawed. The other thing that drew Richard to Atty was his sincerity; the way he looked him in the eyes, the way he nodded his head whenever Richard was talking, and how he squeezed his brow together when he didn't understand something that had been said. There was something genuine and heartfelt about him.

Richard was surprised and pleased when Malcolm showed up at his door the next morning and held it open. "Come on out my man," he said. "You passed the test! You just keep up on your meds and everything will be just fine." Richard stepped through the door and into the open area of the Crazy Wing. For the first time in almost three weeks Richard could walk more than five steps in any direction without running into a wall.

Nineteen

A large group of patients gathered around the television to watch the 10:00 AM airing of "The Price is Right." The commotion in the day room of the psychiatric care wing at Broward was as loud and unruly as the studio audience. Some patients yelled, "Higher!" Others yelled, "Lower!" A pajama clad young man with a shaved head rose from his seat, raised his hands and screamed "Three hundred and seventy two dollars and twenty six cents!" Meanwhile the game show contestant looked back and forth between the studio audience and the showcase, which included a gas grill, a pair of bicycles and an automobile. The nurses and techs enjoyed the two-hour block of back-to-back game shows. It created a diversion for many of the patients whose minds would otherwise be occupied by the demons that fed off their particular illnesses. A few techs hovered about, but steered clear of the rambunctious group.

"Mindless pack of boorish heathens." The British accented voice came from behind Richard and he turned to see who was there. "Allow me to introduce myself. My name is Conrad Hampton the Third, Esquire." The man, who was wearing a gray gown and a red armband, extended a bony hand and Richard shook it. "That sort of debasement is so very dreadful, wouldn't you say old chap? It's almost as if they are completely devoid of even the slightest bit of civility." The man pulled his chair away from the table he was sitting at and turned it towards Richard. He crossed his legs, folded his hands in his lap and continued speaking as if he and Richard had been chatting for hours over ale at a local pub. They had, in fact, not even been introduced to each other.

"Oh, my Sophie would not like it here one bit!" he continued.

Richard stared hard at the man, trying to find anything in his face that might provide even the slightest hint about who he was. "Do I know you?" Richard asked. "Did we--"

"No, she's much more at home with her friends at the ladies auxiliary. Why, there was a time when Lord Worthington himself would have intervened on my behalf, the scoundrel. Sadly that time is long gone. It's dreadful, simply dreadful. You see my mother, the late Duchess of Cornwall, God rest her benevolent soul, was betrothed to Lord Worthington after my father's passing - an untimely death you know. Anyhow, she was set to marry the chap when she discovered that he had been involved in a scandal of cyclopean proportions! Unfortunately, I am not at liberty to speak about it openly. You see, I am sworn to secrecy by the Brotherhood of the Purple Templar. I assure you that common knowledge of it would rock the aristocracy to its very core! But, that shall never happen! Lord Worthington would have me rot here to prevent his dirty little secret from ever seeing the light of day!"

Richard stared blank eyed with his mouth half open. The man dropped his head, smiled and chuckled softly. "Listen to me going on about the past when there is nothing to be done about it; when I'm here with you, who wants only to know about my adventures and perhaps gain a bit of enlightenment. Well, please forgive my dreadful display and know that tomorrow I will regale you with stories of gallantry and chivalry the likes of which you have never known!" The man stood and bowed to Richard. "Good day to you, sir."

Richard turned to watch the man walk away. His gown, which was open in the back, revealed a bare buttock. One of the techs noticed and grabbed him by the arm in an attempt to stop him so the open slit could be tied shut. Conrad Hampton the Third, Esquire ripped his arm from the tech's grasp screaming "Unhand me sir! You ruffian! Unhand me I say!"

Malcolm had wandered over without Richard knowing. He poked Richard with his elbow. "I see you met Dennis," he chuckled. "I always get such a kick out of listenin' to him talk."

"Dennis?" Richard asked, confused and slightly amused. "I thought his name was Conrad Hampton the Third?"

"Well, he certainly thinks so. His name is really Dennis Cooper and he's been here for a while, poor guy. His father took off when he was 13, and his mother killt herself. He's from around Stoughton; some small town, I don't 'member the name. You doin' OK?"

Richard felt sick to his stomach. The same blanket of madness that had wrapped itself around Dennis Cooper seemed suddenly to envelop him. *People think I belong here*, he thought to himself. For the first time since he had arrived at Broward he began to question his own sanity. *Could I be that sick*? He silently questioned.

"COULD I BE THAT SICK?" Author mockingly repeated, seemingly out of nowhere. He followed the insult with a hearty laugh.

"SICK? MORE LIKE TOTALLY DERANGED!" Melissa chided.

Richard turned to Malcolm. "When can I see my family?" he asked, desperately needing the only people he thought would make him feel normal.

Sensing Richard's distress, Malcolm responded in a particularly spirited manner. "Good news Richard, you should be able to see them by Tuesday! Tuesday will be one week. Now that's only two more days! And hey, more good news! Your brother Charlie brung you a few things." Malcolm handed Richard a small plastic bag that held a few items of clothing and his moth book.

"Thanks," Richard said, tugging on the white elastic band wrapped around the upper part of his left arm.

Malcolm patted Richard on his back. "Sure thing, let me know if you need anythin' else," he said before walking towards the nurse's station.

Looking around the day room, Richard saw several yellow armbands, a few that were green, and only one other that was white. Two patients had red armbands like the one Conrad Hampton the Third wore. One, a finely featured woman who was chained to her chair, the other a large olive-skinned man with unruly black hair and an unshaven face. The man stared at Richard, and Richard stared back until it became uncomfortable.

The armband system, which he had learned about during his first stay, was designed to promote good behavior. White bands were reserved for new admissions. If Whites actively participated in workshops and therapy sessions, took all their medications and behaved properly, they graduated to Yellows after three days. That meant visiting privileges, the freedom to wear street clothes, use the gymnasium and attend special events. The green armband was the most coveted and toughest to attain. It meant the patient had full privileges, including the ability to stay up late and even go home for short periods on a pass. Greens were expected to be role models; they helped out during workshops, assisted in cleanup after mealtime, and reported rule infractions to the staff. Reds were the bad boys and girls. The red armband was reserved for those who consistently disobeyed rules, started fights, injured themselves, or had to forcibly be injected with their medications.

Richard had been Yellow before. He had even come close to being Green during one stay a few years back. But that distinction was not granted due to an altercation with another patient who had made a habit of pinching Richard on the behind every chance he got. Richard was relieved to think he might be Yellow in a couple days, if he could manage to play by the rules. The thought occurred to him that he would probably never be Green. *Why*, he asked himself, *would they grant freedom to someone accused of aggravated assault and battery?*

Richard rose and walked away from the day room, down the Plexiglas lined hallway and past the buzz of activity at the nurse's station. Patients were locked out of their rooms and the room lights were turned out every day between the hours of 10:00 AM and 2:00 PM. Light from the hallway filtered through the outer walls of each vacant room, giving them the appearance of zoo exhibits that had been closed. A few feet down the hallway a man stood facing a room, which Richard assumed was his. His hands were pressed against the door. Richard glanced at a clock on the wall and saw that the man would have to wait almost three hours before he was allowed back inside. As he passed him the man mumbled something that sounded like the words to The Star Spangled Banner, but in a monotone voice that made it feel more like a funeral eulogy.

"Code one! Code one in the day room!" The words blared from a loudspeaker overhead. Richard knew it meant there was a patient who needed restraining. He continued walking leisurely around the circle of rooms, listening to the rush of footsteps but never turning to watch as nurses and techs hurried to the site of the commotion. He heard screams, first from what he thought to be the troublesome patient and then from others who he guessed were agitated by the sight of a resident being wrestled to the ground and stuck with a needle.

He stopped to look at a display case full of artwork created by patients. Some were charcoal drawings of flowers and fruit. There were several watercolor paintings of nature scenes, and one of a mother and child. Most were simple and somewhat crude, but one stood out. It was a painting of a stone castle set in a lush countryside and adorned with colorful vegetation, tall stately looking trees and a meandering stream. Its colors were vibrant and its lines and proportions exacting. The sense of depth and dimension and the way light and shadow complemented each other caused Richard to draw in closer. He wondered how a patient could have created such a beautiful thing with nothing but paint and canvas. He smiled as he imagined himself laying next to the stream with a cigarette in one hand and a cup of coffee in the other.

Looking down to the bottom right corner of the painting he noticed a signature scrawled in perfectly written purple cursive letters – "Conrad Hampton III Esquire," it read.

The morning round of medications was beginning to wear on him. He felt sluggish and numb. His feet were heavy as he made his way past room 327, where he spent two weeks during his last stay. He continued on past the last patient room, the buzzing day room and the cafeteria, which held only a small group of techs at the end of one table. He ran his hand along the shiny tan colored tiles that adorned the entrance to the men's bathroom. He turned a corner, knowing that the hallway he had just entered was not meant for residents. *If someone takes notice*, he thought, *I'll just play dumb.* He came upon a door with a sign that read EQUIPMENT ROOM. Adjacent to that door was another that read LAUNDRY ROOM, and a third, a set of double doors with a sign that read NO ADMITTANCE – STAFF ONLY.

He started to turn around and go back, but something stopped him. It happened each time he had stood in front of the NO ADMITTANCE door in the past, and he couldn't help himself. He squinted his eyes and peered through the crack between the two heavy steel doors. The dim light in the room and the limited view from the small space between the doors made it difficult to see exactly what the room held. He made out the hazy outline of one end of a stainless steel table. His throat tightened. Wires protruded from a console containing some sort of electronic equipment, the tangle of colored wires flowing out of his field of vision. Then he saw something that drained the blood from his face - wickedly shaped, shiny silver-colored instruments that were sharply pointed.

This was the lobotomy room.

"It's still here!" he said aloud. Realizing he might have attracted the attention of staff, he looked down the hall but saw no one. Swallowing hard, he placed a hand over his mouth. His palm was cold and sticky with sweat. His heart began to race and his breathing became shallow and quick. Throwing his hand against the door to steady himself, his vision went blurry and his knees began to buckle. *This is it*, he thought. *This time they're going to do it. They're not going to let me walk out of here without operating on my brain. They're going to give me a lobotomy!*

"OF COURSE THEY'RE GOING TO GIVE HIM A LOBOTOMY!" Author screamed. "THEY CAN'T LET HIM OUT THE WAY HE IS!"

"THEY'LL USE THE GERMAN INSTRUMENT!" Melissa said, matching Author's vicious tone. "HE'LL NEVER COME BACK FROM IT IF THEY USE THAT!"

Richard's body trembled and his vision was dimmed to the point where he felt he would lose consciousness. Summoning all his strength, he turned and stumbled back down the hallway towards the public area. Nurses and staff milled about. *One day soon*, he thought, *some of them will be standing over me wielding those wicked shiny instruments, as I lay anesthetized and helpless on that cold stainless steel table!*

Somehow he made it to the day room without drawing attention to himself. Many of the residents were still watching TV. Some were sitting by themselves and others were talking. Several nurses and techs were there. He considered taking a shortcut through the crowd to reach his room but then remembered it was locked. He stopped, still hyperventilating. "Calm down," he said in a whisper. "Don't give them a reason."

He spotted two large upholstered chairs sitting next to each other. One contained a woman who was wringing her hands and rocking back and forth, the other was empty. He made eye contact with a nurse who was standing near the TV crowd. He didn't dare look away for fear that she might wonder what he was hiding and approach him to find out. Instead, he forced a twitching smile at her and began walking as calmly and steadily as he could to the open chair. He was certain she saw his distress, but he couldn't bear even the thought of turning to see if she was following him. When he reached the chair he stopped, his body tensed in anticipation of being grabbed and thrown to the floor. Several seconds went by and the woman sitting in the chair next to him looked up. "My Rodney is a going to take care of those sons o' bitches so they don't bother my feet no more!" she spewed through gray teeth.

Richard turned and dropped down into the chair like a bag of rocks.

"IT'S A GERMAN INSTRUMENT. THE GERMANS KNOW WHAT THEIR DOING. IT'LL GET THE JOB DONE," Melissa taunted.

He closed his eyes trying hard to think of something, anything at all that would take his mind off of the lobotomy room. The stress of the ordeal and the heavy doses of medication he had received earlier had worn him out. His eyes began to grow heavy, and soon they closed and he fell asleep.

Moments later he saw thousands of snowflakes floating around her, like tiny white fairies. Esther stuck out her tongue to catch them, and then she smiled and licked her lips. Her hands were raised high above her head, and smoke colored stone stretched upwards behind her.

"Richard," Malcolm said, waiting for a response but not getting one. "Richard, it's time for lunch," he said again, gently shaking his shoulder.

Richard woke, but it took him a few moments to realize where he was. His mind still held the image of Esther,

Twenty

"Where's Charlie? Where are Isabel and Esther?" Richard asked his mother and father as they pulled out chairs to sit with him at the table in the day room. It was Tuesday, the first day he was allowed visitors.

"Mom, what's wrong? Where is Charlie?"

"Richard, we have something to tell you," Agnes said grabbing his hand.

"What? What happened?"

His mother looked at him soberly and drew a breath. "Esther is missing," she said. Her glistening eyes growing wider upon hearing herself utter the words. Placing a trembling hand over her mouth, she dropped her frightened gaze to the tabletop. She was unable to continue looking at her son's face because it had suddenly lost its color.

"What do you mean she's missing? How could she be missing? Wasn't she with Isabel and Charlie?"

Agnes' mouth twitched as if words would soon come out, but all that passed through her cracked lips were gasps of air.

Edmond cupped her hands in his. "Isabel took Esther to the park, to Tainter Park," he said. "Like they sometimes do on Sundays after church. She likes the merry-go-round and the teeter-totter." His voice began to shake. "She never minded the cold you know."

Richard had never seen his father lose even the slightest amount of control over his emotions. He had always been even-tempered, expressing joy, anger and sadness in a quiet and dignified manner. But looking at him now, Richard saw that the man, who had dutifully tried to take over the conversation for his grieving wife, was unable to force words past the lump in his throat. Edmond shifted in his seat and looked down, his thumb caressing the skin atop Agnes' weathered hand. He swallowed hard, and after a moment he swallowed again. Then he silently nodded his head as if obeying an unspoken command to push forward. "They were playing hide and go seek, and when Isabel went to find her she was gone. That was Sunday afternoon." He exhaled, took another breath and forced himself to continue. "Isabel can't be consoled. And Charlie...well Charlie is..." Edmond's trembling hand covered his mouth and his misty eyes released a single tear, which ran halfway down his cheek before dissolving into the salt and pepper colored stubble on his unshaven face.

Richard's face twisted in anguish. "Does anyone know where she might be? Who's looking for her?" he asked. He didn't wait for a reply before continuing, his voice quivering now. "I just had a dream about her! She was happy!" His mother and father remained silent, so he paused and came up with a question he thought they might be able to answer. "What about the sheriff? What does he think?"

Edmond gathered himself. "Sheriff Langford has all his men looking for her. They've been on it since Isabel and Charlie reported her missing on Sunday."

Richard's head dropped and he covered his face with his hands. "Did someone take her? Is there anyone who would--"

"We're not sure," Agnes interrupted, sniffling and grabbing a handkerchief from her purse. "But everyone seems to think that's probably what happened. Someone took our Esther. Someone took our baby girl." Agnes got up and walked to a sunlit window on the outer wall of the day room, the thick wire mesh covering the window cast a checkered pattern on her body and her haggard face. Richard and his father remained at the table in stunned silence. A throng of residents gathered around the television on the other side of the day room suddenly went quiet when game show theme music blared from the box.

"Dad, what are we going to do?" Richard asked.

"I don't know son. Look. Pray. Wait. I don't know what else there is."

***

The Plexiglas encased wall clock in Richard's room read 3:17 PM when he finally gathered the strength to raise his head. His mother and father had left at 11:30 AM, just before lunch was served. They hugged and kissed him and tried hard to be up beat, offering tight-lipped smiles and weakly reassuring nods. His mother had given him a bag of clothes to wear when he was allowed the privilege. During lunch he sat and stared at his tray, poking fork holes in the flour tortilla encasing his turkey wrap. He ate nothing and couldn't even bring himself to drink his coffee. By 12:30 PM, well before residents were normally allowed back into their rooms, Richard had told Malcolm that he needed to lie down. After conferring with the nurses Malcolm wrapped an arm around Richard's shoulder and walked him to his bedside, trying to comfort him along the way. He had said nothing about the nurse's stipulation that Richard be watched closely, or that his dosage of Diazepam be increased.

His eyes were swollen and red as he lay in bed staring at the wall clock. His stomach was in knots, and it felt like his chest had a hole in it where his heart used to be. A sweat soaked pillow lay crumpled against the wall by his head, and the blanket he had covered himself with was coiled around him like a boa constrictor.

"God, where is Esther? What happened to her?" he pleaded, his hands tightly clenching his blanket. "Talk to me! Tell me where she is so we can bring her back!"

"Richard, you OK?" Malcolm asked, standing outside Richard's door.

Richard stuffed the soggy pillow under his head and rolled over with his back toward the door. "My niece is missing Malcolm. So no, I'm not OK."

"I'm really sorry about that Richard. I know your hurtin'. I'm prayin' that your niece gets found real soon. Real soon. I just wanna make sure you're gonna be OK."

A heavy sigh was Richard's only response.

"OK, I'll leave you alone then. I'll come back to check on ya in a while."

Richard stared at the off-white colored wall only inches from his face. He looked at the pitted texture of the heavily painted concrete blocks and the smoothly mortared joints that connected one block to another. Slowly his vision became hazy, as if he was beginning to daydream, as if images created by his mind were overpowering his eyesight. He saw Esther as he had seen her in his dream, with her hands raised high, funneling snowflakes onto her tongue. He stretched out his hand and caressed the wall as if it were her soft cheek. He began to detect a scent, something noxious that had clung to the floor but was now slowly making its way upward. Again, it was the faint but sickening smell of burnt rubber. He sniffed the air but didn't have the energy to raise his head and look for its source. Closing his eyes, he decided it didn't matter.

"Hey kid. How you holdin' up?" the voice erupted from behind him.

Richard rolled over to see Mr. Lazarus sitting on the floor opposite his bed with his back against the wall. Turning back again, he buried his face in the pillow.

"Get out," he said firmly. His voice was muffled by the pillow but still came through as a direct order. Lazarus said nothing.

Richard turned again to Lazarus. "I don't want you here! Get out!"

"Has it occurred to you that you are locked up?" Lazarus said, his eyes flashing as he spoke and animating his otherwise emotionless face. "Has it occurred to you that you're going to rot in here while your niece is out there hoping that someone will find her?"

"It's all I can think about."

"What if I told you that there was a way for you to help?" Lazarus said slyly. "What if I told you that you could get out of here?"

Richard squinted his puffy, bloodshot eyes. "You're crazy," he said dismissively. "What are you talking about?"

"I'm crazy? Huh. I'm crazy?" Lazarus smirked. "I'm not the one locked up, you are."

"Yeah, I'm locked up!" Richard barked, emphasizing the word *locked* to underscore the ridiculousness of the idea that he could just get up and leave. "I can't get out until they let me out. What do you suggest? Do I just walk up to Malcolm and ask if it's OK if I go out for a while? I'm sure he'd say 'No problem Richard! Here's my key! Come back after you find Esther!'"

"You disappoint me, Richard."

"I disappoint me too," he said in an exhausted tone, grabbing his stomach to untie the ever-tightening knot that seemed to be feeding on his misery.

194

"Don't you remember? Do you really not remember?" asked Lazarus.

"Remember what?"

"Who are you talking to?" Malcolm interjected, standing outside the door once again.

Richard sat up. He looked at Malcolm, then at Lazarus, then back at Malcolm.

"Um, no one. I was just talking to myself. Trying to work this whole thing out, you know?"

Malcolm shook his head. "It's a shame Richard, a real shame. But I'm prayin' for you and your family, especially Esther."

"Thanks Malcolm," Richard said, pausing. "I think I just need to rest for a while."

When Malcolm was gone Richard looked back to Lazarus. "Don't get my hopes up old man, or I swear I'll--"

"You'll what? Tell on me? Hit me? Shut the hell up and listen. I'm the only friend you have right now. Sure Charlie and your mom and dad love you, but they can't help you the way I can. They are as weak and ill fitted to deal with this as you are."

"Then what? Stop playing with me and spit it out. What do you suggest I do?"

"Well, start thinking for one," Lazarus retorted, smirking again. "You don't have to ask what's his face for a key. You don't have to ask him because you already have one."

***

Richard was already up when Malcolm came to his door the next morning. "I got somethin' for ya," Malcolm said, sporting a big grin. He stuck his hand in the pocket of his white tech's coat, pulled out a yellow armband and twirled it on his finger. "You're movin' on up Richard. You're Yellow now but you'll be Green as Kermit the Frog 'fore you know it."

Richard grabbed the brightly colored strip of cloth. "This means I can wear my own clothes, right?"

"That's right! And if you're good I'll let you wear your own shoes too!" Malcolm said, flashing a mouthful of white teeth and laughing heartily. "You know I'm just messin' wicha. You can use the gym and the showers during your free time. And that aint all! You know there's gonna be a sweet little play put on by some kids from the community college? The missus and I saw it over the Fourth of July weekend and we loved it. It's called "The Trouble with Finnegan." I was thinking of asking if I could bring her to see it this time too. It's at 10 o'clock in classroom D, I think."

Richard slipped the yellow band over his arm. "Thanks Malcolm," he said. "You're a good man - an answer to prayer really."

"Well I appreciate that! I really do. You brighten my day some too," Malcolm said, patting Richard's shoulder. "Well, enough chattin'. I got rounds to make." He pointed to the open space outside the door. "I'll see you out there, wearin' that yellow band and actin' like you was from Hollywood or somthin'."

***

"Braham's lullaby, Braham's lullaby, Braham's lullaby. You can't taste the pickle without the sour." The patient standing behind Richard repeated the nonsensical phrase over and over as they shuffled toward the front of the line to receive their morning medications. Richard kept his hands to his sides and counted the moles on the neck of the patient in front of him to keep himself composed. When his turn came he took the small paper cup containing his pills, tilted his head back and emptied the contents into his mouth. He finished by gulping water from another paper cup. When he swallowed he felt something go down. Somehow one of the pills he had maneuvered between his cheek and gum had worked its way out and was now on its way down his throat and into his system. He only hoped that it wasn't the sedative. He smiled and thanked the nurse who gave him the medication. When he rounded the corner leading to the cafeteria he expelled the pills he had not swallowed into his hand during a faked cough.

Richard ignored his lack of appetite during breakfast and ate everything that was on the food tray, the scrambled eggs, sausage, fruit cup and orange juice. The only thing he didn't have to pretend to like was the coffee; he filled his cup four times before he finally got up to leave the table. He waived to nurse Fenstermaker, who ignored him and continued attending to a patient who was refusing to eat. On his way out of the cafeteria he said hello to the dishwashers behind the counter where he placed his tray. He wanted people to believe he was doing well, and didn't require close supervision. Within the hour Richard planned to leave Broward County Mental Hospital and find Esther.

He thought that there were two things that would enable his escape - one was cunning and the other was luck. And while he felt neither cunning nor lucky he reminded himself that he had managed to dupe Francis Tadley, the trickster disguised as a mailman. "I will escape," he said, mouthing the positive affirmation quietly to himself. "I will find Esther and bring her home." He looked at the clock on the wall in the day room. It was 9:07 AM. He would begin his escape at 10 o'clock.

Twenty-One

She reached up and isolated a long hair on the back of her head. With a sharp tug she ripped it out by the roots. Caroline Barry plucked a hair from her head every time she found herself feeling badly. Each dislocated hair was named, this one she called "resignation." She peered out the Plexiglas front wall of her room to make sure no one was looking, and then reached down into the baggy sock that hung loosely around her ankle and removed a dingy white but neatly folded handkerchief. Inside the handkerchief lay a ponytail-sized crop of hair held together on one end by a rubber band. Her bottom lip quivered as she removed the rubber band and softly nestled newly named "resignation" among the hundreds of other long, black symbols of her suffering that had been gathered over the years. She told herself she knew them all by name. "Injustice," she nudged one. "Bitterness," she nudged another. "Apathy. Collusion. Resentment." She stopped suddenly and looked at the long swath of hair beside her on the bed. Grabbing her chest, she thought about the pain it represented. Her eyes began to well with tears and she yanked out another hair, called it "sorrow" and laid it to rest with all the others. A fleeting thought presented itself as it had many time before; if she were ever to have nothing left to pluck, she would simply kill herself.

Caroline wrapped the rubber band around the tuft of hair and began enclosing it in the handkerchief when there was a knock on her door. She quickly slid the handkerchief under her pillow before looking up to see a man standing there, a man she had seen before but had never talked with. She wiped her eyes and walked to the door.

"Yes?" she said, standing close to the speaking holes.

"Hi, I'm Richard. Richard Buell."

She hesitated. "Yes, how may I help you?"

"Um, I was wondering if I could ask you something."

"What is it that you want?" she asked, nervously stroking her hair.

"Well, I was kind of hoping I could come in and talk with you."

Caroline looked past Richard to a group of nurses who were talking halfway between her room and the nurse's station. They were too far away to hear Richard's request, and she thought about yelling for help.

"May I come in?" Richard asked again.

Caroline shook her head no. Her lips were tightly pursed and her eyes darted nervously between Richard and the group of nurses.

Richard looked around to see if he was being watched. "I have something you might like," he said. He reached into his pant pocket and then withdrew his hand, keeping it close to his waist. Slowly, he opened his fingers to reveal a single stick of white chalk.

Caroline gasped audibly. She covered her mouth to prevent giving further voice to the intense desire that had exploded inside her like a clap of thunder. She looked at the chalk, then at Richard, then back at the chalk. Dropping her hand, her face lit as if a dear old friend had unexpectedly appeared at her door. Richard knew he was in. Caroline opened the door to her room and began rubbing her hands together. He walked past her and stood facing the side of her bed. Scurrying in front of him, she sat on the mattress. Submissively she lowered her head and turned her eyes upward, like a slave in the overpowering presence of her master. Then she cupped both hands and held them in front of her.

Richard snapped the stick of chalk in half and placed one chunk in her hands. Caroline shoved it in her mouth and began chewing. "Mmm," she moaned, crunching down and grinding the chalk into a gritty paste. "Mmm. So good. Sooo very good." She smacked her lips and swallowed and then held out her hand again. When Richard didn't immediately place another piece into it she jerked her fingers towards her open mouth. "More! I want more!"

"Shhhh!" Richard responded, glancing back toward the door to make sure no one had noticed her passionate demand. "I'll give you the chalk, but I need something from you first."

Caroline cocked her head to one side as a dog does when it hears a strange sound it doesn't understand. She turned her head again as if finding the correct angle would funnel his words into her ear canal, through the correct neural pathways and into the precise part of her brain that would produce the response needed to get the second half of the stick of chalk. After some consideration she thought she knew what he was asking, but she didn't know how to fulfill his request without drawing the attention of the nurses and techs. It took only moments for her to decide that it didn't matter as long as she was able to feed the previously dormant but now ravenous animal inside her, which was screaming for more of the tube-shaped opiate. She smiled at the thought of the next bite and began unbuttoning her blouse.

"No-no-no! Not that!" Richard said, holding up his hand in a halting motion. "I didn't mean that! I'm not asking for -- Never mind, just stop!"

Caroline froze with a confused look on her face. Its appetite whetted, the beast inside her ordered her to grab him and get on with it, but the desperation in Richard's eyes stopped her. After a moment of silent consideration she re-buttoned her blouse and rested her quivering hands on her lap. Richard looked down at her face, the features of which were youthful but weathered. Her skin was a flawless ivory color and her cheeks were plump and slightly flushed. But, heavy lines etched the corners of her eyes and stretched across her forehead in furrows. Full, parted lips revealed a row of perfectly formed white teeth set into a firm jaw. A few strands of gray-black hair hung over large eyeglasses, the lenses of which were so scratched and worn it appeared they had been rubbed with sandpaper. The damaged lenses obscured her stunning blue-green eyes. But Richard could still see that they were beautiful and vulnerable, like the eyes of an innocent child who had a chance to satisfy her unceasing appetite. He thought of Judith, and that made him feel badly for taking advantage of Caroline's weakness. But his need for freedom was greater than the nagging compulsion to act decently.

Caroline Barry had been at Broward for a long time. During one of his previous stays some years ago, Richard sat with her in a group therapy session where she openly admitted her love of chalk. When asked by the therapist to describe the problems caused by her addiction, she mournfully recalled a situation where staff had wrestled her to the floor in one of the older classrooms. She fought and screamed and stuffed as much chalk into her mouth as she could before being forcibly removed from what she called the "Black slate garden," the blackboard from which she thought the chalk grew. Richard had forgotten about Carolyn's problem until Lazarus reminded him of it during their discussion about the escape plan. He dwelled for a moment on vague memories of Carolyn and the few interactions they shared. Then, the current predicament pulled him back to the present.

"I'm sorry if I frightened you. Are you OK?" he asked.

Still looking into his eyes she nodded yes and licked her lips, taking in whatever chalk residue had clung there.

"HE SHOULD JUMP ON THIS!" Author screamed, pushing his way into Richard's consciousness like a bulldozer.

"YEAH! SHE'S RIPE! SHE'S RIPE FOR THE TAKING!" Melissa joined in, giving no consideration to the fact that anyone outside the room could watch what they were doing.

Author and Melissa's comments, while distracting, gave him a sudden and delightfully greedy sense of power. Richard felt a surge radiate through his body, and his mind registered it like a Geiger counter that clicked faster and louder with each passing moment. He felt strong and confident in ways he was not accustomed to, and he considered what his newfound power could do for him. He had complete control over Carolyn Barry and she would do whatever he asked. What's more she would do it willingly, even gladly. He inhaled deeply as if drawing power from the very air around him. He was keenly aware of his body and his presence in the room, which seemed to dwarf everything else, especially the subservient woman sitting at his feet.

"GO FOR IT!" Author said permissively, attempting to remove any reluctance that remained in Richard's mind.

He blinked several times and looked at the wall above Caroline's head. Judith had been standing silently in the back of his mind since he had walked into Carolyn's room. He could see her clearly now, clutching her handbag and peering at him expectantly. The image of her caused him to feel a pang of guilt and shame for even having considered abusing his newfound power. It pulled him out of his fantasy and back to the reason he had come to Carolyn in the first place - to aid in his escape from Broward and get to Esther.

Richard opened his hand revealing the remaining half stick of chalk, but he held it far enough away from Carolyn to let her know that it was not yet hers. Caroline's unblinking eyes were fixed on it.

"I need something in this room," he said.

She shook her head. "Take it. Take whatever you need," she answered, parting her lips and caressing them with her fingertips.

"I need you to do something for me."

"Uh huh. Whatever you need. Just tell me."

"I need you to stand by the door and tell me if anyone walks this way."

"May I please have one first?" she begged. The desperate, pleading tone in her voice told Richard that denying her would not go over well. The last thing he wanted was to draw attention, so he handed her the chalk. She closed her eyes and chewed, slower this time, taking deep breaths in and out of her nose like a drug addict whose needle had just released the warm embrace of heroin into her veins. She finished chewing and swallowed. Slowly opening her eyes, she glanced up at Richard. "How much do you have?" she asked. Her eyes were serene, but her voice had an edge. Richard reached into his pocket and pulled out a box about the size of a pack of cigarettes. He opened the cardboard flap to reveal nine perfectly formed pale white sticks.

"Oooh! Oh yes!" she mewed, straightening her posture and running her fingers through her hair in a hasty attempt to comb it. She stood up and brushed the wrinkles from her gown. "I'll tell you if I see anyone," she said, hurrying to the door.

Richard didn't bother explaining what he was after because he knew she didn't care. "I'll give you the rest when I have what I need," he said, walking to a small round bedside table and kneeling beside it.

The excitement and quick sprint to the front of her room caused Caroline to feel light-headed. She closed her eyes and took a few deep breaths to gather herself. When she opened them, nurse Fenstermaker was within a few steps of the door.

"Oh! She's here!" Caroline hissed.

Richard looked up, saw the white of her uniform and immediately grabbed his shoelaces.

"Caroline, what are you doing?" Nurse Fenstermaker asked, the high-pitched squeak of her voice causing Richard to bite his lip. He untied a shoelace and immediately began to retie it.

"Oh hello!" Carolyn bellowed, her smile revealing a chalky white residue in the corners of her mouth. "Yes, um, nothing," she said. "Just visiting with, um, ah…"

"Richard," he said, finishing her sentence and walking towards the door. Nurse Fenstermaker eyed them both suspiciously.

"I was just asking Caroline if she wanted to go with me to the play….wasn't I Caroline?"

"Yup…and I said yes…so we are going to the play." Carolyn glanced at her wrist, which had no watch strapped to it. "What time is it anyway? Doesn't it start soon?" she asked nervously, looking nurse Fenstermaker directly in the eyes and smiling politely.

Throwing squinty glances back and forth between the two, nurse Fenstermaker raised her arm and looked down at her wristwatch, which was as white as her outfit. "It's 9:47 AM. Play starts in thirteen minutes. So does lockout," she said, her eyes connecting with Richard's. "Mr. Buell," she squeaked. "How are you getting along?"

Silently giggling to himself he responded. "I'm fine, I'm fine. And hey, I wanted to thank you and Atty for not keeping me locked in my room. It's nice being able to walk around and talk with people and stuff."

"That was Doctor Dorjee's doing, not mine," Nurse Fenstermaker interjected as she turned to go.

When she had walked away Caroline grabbed her chest and started to hyperventilate. Richard retrieved the box of chalk from his pocket and extracted a whole stick. "You can't let anyone see you eating," he said, slipping her the slim, white drug.

"I won't," she responded. Then she faked a cough and immediately covered her mouth with the hand that held the chalk. Richard heard the chalk snap in her mouth, and then turned and walked back to the bedside table. Kneeling once again he lifted one of the metal table legs a few inches off the ground. With his other hand he began working the foot at the end of the leg back and forth. Little by little the foot loosened and slid off the leg. Richard heard a soft metallic clinking sound and reached down to pick up a brass colored key. He couldn't believe his luck. It was still there after all this time. He picked up the key and looked at it, thinking back to the time he had placed it there. The memory of it was weak, and he would not have remembered it at all if Mr. Lazarus had not reminded him.

Recollections of an incident during his last stay at Broward began to unfold in his mind like snapshots from a camera, fragmented and incomplete, but sufficient to relive the foggy memory. One of the patients, a large hairy man named Liam Pinto, stood in line to receive his morning medications. When his turn came he took the paper cup filled with pills and dropped it on the floor. Then he proceeded to snap the neck of a male nurse who had the unfortunate duty of handing him his medication. The nurse dropped limply to the floor and Pinto began kicking his torso. The other patients in line scattered like cockroaches. Richard, who had received a heavy dose of medications almost thirty minutes earlier, rose groggily from his chair in the day room and moved towards the commotion. One tech grabbed Pinto, but was soon flung head first against a nearby wall. Afraid they'd end up the same way, the other techs and nurses did nothing but yell at him until one was able to retrieve a syringe loaded with sedative. It took three techs and a nurse to bring Pinto to his knees so the one with the syringe could make the injection. Three techs lay atop him while the drug began to take effect. When he was unconscious the rest of the staff began attending to the injured.

Patients moved in closer once the madman was out. Standing only a few steps away, Richard looked down to the floor and saw a key ring that had been ejected from the injured nurse's coat pocket when he was being kicked. He picked it up and stepped to the back of the group of gawking patients. The ring held an assortment of keys, but one stood out; it had the letter M stamped on it. He had seen the M stamp a few years back when he did janitorial work at a small office complex back in Cutter's Mill. The M meant it was a master key that would open any door in the facility. He looked up and saw that everyone was still facing away from him, so he removed the key and placed it in his pocket. Then he moved up close to the group, set the remaining keys on the floor and walked away.

The head nurse gave an order to have all patients confined to their rooms until the situation was under control. Once back in his room, the room that was now occupied by Carolyn Barry, Richard looked around for several minutes before deciding to try hiding the key in the leg of the table that sat beside the bed. It worked. The key was in place and soon Richard lay on his bed, his eyes heavy and his mind numbed. The medication in his system and the events of the morning had tired him so greatly that he dozed off and slept until just before lunch. He later learned that the nurse whose neck was broken was confined to a wheel chair for the rest of his life. And the tech that was thrown against the wall recovered completely, but could not bring himself to return to work.

Drawing himself back to the present, Richard looked up to see Caroline dutifully standing guard at the front of his old room. He stood and removed the box of chalk from his pocket. "Psst," he said, getting her attention.

When she turned around she saw him slide the box under her bed pillow. She smiled at him and stroked her hair. "Thank you for doing that," she said kindly. "Thank you so very much."

Richard moved to her side. "Make it last," he said pointedly. "I won't be able to give you any more." Squeezing her arm softly, he left the room. As he walked past the nurse's station he glanced back to see her sitting on the edge of her bed clutching the small box.

Twenty-Two

The clock on the wall in the day room read 9:53 AM. Patients and staff would soon begin making their way to Classroom D to see the play. Richard didn't have much time and he had to move without being noticed. He opened the closet door in his room and grabbed a loose fitting and lightly insulated plaid shirt his mother had brought him. He pulled off his sweatshirt, threw it on the bed and quickly changed. His heart rate and breathing began to quicken and his hands were shaking. Tiny beads of sweat clung to his upper lip, and his eyes darted around the room as he tried to think of anything else that he needed to take with him. He thought about the moth book, how it symbolized his ongoing transformation from loathsome worm to beautiful creature. He hated to leave it behind, but quickly decided that it would be impractical to take so he started walking towards the door.

"Hey my man! You goin' to the play?"

Richard stopped in his tracks when he saw Malcolm at the door. "Ah, yeah," he said. "I was just, ah, I was just on my way to the bathroom." *Not now Malcolm! There is no time!* he screamed to himself. *I need to leave now!* Richard moved forward, opened the door to his room and walked out.

"Where's your armband my brotha? You earned it! You should be wearin' it!"

"Oh yeah, the armband," Richard said, walking back to the bed. He picked up the sweatshirt he had just thrown there and removed the yellow band from the sleeve. "OK, well I guess I'll see you at the play." He motioned in the general direction of classroom

D, hoping that Malcolm would take the hint and leave. Richard hurried back to the door, painfully aware that the clock was ticking.

Malcolm placed a hand on Richard's shoulder. "You OK?" he asked. "You seem a bit out of sorts."

"Oh yeah, I just have to pee so badly. I need to go. I'll see you soon, OK?"

"Lookin' forward to it my man. I'll see you soon."

Richard walked away from Malcolm and through a throng of people walking past his room on their way to Classroom D. He made his way past the nurses' station, rounded the corner and started down the hallway that led to the bathroom. Midway down the hall he saw the man who called himself Conrad Hampton the Third coming his way. Richard looked at the floor to avoid making eye contact.

"Greetings old chap! How do you do on this most glorious of days?" Conrad bellowed, stopping in his tracks and hoping to talk at Richard for a while.

"Gotta go Conrad. Gotta go," Richard said, rushing past him and ducking into the bathroom. Two patients and a tech were washing their hands, so Richard stood at the urinal pretending to pee. *Leave!* he yelled at them in his head over and over while they took their time rinsing and drying. Finally they left and Richard hurried to the entrance, peeking around the corner to see if anyone else was coming. The hallway was clearing quickly. When the last person was out of sight, he reached into his pocket and pulled out the key.

"Please let this be a master key. Please let this be a master key," he pleaded as he approached the door marked LAUNDRY ROOM. Slipping the key into the lock he tried turning it, but it didn't budge. "God please open this door; please let this be the key that opens this door." He tried turning it and felt it catch again. "No, please no!" he hissed, removing the key and looking at it, hoping to find something to explain why it wasn't working. He saw nothing. "God, Esther needs me. Pleeeeease open this door!" He stuck the key back into the lock and jiggled it with his trembling hands. Suddenly it turned and he heard a click. He gasped as the door handle turned and the door swung open. He quickly stepped inside and closed the door behind him. As soon as he got inside he realized that he forgot to look down the hallway to see if anyone may have entered it while he was fidgeting with the lock. *It's too late now*, he thought. *If they catch me, that's it. It's over.*

Two large fabric baskets on wheels sat near the door so staff could easily throw in soiled items that needed washing. Richard reached into the one nearest him and began pulling out handfuls of towels, bed sheets and gowns. He didn't find what he needed. He went to the next basket and threw its contents on the floor. Again he found nothing. Frantic now, he stood and wiped the sweat pouring from his face. Then, looking to a shelf in front of him, he saw them; stacks of tech uniforms, tops and bottoms of all sizes and colors. He wrestled out of his plaid shirt and blue jeans, grabbed a set of trousers and began pulling them on. He only got them up to his knees when he realized they were too small, so he pulled them off again.

"HE CAN'T DO THAT! HE'S IN TROUBLE, BIG TROUBLE!"

Richard jerked to his left and right before realizing that the voice had come from inside his head. Relieved but agitated, he grabbed a pair of trousers from the shelf marked LARGE. They fit perfectly as did the top.

"HE THINKS HE'S GOING TO FIND ESTHER! HE THINKS HE CAN SAVE HER! WHAT A CHUMP!"

Richard paid no attention to the verbal attack. Instead he placed his blue jeans at the bottom of one of the fabric baskets and piled the laundry he had removed earlier on top. He folded the plaid shirt over his arm and quietly opened the laundry room door just enough for his head to fit through. He looked down the hall both ways and saw no one. Directly across the hall was the set of double doors leading to the lobotomy room. Leaving that behind would be a bonus. Just a few feet to his right was the way out. He reached into his pocket where the master key was supposed to be, but it was not there. He patted his pants frantically trying to locate it. Then he realized he had left the key in the pocket of his blue jeans. Digging through the laundry basket again, he located his pants and retrieved the key. He thought about how lucky he was that he hadn't closed the laundry room door behind him before discovering that the key was missing. *This is it*, he thought. *It's time to get out of here and go find Esther. God be with me.*

Richard eased out of the laundry room and into the hallway. He wasted no time fitting the key into the door that led out of the Crazy Wing. He jiggled it until it opened. Keeping his head down, he moved with purpose, hoping to not run into anyone who would recognize him. The hallway he was now in was long, and the first part was bordered on both sides with windowless doors, all of which were closed. Looking further down the hallway he saw people milling around and walking in and out of rooms. They were not patients - they were staff. His stomach tightened and he slowed his pace.

"THEY'RE GOING TO CATCH HIM! HE'S GOING TO PAY FOR THIS!" a voice screamed.

Dizzy with anxiety, Richard paid no attention to whether it was Author or Melissa who had spoken. He felt bile rising up his esophagus and he was sure he'd vomit. Immediately to his left he spotted a tiny alcove that held two chairs and a small table. He could think of nothing but getting out of sight of the people down the hall, so he ducked in and stood, fists clenched and facing the table.

"HE'S GOING TO BE SICK!" a voice jeered.

LOOK AT HIS FACE! HE'S AS PALE AS A GHOST!" the other added coldly, and for the sole purpose of making him feel worse than he already did.

Richard shut his eyes tight. "You can do this," he said aloud. "You have to do this."

Reaching down, he grabbed a magazine from an assortment that was fanned out on the table. Author and Melissa screamed at each other about how he was crazy for moving, but he willed himself to turn around and reenter the hallway. His feet felt like they were set in concrete, each step heavy and sluggish, as if his own body was resisting movement. Sensing the searing gaze of curious onlookers he willed himself forward, closer and closer to the group. He felt he was moving headlong into a den of ravenous lions that would rip him apart once they realized who he was. He kept his head down and the magazine open, hoping no one would notice him. *Just keep putting one foot in front of the other*, he told himself. The tension in his body caused every inch of his flesh to vibrate. A metallic hum in his ears grew louder and louder, like a siren warning him to run away from the danger he was approaching. Relentless, he resisted what his body and mind and the voices were telling him to do; he kept walking forward.

The image of Esther flashed before him; her hands raised high and her long curly hair blowing lazily in the wind. He was determined to get her back, and he was not about to allow his anxiety, no matter how intense, to prevent him from doing it. Within only a few steps of the bustle of people he closed the magazine. Looking up, he smiled and made eye contact with those closest to him.

"Hello," he said to one, pleasantly. "How are you?" he asked another.

Passing a nurse that looked a lot like Nurse Fenstermaker he said "Looks like a great day out there!" For added theatrical effect he smiled and pointed to a window revealing a sun filled sky.

"Sure does. You have a good day now," she replied.

He continued on, cordially nodding to and greeting those he passed until he reached a bank of elevators on his right. Instinctively, he reached for the elevator button, ready to board and ride down to the first floor. But he decided against it at the last moment. *Being held captive inside a metal box with other people is too risky*, he told himself. Instead, he turned and went into a stairwell and began descending three flights of stairs that would end on the ground floor. Now that he was alone, he felt ill again. Sweat dripped down the sides of his face and his stomach was in knots. Each step he took echoed off the dimly lit concrete walls as he went downward. When he reached the bottom he wiped his face, swallowed hard and opened the door leading to the first floor. When he exited the stairwell he stopped to get his bearings. "Which way? Which way?" he softly mouthed the words as he looked left and then right. *Go towards the sunlight*, he thought. He turned left and began looking for signs of daylight.

Hurriedly, he rounded a corner and crashed hard into something that knocked him back a few steps. It took only a fraction of a second to realize that it was a man, a very annoyed looking man wearing a gray suit and brightly colored tie. The folders he was carrying were strewn about the floor, and he looked at Richard with a scowl on his face.

"Oh, I'm so sorry," Richard said, kneeling to pick up sheets of paper and manila folders. *Oh no! This is it!* he thought. *I'm done! They'll put me away forever and I'll never see Esther again.*

"I, I was just looking for the way out. I'm new here and it's such a maze," Richard said apologetically.

Seeing that Richard was flustered, the man's countenance softened. "Oh that's fine. Don't worry about it. Let me get that," he said, kneeling alongside Richard and helping to gather his papers. Richard handed him the pile he had gathered and they both stood up. "What's your name?" the man asked, smiling.

"Richard Buell," he responded instinctively. *Why did you use your real name you idiot?* he screamed to himself.

"Hello Richard, I'm Ben Rosenberg." Ben extended his hand and Richard shook it. "I'm the Chief Executive Officer here at Broward."

Richard let out a moan and his eyes fluttered involuntarily as if he had taken a hard kick to the groin. "I...I...I hope you can--"

"Don't give it a second thought!" Ben said, patting Richard's shoulder heartily. "I'm fine. Are you OK?"

"Well, yes. I'm just a little lost."

"I was too when I started here some 23 years ago. What department do you work in?"

Richard was stunned into silence at the thought of having to answer employment questions from the CEO of the hospital where he was committed for aggravated assault and battery. *OK, this really is it,* he thought. *There's no way I'm leaving here alive. I'll be lying on that stainless steel table in the lobotomy room before the end of the day.* He considered crossing his hands in front of him, as if to indicate that handcuffs could now be applied with no resistance on his part. He even felt his arms flinch like they would take the action on their own. Instead he opened his mouth, praying that something coherent would come out.

"I'm sorry - I'm still a little stunned. I'm ah, I'm a tech up in D wing. Nurse Fenstermaker has been taunting – I, I mean training me."

Ben laughed loudly. "Nurse Fenstermaker, huh? She's been here as long as I have, maybe longer. She's a bit tightly wound, but she really is a sweetheart."

"Yes, that's exactly what I said to Malcolm. Do you know Malcolm," Richard asked, continuing the charade and for the first time realizing that he didn't know Malcolm's last name.

Ben chuckled again, "I can't say that I do, but I'm glad that you're here working with us. We need good conscientious people like you." Ben paused, eyeing Richard sympathetically. "But I must say, you look pretty worn out. It's time we get you on your way. Go home and get some rest. Tomorrow will be better."

"Thanks Mr. Rosenberg, I'll do that."

"Please, call me Ben. Let me show you how to get out of here."

Beginnings lead to endings

And endings start anew

The flesh he wears in this life

Is just an anteroom

———————————

In silken shroud he wraps himself

To make his earthly tomb

But grave it's not

For providence makes

A warm and restful womb

———————————

Upon the light he breaks away

In lofty flight above

And upward flutters on his wings

Toward beauty, joy, and love

Twenty-Three

Daylight flooded Richard's face and it made him squint. He stepped onto the sidewalk leading to the hospital parking lot and buttoned up the navy blue, wool pea coat he took from a coat rack sitting in the main hallway at the front of the building. He had no car or bike to get him where he needed to go, and time was not on his side. Soon someone would discover he was missing. He figured it would be Malcolm since he would probably notice his absence at the play. He prayed that Caroline wouldn't reveal to anyone that he had taken the key. But he knew she might if they discovered her chalk and threatened to take it away. Nurse Fenstermaker seemed always to be on the prowl, so it wouldn't surprise him if she were the one to sound the alarm and send out the hounds. Thoughts about what could go wrong plowed through his mind like bulls running the streets of Pamplona. He imagined police cars with their sirens blaring and lights flashing and decided it would be best to stay away from the main roads.

As soon as he stepped onto the parking lot he headed towards a line of trees bordering a small creek that meandered through the hospital property. *Maybe if I follow the stream it will cross a road*, he thought. *Maybe I can hitch a ride from someone. Or, maybe I'll find a bicycle somewhere.* There were many uncertainties, and they began to weigh on him. But they didn't keep him from moving forward. He knew where he needed to go, and by God's grace he would get there. No matter what the cost.

He wished he had thought to bring his stocking cap and gloves. The air was cold and dry and it stung his face and hands. He figured he had 40 minutes before the play was over and someone would notice him missing. So he picked up his pace, crashing through brambles and stepping over toppled trees strewn about the forest that bordered the stream. It would have been easier for him if Broward Hospital were set within the town limits instead of five miles outside of town and on a thirty-acre lot surrounded by miles of countryside. Stealing a bike or thumbing a ride would take less time if he were in town. He thought about the prospect of stealing a car. For a brief moment he imagined himself leaning underneath the dashboard, grappling with the ignition wires the way they did in movies he had seen long ago. Then it dawned on him that he couldn't tell an ignition wire from a string of spaghetti, so he dumped the idea.

Looking ahead he saw only trees and underbrush. He heard no noises that would indicate the presence of people. His body was heated now; even his hands and ears were warm. A crash of breaking branches startled him, and he looked up to see three deer bounding away with their white tails switching back and forth like warning flags. He plodded alongside the creek for what seemed to be another twenty minutes. He was sure he would have come across something by now, a road or field or farm. Still there was nothing but wilderness. He felt time was running out. Soon the police would be alerted and everyone would be on the hunt for a madman they undoubtedly would consider to be desperate and dangerous.

He stopped to catch his breath, telling himself he would rest for only a moment. Then something caught his ear. Off to his right, far beyond the stream, he heard the faint mooing of a cow. He stopped breathing for a moment and heard it again. A flicker of hope grew inside him. Moving quickly along the stream, he stopped at a place that looked narrow enough to jump across. Getting wet would almost certainly mean frostbite, hypothermia or both. But he needed to cross and he would have to find a way to endure whatever happened. *A good leap with the right speed and height might propel me over the water*, he reasoned to himself, giving no thought to what would happen when he landed. With a burst of energy he ran hard until he reached the bank. He left the ground with his legs swinging wildly, trying to propel his body over the frigid water. The frozen ground approached fast and he failed to get both feet under him before he hit. He landed with a thud and tumbled forward onto the ground, which felt like solid concrete. For a moment he lay still, wincing from a searing pain in his left ankle. He didn't hear anything snap, but it sure felt broken. His face buried in his arms, he closed his eyes and gritted his teeth. He was hurt, but thankful to be dry.

While he was sprawled on the hard ground, Esther's smiling face appeared once again. She lit the darkness behind his closed eyes like a full moon in a pitch-black sky. He enjoyed the sight of her for a moment and then leapt to his feet. He made it only a few yards before crashing to the ground again. Pulling himself upward with a grunt, he rested his weight on his right leg and hopped another few feet to a sturdy looking branch lying on the ground. He held it at his side, peeling away some of its bark to make a mark at armpit height. Then he stuck it in the crotch of a tree and used his weight to snap off the portion he didn't need. The makeshift crutch dug into his armpit when he put his weight on it, but he was able to hobble forward with less pain.

Walking on, the woods soon thinned and opened to a large field. The stubby remnants of corn stalks stretched onward for a great distance. Like strings of lights on an airport runway, they beckoned him forward. He saw a line of trees and a barbed wire fence bordering the right side of the field. The trees and fence ran parallel to the rows of harvested corn. On the other side of the fence was a pasture, and that's where Richard spotted the cows off in the distance. *Where there are cows*, he reasoned, *there will be a farm.* It was his only hope, so he limped forward and followed the fence line toward the horizon.

The farm came into view within minutes. It was a ways off, a little more than a mile perhaps. Trees bordering the farm property obscured his vision. Still he could see what appeared to be a large barn, two smaller outbuildings and a house. All were painted white except the barn, which was a blood red. Richard stayed close to the tree-lined fence for cover. He stopped periodically to see if there was any sort of movement, but saw none. Even the cows were standing still. He tried crouching down to further reduce the likelihood of being spotted, but it was difficult to bend his body downward and still support his weight on the crutch. So, he remained upright and continued forward, stopping behind larger trees as he scanned the landscape. *I'm close now. Maybe 10 more minutes*, he thought.

As he inched forward a cow started mooing when it spotted him. Several others, a dozen or so, turned and joined in sounding the alarm. Richard's nerves were shot. The events of the day had worn him down. Now he faced being exposed by a herd of cows. He feared they would start to run and further attract the attention of anyone who might be in the vicinity. Fortunately they just stood in place and mooed. He crept forward until he was within 50 yards of the barn, standing next to the last tree along the fence line. He bolted across the clearing in jerky motions, clenching his jaw to prevent the screams that were pushing on his front teeth from escaping his lips. His back hit the barn with a hollow thud that reverberated inside the huge wooden structure. Sweat seeped from every pore in his body, and his face burned like steaming asphalt.

Inching along the side of the barn he peered around the corner and saw a large shed with an open door, which revealed different kinds of farm equipment. The back of the white, two story farmhouse held rows of windows, a use-worn back door and a set of steps that led to the yard. The barn had a small room jutting out its side, which Richard thought was the milk house. It was just a short jaunt away from where he stood. The milk house door would be his way into the barn. He looked around again to make sure he saw no one. Then he rounded the corner and scurried with his back against the barn wall until he reached the side of the milk house. The cows had stopped mooing, which made him feel better. But now he was about to step around the corner in plain view of the house and the back yard. He breathed deep, peered around the corner and quickly stepped out to face the milk house door. Thankfully, it was already wide open. He jumped inside and froze, listening for the slightest sound that might indicate he had been seen or heard. Trying to suppress his heavy breathing, he covered his mouth with his hand. His wide, watery eyes scanning left and right, he stepped past bulk tanks and hoses to the back of the milk house and to a door that opened to the inside of the barn.

The cavernous room held cow stalls on both sides, but was empty except for a large calico cat with matted fur that bolted from under a wooden bench towards the far end of the building. The smell of cow manure was strong, but it was something Richard had grown accustomed to in his childhood. It brought back memories of a time when his life was simple and carefree, strikingly different from the mess he found himself in now. He spotted a set of crudely built wooden stairs ascending to a hayloft. The climb upwards was slow and painful, and when he reached the top he stood at one end of a huge room. It was filled with stacks upon stacks of hay bales, stepped, pyramid-like, one on top of another. The smell was musty but pleasantly sweet and earthy, and for a brief moment it brought him back to the times he had bailed hay at the Hansen farm as a kid. Pigeons fluttered about overhead, flying from one large roof timber to the next. Patchy sunlight filtered through the barn's wallboards, illuminating fine particles of dust that hung in the air.

He saw a light switch mounted on a nearby post, but knew he didn't dare turn it on. A dirty cloth tarp sat in a rumpled mass on the floor at the bottom of the hay mound. Next to the tarp was a large man-made hole in the floor that Richard knew was the hay chute. He grabbed the tarp and began climbing the large stepped pile of hay, clawing his way to the top. The pain in his leg had intensified, making the trek upwards difficult enough to require several stops to rest and regain his strength. When he finally reached the top, the hay mound flattened out. He removed two hay bales and set them in front of the hole that he had created. Climbing into the narrow burrow he covered himself head to toe with the tarp, which shut out the little bit of light coming into the loft.

It was dark and eerily still. He was hot from exertion, but the icy tarp pressing against his face and body reminded him that the cold would soon set in. *This must be what it feels like to lay in a tomb*, he thought. *And if the owner of this place finds me here, that's just what it could become.*

Ironically, while his fears were still present, the rest and temporary safety provided by the little hay coffin he had created eased his mind and he began to shed some of the weight of the day. He was completely drained. He could do nothing but breathe, and if that had required any conscious effort he would have failed to produce it. Richard's eyes eased shut, and the world around him ceased to exist.

Twenty-Four

"Come Bos! Come Bosy!" the shrill voice called out, jerking Richard from his sleep. His eyes sprung open and he wondered if he had dreamt it. Peeking out from under the tarp that covered him, he saw that the sunlight coming through the barn walls was weaker than before. He wondered how long he had been out.

Again the command cut through the chilled dusk air. "Come Bos! Come Bos!"

Bos, Richard remembered, was a term farmers sometimes used when they were calling their cows. Normally, they were put to pasture after morning milking and brought back towards the end of the day. Within a few moments he heard the sound of hoof beats in the distance. It grew louder and louder as the cows came closer. It was clear that people were approaching the barn along with the cows.

"Hya! Hya!"

"In! In with you now!"

Low, guttural lowing was accompanied by hoof beats from the herd, and the previously quiet barn suddenly came to life. Richard didn't have to see what was going on to know what was happening. Each cow knew which stall was theirs, and they all looked forward to the savory hay that would be placed in the feeding trough in front of them. They hurried to take their places in anticipation of the effortless meal that was about to be served.

"Hurry up, Brian!" a voice rang out, followed by footsteps pounding up the wooden staircase leading to the hayloft.

"I'm coming, hold your horses!" another replied.

Richard saw a shaft of light stream through the edge of the tarp closest to his head, and he knew that the loft lights had been turned on. Another set of footsteps ascended the stairs. Based on the high pitch of their voices it seemed there were two young boys in the hayloft just a short distance from where he lay. He heard the scraping of feet against the wooden loft floor, followed by a swooshing sound and then a thud. Having done it himself as a kid, Richard knew that the boys were grabbing bales and dropping them down the hay chute to the barn floor below. There they would be placed in hay troughs set in front of each stable.

"Get the ones on top," one of the boys ordered to the other.

Richard held his breath. He heard a boy climbing, getting closer and closer to his little hay coffin.

"How many?"

"Four should be good."

He heard the rustle of hay as the first bale was removed from its spot in the pile just a few feet from where he lay, and then a hollow thud echoed throughout the loft when it hit the floor below. He heard it a second and third time, each a little closer than the one before. Bale number four came from right above him. He was certain it was one he had removed to make the hole in which he now lay, helpless and completely frozen with fear.

There was a pause. He didn't hear the fourth hay bale hit the loft floor. Richard was certain the boy was standing over him ready to reach down and pull the tarp away. Adrenaline shot through his body like electricity from a high voltage wire. His muscles reached the peak of tenseness. He was cocked and ready to lung upward and leap off the great hay mound and onto the floor below. He grabbed the tarp tightly, ready to throw it off. Then he heard the thud.

"Is that it?" asked the boy who was dangerously close to Richard.

"Yeah, that's enough."

The boy descended the hay pile and stepped onto the wooden floor. The loft lights went out and Richard breathed a sigh of relief, hearing the boys climb down the stairs to the first floor of the barn. He peeled back the tarp from his face, quietly gasping for air and staring upwards at the soft light projected onto the rafters from the barn below. Another 30 minutes went by while he listened to them work, banging, clanking, and scraping as they fed the cows. The sounds were punctuated by muted conversations between the boys and an adult Richard assumed was their father. Soon, the noise died down and the lights below went out.

The sun had set and a quiet darkness surrounded him. He waited fifteen minutes more before moving. Then he pulled himself upward, rolled onto his stomach and slid feet first down the pile of hay. Inch by inch he felt his way, dragging his makeshift crutch along with him. When he reached the loft floor he groped his way through the blackness, which seemed as thick as molasses and as unending as the sea. Finally, he located the wall against which the stairs were set. Working his way in the direction of the stairs he cautiously slid his feet along the floor until he felt it drop off, indicating he had reached the top of the stairs. Slowly, he worked his way down to the barn floor, which was softly illuminated by moonlight coming in through the windows lining one of the two longest walls. A few cows stirred a little when he stepped into the barn, but none of them made a sound. He made his way back through the milk house and saw that the door, which was open before, had been shut. It creaked when he pushed on it, so he slowly opened it only wide enough to squeeze through.

At risk of being seen in the open area outside the milk house, he hobbled towards the equipment shed as quickly as he could. The farm house lights were on, but he saw no movement. A flicker of light from one window indicated that a television was probably on, and he hoped that at least some of the family was sitting in front of it. Entering the machine shed he was relieved at the sight of two bicycles, which were illuminated by moonlight coming in through the open door. Grabbing what seemed to be the larger of the two, he wheeled it outside. Concealing his crutch in a nearby bush, he mounted the bike and began peddling down the driveway. The tires made a loud crunching sound as they rolled across the snow covered gravel. He thought that perhaps walking next to the bike might make less noise than riding on it, but before he could dismount a violent sound burst at his side. A dog with a head the size of a watermelon came directly at him in great leaps, barking ferociously and ready to pounce. Its viciously snapping teeth came within inches of Richard's leg when the chain the dog was tethered to reached its end and halted the seething animal in its tracks.

Peddling as fast as his legs would carry him, Richard zoomed past the farmhouse and the front yard and onto a paved road. Instinctively he turned right and kept peddling hard, never turning to see if he had been discovered. The adrenalin running through him numbed his body and he didn't feel the cold. It seemed that he had been riding for a half-mile or so before reaching an intersection. Certain of his destination and the route that would get him there, he turned right again.

He thought about the family in the farmhouse and hoped that they had attributed their dog's barking to a raccoon or some other nocturnal animal. A tinge of guilt poked at him for stealing the bike, but that was soon washed away by a strange mix of courage and anguished uncertainty. He had been through a lot in the few hours since his escape, and he was determined to deal with whatever else stood in the way of finding Esther. What he didn't know was what would be waiting for him when he arrived at his destination.

***

Richard turned onto the gravel road at Mueller's Quarry. He wasn't sure how much time had passed, but his gloveless hands were well beyond the point of stinging from the frigid air; they were completely numb. He felt no sensation when he stopped and stuffed them into his coat pockets, not warmth or even the brush of fabric against his skin. But when he drew them out to warm them with his breath, he noticed something fall out of the right pocket and onto the ground. He bent over and picked up a black leather glove. Reaching into his left pocket he retrieved another and put them on his hands, cursing himself for not having searched the deep recesses of the pockets earlier.

Looking down the deeply sloped quarry road he saw that it turned to the left a short distance off, bordered by a guardrail. Beyond the guardrail was a massive stretch of open and unbroken blackness, the depths of which seemed to swallow the bright moonlight. Richard knew it was the massive pit of the abandoned quarry.

He closed his eyes and reimagined Esther as he had seen her in his dream, smiling with her hands reaching upwards against a backdrop of gray, jagged rock. He knew this was the place. He knew his dream was meant to show him that she had been taken here. The sweetly perfumed smell of her hair seemed to ride on the winter wind, and he raised his nose to take it in. Gripping the handlebars of his bike, he relived the kiss she had planted on his cheek at his parent's anniversary party, and the gentle tug on his hand as she plucked him from his chair and led him to Thanksgiving dinner at his parent's home. He opened his eyes, which were now focused and hard set. His mind was strangely uncluttered, no voices or phantoms distracted him. Focused only on finding Esther, he began coasting down the road.

Rounding the corner, the road straightened for a short distance and then took a sharp turn to the right, which Richard assumed led to the bottom of the pit. Just beyond the turn sat a small, dilapidated metal shack that served as the office when the quarry had been in operation. The building looked like it had died slowly. Its sagging and rusted corrugated steel roof and weathered walls were stained red as if its lifeblood had oozed out over years of neglect. A small bare rock clearing at the front of the shack gave way to a sheer vertical drop to the bottom of the quarry pit some 80 feet below.

Richard dismounted the bike and wheeled it to the bushes along the side of the road. Stealthily he made his way to the edge of the building, walking softly and in small steps. He stopped to listen but heard no sound coming from the shack. Rounding the corner to the front there was a door with two small curtain-covered windows on either side. The first wooden step leading to the door creaked when he put his weight on it. He froze expecting to have aroused the attention of whoever might be inside, but again he heard nothing. Climbing the remaining two steps he reached for the door handle but discovered that it was missing. Then he saw the padlock.

The wooden frame around the door seemed weathered and flimsy. Grabbing the padlock, he pulled hard and immediately knew that his strength alone would not be enough to tear it away. No longer concerned with being quiet, he grabbed a rock from the ground at the bottom of the steps and swung hard. The hasp loosened its hold on the doorframe but remained in place. It took two more powerful strikes before it dislodged, allowing him to open the door. Inside now, he opened the drapes to let moonlight into the room. Scanning left and right he saw an empty, crudely made bookshelf, what appeared to be an electric heater, several stacks of old newspapers and a cardboard box. The floor groaned as he stepped towards the box. Reaching inside he felt something hard and pulled it out; it was a can of peas. He reached in again and pulled out a can of corned beef hash and another of Spam.

Someone has been here! he screamed to himself. He whipped his head around, expecting the owner of the food to come lurching out of the shadows and attack him. But the room remained still and quiet. Then he heard a soft rustle from behind a door to his right; a door that led to another room. Blood rushed to his face and his body tensed. He slowly turned the doorknob but it was locked. With brute force he hurled himself at the door and the frame splintered and broke free. He rushed into the room wielding the can of Spam above his head, ready to strike hard at anything that got in his way.

"No! Please! Don't hurt me!" a little voice pleaded from a corner of the room.

"Esther! Esther!" Richard yelled, plunging to his knees near the dull outline of a mattress lying on the floor. He clawed at a rumpled mass of blankets trying to uncover the little girl.

"No! I didn't do anything bad! Leave me alone!"

Grabbing her by the shoulders, he turned her away from the wall against which she was huddled. Her tiny body was shaking violently. He drew her into his chest and hugged her desperately, as if she were a spirit that would evaporate if he let go.

"Are you alright? Are you hurt?"

She did not answer.

"Esther? It's me. It's Uncle Richard. Do you hear me? Esther?"

Moments of silence followed as the little girl quivered in his arms. Then, she spoke words that rocked Richard to his core.

"I'm not Esther," the tiny, frightened voice said.

The words hollowed out Richard's insides like a Halloween pumpkin. He gasped and drew her closer, as if his niece was being taken from him all over again. His mind raced, trying to resolve the unthinkable. *How could you not be Esther? I saw you in my dream! I came here to rescue you!*

Reeling in disbelief, he ran to the other room and held her up to the moonlit window. A whimper escaped his lips when he saw her face. His heart sank as he turned her this way and that, hoping that a new angle might prove him wrong. But it didn't. The girl in his arms was not Esther. She appeared to be about the same age as Esther but her hair was straight, lighter in color and shoulder length. The room was too dark to tell much else. He didn't know who she was, but her twisted face and rigid body told him that she was terrified.

"It's OK. I won't hurt you. You're OK now," he whispered into her ear, drawing her to his chest. "What's your name?"

Her tiny body relaxed a little, and she paused to consider whether or not she should answer. "Naomi," she finally relented.

"How long have you been here?"

"I don't know, but I want to go home now," she pleaded, her voice quivering at the word *home*.

"You're OK now. I'm going to bring you home," Richard said. He paused to think carefully about how to ask the next question. Part of him was afraid to hear the answer. A much bigger part of him had to know. "You know Esther?" he asked. "You know where she is?"

"Yes, I know Esther. She was here, but now she's gone," Naomi said, her tiny voice still strained by fear. Every inch of her body was fighting to hold back tears pushed forward by the sense of relief she felt welling up within her.

"Where did she go?"

"I don't know. He took her yesterday."

"Who? Who took her yesterday?" Richard asked, loosening his embrace and holding her face in front of his.

"The man," she whimpered. "The bad man."

Richard felt dizziness overtaking him and he widened his stance to prevent losing his balance. Swallowing hard, he looked into her frightened eyes. His bottom lip quivered like jelly.

"What...What did the bad man..." He couldn't complete the sentence. The words would simply not come out. The only thing he could do was to hug Naomi again, which he did tightly and in trembling arms. She buried her dirt-smudged face in his neck, and her soft whimpers escalated to unrestrained sobs as she began to realize that her ordeal might be over.

Twenty-Five

The blow to Richard's head came as soon as he stepped out the front door of the shack with Naomi in his arms. Instinctively, he ran forward, but his legs buckled under him before he made it off the wooden steps. His vision went black, but Naomi's screams brought him back to consciousness only moments later. She was lying next to him on the ground at the foot of the steps. He stretched his hand toward her, summoning his body to move, but it did nothing. Turning to where her screams were directed, he saw an imposing figure. A large hood concealed the attacker's face, and the assailant was poised to strike again with what looked like a metal pipe. Richard rolled to his right and the pipe pinged off the hard earth just inches from his face. He rolled again, but this time he heard a thud and a wave of pain shot through his left arm. The attacker lost hold of the pipe during the next swing. It flew to the ground only a few feet from where Richard lay, and he made it to his feet in the few seconds it took for the phantom to retrieve it. Richard was now face to face with a person poised as a batter, and he knew that his head was intended to be the ball.

"You're gonna wish you never came here!" the assailant yelled, revealing the tenor of a man's voice.

"You're gonna wish that too!" Richard hollered back defiantly. He rushed forward and raised his already wounded left arm to intercept another blow. Shocked by Richard's fearless aggression, the man retreated backward before attempting another swing. The pipe whistled as it passed only inches from Richard's face. Ignoring the pain that racked his body, he rushed forward and grabbed the man around the neck, squeezing as hard as he could. Richard's hold prevented the man from swinging the pipe, so he repeatedly thrust spear like jabs into Richard's torso. His pain masked by intense anger, the man's viscous jabs only forced Richard to bear down harder. Like a bulldozer he pushed the flailing man away from Naomi, who was still lying on the ground at the foot of the steps. The assailant fell to the ground with a thump. By the time he was upright again Richard had grabbed handfuls of his coat, forcing him backward and ever closer to the edge of the deep pit.

"Aaahhh!" Richard's scream cut through the air like a steam whistle on a locomotive, born of pure, blinding rage. The burst of violent energy that accompanied it was like a detonation, and it hurled the man so forcefully that his feet left the ground. When he landed the lower half of his body dangled over the edge of the dark precipice. Clawing frantically at the surface of the bare rock, the thug tried to find something to grab that would prevent him from falling to his death.

"Help! Help me please!" he pleaded, pressing his feet against the sheer rock wall to find a protrusion that could hold his weight. His body continued to slip backward, the tips of his fingernails ripping off as he tried sinking his fingers into the impenetrable surface.

Richard stood over the man knowing it would be only moments before it was over, before the monster would fall and his body would be split open on the jagged rocks at the bottom of the pit. He thought about Esther and then turned to see Naomi still lying in a desperate, crying heap. He was done waiting; it was time for the monster to die.

Richard stepped closer and raised his foot, poised to bring it down on the man's hand and send him to his death. Then, he heard a familiar voice inside his head. "YOU ARE MY CHILDREN, AND I LOVE YOU BOTH. WHAT YOU DO TO HIM, YOU DO TO ME."

It took only a moment for Richard to know that he was hearing the same voice that had spoken to him at the cabin. It was the good voice, the voice of God. And as soon as he absorbed the meaning of His message Richard's legs gave out. He fell to his knees directly in front of the fiend, who had managed to stop sliding but could hang on for only moments without Richard's aid. Richard had no doubt that this was the bad man that Naomi had spoken about; he was the one who had taken Esther.

"Where is Esther?" Richard screamed. "Tell me where she is!"

A blood-curdling shriek was the man's last response as he slipped backward. Richard lunged forward to grab his hand, but he disappeared over the edge and out of sight.

Scurrying on his belly, Richard looked into the pit expecting to see a broken and lifeless body at the bottom. Instead he saw the man he had wanted to kill hanging tenuously onto a root protruding from the rock wall. The hood that had previously obscured his face had fallen away to reveal his identity. Mark Valjean, the Alpha House orderly, stared terror-stricken into Richard's eyes.

Richard blinked his eyes repeatedly as if clearing a fog of disbelief. Then, without conscious thought he stretched his hand downward. "Take my hand!" he commanded.

"I can't! I'll fall!" Valjean whimpered, pressing his face against the cold rock.

"Look at me!"

"I can't I--"

"Look at me Mark!" Richard cried.

The sound of his name caused Mark Valjean to turn his head upward and look into Richard's eyes. His grotesquely contorted face was painfully familiar to Richard; he had seen it many times in the reflection of his own bathroom mirror. It was the look of a tormented and desperate soul who had lost his connection with the goodness in the world; it was the look of a person who battled something evil living inside him, something that taunted him and told him to do unspeakable things.

Richard fixed his hard-set eyes on Valjean. He wanted him dead. But for reasons he did not fully understand, he knew that the decision to send him to his death was not his to make. He bit the tip of his right glove with his teeth and pulled it off.

"Take my hand," Richard said. "I understand. I know what's happening to you, but it's time to do what's right."

Acting on his only chance to live, Valjean lurched upward and grabbed Richard's hand. But Richard's body slid forward against Valjean's weight. Using his left hand, Richard tried pushing himself backwards but was unable. He was losing his grip and he felt he had no choice but to extend his free hand over the edge and offer it to Valjean.

"Take my other hand," he said in a strained whisper, the air forced from his lungs by the immense weight of Valjean's body. In an act of sheer faith, Valjean let go of the root and grabbed onto Richard's other hand, now the only thing preventing him from plummeting to his death.

"Why are you doing this for me?" Valjean asked, astonished to the point of confusion.

It was not a question Richard was prepared to answer; yet the answer came effortlessly. "Because God loves us all, every sick and hopeless one of us," he said.

Valjean was stunned, and for a moment his lips moved but no words came out. He needed more than anything to speak, even as he was facing death, even as the last remaining bit of energy to hold on was leaving his body. The need to purge himself and perhaps ransom his soul was greater than his need to go on living. "I'm sorry for what I've done," he finally relented. "I don't deserve this."

"I know," Richard said empathetically. "None of us do." Then, taking a deep breath and summoning all the energy that was in him, he lifted Valjean's massive body upwards to a point where Valjean was able to get a foothold and propel himself to the very top of the ledge. It took a moment for Valjean to realize he was on firm ground, and when he did he turned back towards Richard. But, Richard was gone.

"No!" Valjean screamed, slithering back to the edge on his belly. Looking into the moonlit pit he saw Richard's body laying at the bottom of the abyss atop a snow-covered sheet of ice that had cracked upon impact. His feet lay one on top of the other and his arms were spread wide-open, palms outward. Little by little the ice gave way and his broken body disappeared into a cross-shaped black hole and down to the icy depths of the quarry pond.

Twenty-Six

It registered first in his torso and limbs. Comfort. Warmth. Life energy.

Then it registered in his mind and, deeper still, in his spirit. Contentment. Fulfillment. Boundless love.

A warm breeze washed over him and he felt the hair on his arms and legs stand at attention, softly tingling like tiny electrical charges danced around each one. The breeze carried a refreshing aroma, something like ripened grapefruit and eucalyptus but with other delicious qualities that were subtle and indistinguishable. Leaves rustled like whispering angels, and gently undulating yellow and blue light filtered through his closed eyelids. He would have been content to remain this way forever.

Then Richard opened his eyes. What he saw was shockingly beautiful, and intensified his sensory experience to a point that made the whole thing seem otherworldly. A field of dazzling wheat encircled him in every direction, ceaseless and unbroken all the way to the horizon. It danced and rolled with the breeze like luminescent waves on a golden ocean. Nothing interrupted its flow.

Looking into the distance directly in front of him, a massive mountain rose from the horizon and dominated the skyline. Blue-green at its base, it melted into a lush green as it reached upwards. Its crown was a glimmering amber color that reflected the light like a precious stone. The outline of the mountain was offset by a cloudless, azure blue sky.

For the first time he became aware that he was sitting on the ground with his back against the trunk of a tree. The tree grew on a hill that was just high enough to allow him to clearly see everything else that lay before him: the golden field, the mountain, and the clear blue sky.

He had never seen light the way he saw it now. Brilliantly illuminating and unwavering light was everywhere. The distinctions between foreground and background, between one object and another were vividly pronounced, yet he saw no sun and no shadows.

Bird songs came from above, and now and then brightly colored pairs whizzed past him in a playful chase. The breeze seemed not only to blow over him, but through him. And the light, while all around him, seemed also to come from within him. He held out his hand, marveling at a subtle glow emanating from his palm and fingers. Noticing a faint movement, Richard looked up to see a beautifully colored butterfly-like creature floating towards him. Its graceful wings gliding on air, it landed on his outstretched hand. He smiled when he realized that it was the Polyphemus Moth he had admired in the moth book, the one that had inspired his dream about transformation. It was as big as his hand, and its brilliant purple and yellow eyespots moved back and forth gracefully as the dazzling creature flexed its wings.

"What is this place?" he asked out loud. His voice was clear and bright and filled with wonder. "Am I dreaming?" After a moment the beautiful moth floated from his hand just as gracefully as it had landed, rising into the blue sky in the direction of the mountain. Watching in amazement as the moth fluttered upward, Richard rubbed one hand to the other and then stroked his cheek just to feel his own touch and confirm that what he was experiencing was real.

Far off in the distance, in the direction of the mountain, he heard what sounded like the blast of a multitude of trumpets. Moments later the announcement grew louder and more intense.

The birds and rustling leaves went quiet and the flowing field of wheat went still, each glowing head of grain standing at attention. The announcement burst forth again, reaching a harmonious crescendo that caused Richard's skin to tingle more and his eyes to open wider in anticipation.

He saw movement on the carpet like surface of the wheat field at the base of the mountain. Something seemed headed in his direction. As it got closer he could see that the stalks of wheat were being parted like the hull of an invisible ship was cutting through it as it sailed toward him. Richard looked to his left and right to see if there was movement elsewhere, but everything was completely still. He turned his attention forward again; it would be only moments before the mysterious trail reached the edge of the field, and whatever had made it would be visible in the clearing not 50 feet from where he sat. He held his breath.

His anticipation peaked when the commotion stopped just short of the edge of wheat field. Moments passed. Richard didn't know if he was standing, sitting, or floating when a tiny hand reached through the wall of golden grass, pulling it to one side. Then a small human form stepped out. Richard couldn't believe what he was seeing. He rubbed his eyes vigorously and looked again. It was Esther!

"Uncle Richie!" she squealed joyfully, waiving her hands above her head.

Richard ran down the hill, his heart pounding. Within the few seconds it took for them to run into each other's arms, he knew in his heart where they were.

"I found you Uncle Richie! I found you! I found you!" she exclaimed, wrapping her arms around his neck and kissing his cheeks over and over.

"You did find me Esther, and I'm so happy!" he cried, hugging her tightly and then loosening his embrace, fearing that he might hurt her.

"No, you won't hurt me! Hug me harder!" she whooped, somehow aware of his unspoken concern.

"OK! OK!" Richard replied, choking out the words. "I'll hug you as hard as I can and never let you go!"

"Hey, there's no crying here," she said with pretend sternness, followed seconds later by screams of delight that spilled forth like candy from a piñata.

"Well, I don't know how things are supposed to work here but I can tell you that these are tears of joy, not sadness," he chuckled. "Are those OK?"

"Happiness and joy are abundant here," she said, grabbing his hand. "And, I can't tell how happy it makes me to know that you're here with me. Now come," she commanded, tugging on his hand and leading him back up the hill and under the tree. Esther spread out her blue and yellow gingham dress in a perfect circle on the green grass. "Let's sit and talk a while," she said, patting the ground with her hand until Richard sat.

"You have questions," she stated.

Richard paused for a moment, "Yes, I do have questions," he said, not quite sure if he should ask what he already thought to be true. But it seemed so fantastic that he had to. "Is this heaven? Are we…I mean did we…"

"Yes, our earthly bodies perished, and yes this is heaven. Isn't it wonderful?" she smiled and reached for his hand again.

"Um, yes. It is wonderful, but… OK wait…so I died and now I'm in heaven."

"Yup!"

Richard shook his head approvingly and then smiled. He looked into the blue sky and then down to the rich earth. "Cool," he said.

His mind percolated with questions. One bubbled to the top and he blurted it out. "It feels so different here. I feel God everywhere, but I don't see him. Where is he?"

"You feel him in everything because he is in everything, just like on earth. But here there is nothing standing between God and us. No distractions. Nothing bad. The place we call home is over there," she said, pointing to the mountain.

"When will I see him?"

"In a while. We'll talk about that in a bit."

Another question popped out. "I figured there would be more people here, where is everybody?"

Esther giggled. "They're over there," she replied, pointing to the mountain again. "I need to be with you now. You'll see them later."

"Your mom and dad, Charlie and Isabel, they must be--"

"Mommy and daddy are terribly sad right now, but they don't know I'm here. They'll feel a lot better once they know that," Esther replied, running her hand over the lush green grass that grew all around them.

"Why did we die?"

"Everyone dies, Uncle Richie. The more important question is why we live, and what God wants us to do with our lives."

Richard shook his head. "Those are great questions. But, I don't have the answers."

"You will." Her voice was certain, and Richard was too amazed to not believe her.

"I know what happened to me," he said, squeezing her hand. "What happened to you? Why did you... Why did you have to die?"

"The world is an imperfect place. People are imperfect, and they do bad things. It's really no more complicated than that."

"But you were so young and full of life. It doesn't make sense."

"I know this is hard to understand Uncle Richie, and I can't explain it all now because it's not time yet. Just know that God reasons differently than people. He loves us all in ways you can't begin to imagine, and the beauty and joy of this place is far beyond what I can describe to you in words."

"So there's more than this?" Richard asked, pointing to the beauty surrounding them.

"So much more. Very, very much more."

Richard looked at Esther, the breeze gently tossing ringlets of her hair, her olive skinned face serene and all knowing. He leaned over, grabbed her around the waist and hoisted her onto his lap.

"How did you get to be so smart?" he asked, smiling and stroking her hair.

She smiled back and hugged him. "Being here makes everything clear," she replied.

"OK, I've waited long enough. Can we go over there now - to the mountain?" he said, pointing at the place she called home, and looking expectantly into her eyes.

"Not yet. There's something you need to do first."

"What? Do I have to pass some sort of test or something?" he asked, concern shading his face. "I'm not good at taking tests."

She smiled. "No, Uncle Richie. There is no test."

"Then what? What do I have to do?"

Esther cupped his face in her hands and looked into his eyes. "Go back," she said.

Richard was stunned into silence. After a few moments he began to mumble a string of unintelligible words, and that continued until his mind had cleared enough to ask a coherent question. "What do you mean, back? Back where?"

"Back to the life you just left behind."

"But why? I just got here!"

"You're funny," Esther giggled.

"I'm serious! I don't want to go back there. I want to stay here with you. I like it here!"

Esther thought for a moment, shifting in her uncle's lap. "Uncle Richie, what do you want more than anything?"

"I just told you - I want to be here with you."

"That's good. I want that too, but think bigger. Think about the people you left behind."

Richard said nothing for a long while. Esther laid her head on his chest and fiddled with the large black buttons on his coat to give him time to think. The gentle breeze blew once again and the golden field of wheat swayed and whirled in response, as if the wind and the wheat were dance partners. The hushed birds started to warble and sing again and amazingly, in the midst of the most beautiful place he'd ever been, Richard's thoughts were completely focused elsewhere.

He thought about Charlie and Isabel and the pain they felt. He thought about Judith and, for the first time since he arrived in heaven, felt a trace of sadness for what might become of her if he wasn't there. Conrad Hampton the Third, nurse Fenstermaker and Carl Maznik flashed in his mind. Finally, he thought about Mark Valjean and what had happened between the two of them just before he fell into the quarry pond.

He longed for his own peace, comfort, and happiness. But he also wanted something more – something he had never even considered before. Maybe going back to live for a while longer in the world he had just left behind wouldn't be so bad. Not if he knew that God wanted him there. Not if he knew he would eventually end up back in heaven, with God and with Esther.

Richard drew a deep breath and exhaled. Then, he lifted Esther's chin until her eyes met his. "I want to help people conquer their demons," he said. "And, when life is over I want them all to come home to this place."

Esther smiled broadly and clapped her hands in applause. "You are a good man Richard Aaron Buell. And you have a big heart; big enough to do everything you just said, with God's help of course." She stroked his cheek and kissed his nose. "I love you Uncle Richie. God loves you too, and he'll be with you every step of the way. Please tell mommy and daddy that I'm happy. Tell them that God loves them. Tell them that he wants them to be here with him, and with me."

Twenty-Seven

An Emergency Medical Technician hovered over the body. "Clear!" he said in an urgent but controlled manner. When his female counterpart had pulled away he depressed the switch on the defibrillation paddles, releasing one thousand volts of electricity into Richard's chest cavity. His body heaved violently upward and then slammed back down onto the ambulance stretcher with a thud.

"I've got nothing!" she said looking sharply at the heart monitor. "Epinephrine?" She posed the question even though she knew it was necessary, given that the two previous defibrillations had failed to produce a heartbeat.

"Yes, 1 milligram!"

She sank the needle into Richard's arm at the same time her partner started chest compressions. Moments later the paddles were once again pressed against his chest. "We're going again! Clear!" The electrical shock tore through Richard's body. Again he convulsed and then lay still. Medically he was dead.

"Still nothing!"

"Come on man, come on!" the EMT pleaded, setting the paddles aside and forcing his weight onto Richard's chest. His lifeless eyes stared blankly at the ceiling and his head bobbed forward with each thrust.

"How long? 11 minutes? 12?"

"We're at just over 12 minutes."

"OK, one more time," he said, grabbing the paddles and knowing it would be his last attempt to restart Richard's heart. "Come on now! This is the one! This is the one! Clear!"

The familiar pain of life on earth started for Richard as soon as Esther had kissed his nose and said goodbye. His body burned as if napalm had ignited inside him. His eyes flew open and flashes of yellow and blue attacked him like tongues of fire licking at his face. He began to cough and choke simultaneously as the water in his lungs sprayed out his mouth and over his face.

"I've got a rhythm but it's weak!" the EMT yelled.

Richard's eyes slammed shut in response to the searing pain. Instinctively he raised his hands in a defensive gesture, but the technicians forced them back down. Survival impulse forced his eyes open again. He saw two hazy blue silhouettes, each one restraining him. An immense weight crushed his chest. The glinting stainless steel of the lobotomy room flashed in his mind.

"Aaahhh! Get off of meee!" he screamed, not knowing that the intense pressure on his chest was the result of trauma caused by the massive amount of electricity that had violently surged through his body just moments before.

"You're OK! You're OK now! Nobody is trying to hurt you! We're here to help you!" the male technician yelled, still restraining Richard's arms while his partner forced her weight onto his legs.

Richard began to hyperventilate, and a new kind of desperation overtook him. He could feel himself slipping away – dying for the second time. The scream of the ambulance siren faded away and his world turned to black. Then he saw Esther, cupping his face in her hands and kissing his nose. His body and breathing relaxed and he was aware of only one wonderful and unexpected thing - the steady, and solid pounding of his heart.

***

Charlie and Isabel stood on the left side of Richard's bed at Sacred Heart hospital. His mother and father stood on the right. There were hugs and kisses and reassurances, but no one smiled. All four had been without sleep and hope for days and their eyes showed it, blood shot and weary. Charlie stared blankly at the floor. And Isabel, whose appearance had always been fresh and feminine, looked like she had just spent a week living in a cardboard box. Her normally full and cascading head of hair hung limply in a frazzled looking ponytail, and her olive colored skin was pale and blotchy. The rumpled gray fabric of a sweat suit hung like sackcloth on her hunched body. Frames of red swollen skin surrounded her eyes, which were downcast and unblinking.

Richard had casts on his broken right leg and arm. He slowly extended his weak but functional left arm and grasped Charlie's hand. "Tell me what you know," he said.

Moments went by and Charles said nothing. Richard's request registered in his ears, but he couldn't bear to utter the words that had been pounding his insides like a relentless hurricane. Finally he opened his mouth. "Esther is..." he whimpered and then halted, unable to give voice to the unimaginable, as if speaking it would make it so, as if not speaking it would make it a lie. "Esther is dead," he finally let go. The others choked up at the acknowledgment, which stung even more when it was spoken aloud. A brief silence followed the excruciating words, and then it was broken by the soft pat, pat, pat of Charles' tears splashing onto the flecked linoleum floor.

Isabel took Charlie's other hand, her face puckered in pain. She had stopped asking God to forgive her for cursing him in her grief and desperation. She had even decided to stop asking God to bring Esther back to life. Polite requests were not working. She knew it was time to make demands, which she did silently and sternly. And, for what seemed to be the hundredth time since Esther's disappearance, she lifted her eyes and looked around the room to see that her baby was still gone. She clenched her jaw and her chapped and peeling lips tightened as the corners of her mouth dipped downward.

Her prayers had resulted in nothing but diminished hope and wounded faith. Like opening a hollow wooden doll because it held the promise of something good, only to find another identical but smaller one nestled inside, and opening that one to reveal yet another still smaller doll, and so on, and so on. Hope and faith were dashed for Isabel when her final demand went unanswered, like opening the last little doll to discover it was hollow and empty.

A new truth had slowly been revealing itself to her since Esther's disappearance. For the first time she saw it in full view. Her precious little girl died at the bottom of a frozen pond next to her uncle. Monsters like Mark Valjean roamed the earth and preyed in the most sickening ways upon innocent children. God could not keep bad things from happening because God, at least the one she had believed in, did not exist. The object of her faith was, like the last little wooden doll, nothing but an empty shell - beautifully painted on the outside by those who created him, but deceptively void of any substance or ability.

Richard's newly beating heart felt as if it would once again stop beating. Before his eyes the family he loved sank deeper and deeper into the most desperate anguish he had ever witnessed in other human beings. He wanted more than anything to help. His mouth opened to speak but he stopped himself before uttering a word. He knew with certainty that now was not the time to tell them about what had happened. As painful as it was to allow his family to remain in such a terrible place, the disbelief and utter resentment he feared he would cause by telling everyone that he had been with Esther in heaven would only make matters worse. He would be telling the grief stricken parents and grandparents of a murdered child to look on the bright side; to take the consolation prize when what they needed was the grand prize, their living, breathing baby girl. Then there was the very real possibility that they wouldn't believe him at all, that dying and being brought back to life had somehow produced yet another delusion in his already delusional mind. It just wasn't right.

All he could think to do was squeeze Charlie's hand and tell them how he felt. "I'm so sorry that Esther has gone away. And my heart hurts so, I can barely breath," Richard said, as the pain of knowing he would not be with Esther in this life stabbed at his heart. "But when I close my eyes," he added softly, "when I close my eyes, I can see her. I can feel her and smell her hair." He held his open hand in front of his face as if caressing the back of her tiny head. "Charlie," his voice cracked. "I can feel her kissing my nose."

***

"What's not to like?" Sheriff Langford asked, prodding Charles for an answer as they stood in the living room of Charles and Isabel's home.

"You make it sound like I just won the prize behind door number three," Charles retorted, sarcastically. "You know as well as I do that Richie doesn't belong -- I mean doesn't deserve to be in there," Charles said, referring to the Sheriff's proposal that his brother be sent back to Broward Mental Hospital. "He caught Esther's killer and saved that little girl who would surely have ended up dead. Doesn't that count for anything?"

"Technically, Valjean turned himself in," the sheriff countered, regretting the comment as soon as the words escaped his lips.

Charles spun around to face him; his eyes cutting into him like steel daggers. "Go to hell! Go to hell!" he spewed through gritted teeth. Grabbing fists full of the sheriff's coat collar he pulled him in, nose to nose. Torrents of his hot, alcohol soaked breath blasted the sheriff's face. "Don't EVER speak that name to me again!"

The sheriff's hand, which had instinctively reached for his holstered pistol, was ripped away from its grip when Charles thrust him against the wall with crushing force. The sound of crumbling plaster broke the taught silence while Charles drew his next breath. "You can't begin to imagine what I'll do to you if you utter that name again," he said, thrusting the sheriff still deeper into the broken wall before releasing his iron grip. Then Charles turned and, without looking at Isabel, walked out the front door of their home.

Isabel sat in stunned silence as the sheriff pulled himself and his bruised ego out of the torso shaped hole in the wall. He swept the pulverized plaster from his coat and brushed back his disheveled hair. "Do you know where he is going?" the sheriff asked, still stunned from the attack. The blank stare on Isabel's face told him she had no idea.

Isabel knew Charles' anger towards the sheriff wasn't only about Richard. He was understandably grief stricken, but he had withdrawn from her and everyone else in the family. He spoke only when spoken to and then only in short monotone spurts. The thing that hurt most was that he no longer looked at her. He kept his eyes cast downward, even when she stood in front of him. There was one exception. The day before as they sat in silence at opposite ends of the dinner table picking at a late evening meal, Charles looked up from his plate and stared coldly and silently at Isabel. When she asked what was wrong his face became contorted with anger and disbelief. He threw his napkin on the table and left the room. He hadn't spoken to her since.

Tiny pebbles of wet sleet pelted the living room window. Isabel sat curled on the corner of the couch with her arms wrapped around her legs. She needed to be held, but a self-embrace would have to do. *I've lost my daughter and the god I believed in*, she thought. *Could I loose my husband too*? *Does he blame me for Esther's death*? The room began to spin. *What if he doesn't come back*? *What if I never see him again*? Closing her eyes she pressed her face into her knees. *What if I am to blame*? *What if Esther died because of me*? The last question landed like a punch, it left her mouth open and she covered it with a trembling hand. She didn't think it was possible to feel anything but searing pain in her heart, but she was wrong. The agony of losing her child was terrible beyond words, but the guilt she now felt for having caused Esther's death was simply unbearable. She was unable to draw breath. Muffled gasps for air escaped through the hand that cupped her mouth. She collapsed to the floor and Sheriff Langford rushed over to lift her into his arms. He cradled her rigid, trembling body. "Charlie, come back! Charlie! Esther's dead!" she shrieked. "I'm sorry! It's my fault! I killed her! I Kill--"

Isabel's body went limp, and the Sheriff retrieved his cell phone and dialed 911.

Twenty-Eight

It had been one week to the day since Richard had entered the Sacred Heart Hospital emergency room, having died and been brought back to life. He stretched out his hands toward the Sheriff, who reached around to his back and unsnapped the black leather handcuff holster strapped to his belt. "I'm sorry I have to do this," he said frowning. "But the judge thought you'd be a flight risk." The cuffs made a ratcheting sound as they closed around Richard's left wrist and then around the arm of the wheel chair upon which he sat. It was a sound he had heard before and always disliked. It had made him feel like an animal that had to be restrained for the safety of others. But this time it did not bother him.

"It's OK Jim. I understand," Richard said, testing the cuffs to make sure they were secure.

Previous encounters with Richard had taught the sheriff that he could be uncooperative when he was being hauled away. Half expecting a struggle the sheriff looked at him with curiosity, trying to find anything that might indicate he was about to lash out. The sheriff was caught off guard when Richard smiled. He took a small step backward thinking that the smile was a ruse and, more likely than not, a precursor to Richard's clenched fist traveling at a high velocity towards his jaw. But, Richard remained calm, even peaceful.

"You seem to be doing OK considering the circumstances," the sheriff said cautiously. "But I've been in this line of work long enough to know that appearances can be deceiving. How do you feel?"

Richard glanced away from the sheriff, his eyes falling upon his shackled hand. "I'm doing OK. But I hurt for Charlie and Isabel." Richard paused and looked again at the sheriff. "I'm sorry for the problems I've caused," he said. "What I did to Connie and the whole mess with my escape from Broward. I'm not sorry I escaped, but I realize it caused problems for a lot of people."

Sheriff Langford nodded in agreement, "You did cause quite a stir, but I'm glad you are taking responsibility for it." He paused and then smirked. "There's someone here to see you."

Leaving the room he returned seconds later with someone following close behind. Richard heard the shuffle of tiny feet across the floor, but the visitor was hidden from view until the sheriff stepped aside. The smile returned to Richard's face when he saw Judith. In usual form her eyes were cast to the floor and both her hands grasped the large hoop-shaped wooden handles of her purse, which she held at chest level like a shield.

Richard spoke her name and their eyes met. The icy tension Judith felt by being in a hospital, a place the family had told her to stay away from, melted like snow on a roaring campfire. Dropping her purse to the floor she scurried forward, kneeling in front of him. She wrapped one hand around Richard's waist and placing the other over her glistening eyes. She pressed her cheek hard against his chest and nudged it back and forth, every stroke reassuring her that he was really there; that he had come back to her. "I thought I would never see you again," she said, her voice trembling. "I thought I'd have to live without you."

Richard stroked her hair. "You don't have to live without me. It's OK. We're together, and we're going to be OK."

Judith looked down to see Richard's hand cuffed to the arm of wheelchair. "But you're going away again," she sobbed. "What am I going to do? When will you come back?"

Richard nudged her chin upward with his injured right arm until their eyes met once again. "Yes, I am going away for a while, but that doesn't mean we can't see each other. The judge asked the people at Broward if they would allow me to have visitors. He said it would help the healing process for all of us," he said, stretching his cuffed hand to brush the hair from her eyes. "I'll be there for a while - I'm not sure how long. But that's OK." He drew a deep breath and exhaled slowly. "I did something to Connie that I shouldn't have done. Something terrible. I also left Broward before I was supposed to. And even though I don't regret it for a moment because I did it for Esther, I have to face the consequences. I'm OK with that," he said, smiling. "And you will be too."

Judith shuffled alongside Richard as the orderly, who was instructed by the sheriff to move slow enough to allow Judith to keep her hand on Richard's shoulder, pushed the wheel chair towards the hospital entrance where the police car was parked. The sheriff walked behind them, smiling at the tender scene and the hopes he had for their future.

Nurse Fenstermaker was among the first to see Richard after he was admitted back into Broward Mental Hospital. He rose, balancing his weight on his good leg as she entered the room. "Mr. Buell," she said in the tone of a disgruntled munchkin. "I see you're back again. We need to get a few things straight this time around." Before she could utter another word Richard stepped forward and embraced her cheek-to-cheek, with his good arm reaching as far around her amply sized body as it would go.

"This is... well this is simply not allowed," she protested, her arms set rigidly at her sides. "There is a policy against intimate physical contact between patients and staff and I think we should--"

"I'm sorry for how I've treated you," Richard interrupted, still hugging her. "You're a wonderful and caring person, and I want you to know that I appreciate who you are."

Nurse Fenstermaker tried to formulate a response to help regain control, which she felt was quickly slipping away. "PULL AWAY!" a voice inside her head warned. But she was unable. Her mouth hung open but no words came out.

Richard hugged her tighter and stroked her back. "I want you to know that I consider you a friend," he added.

Nurse Fenstermaker had, for most of her life, been unfamiliar with intimacy. She had no close friends to speak of and her immediate family was distant, both geographically and emotionally. She had never seriously considered marriage, but had on several occasions begrudgingly agreed to dates. Unfortunately she seemed only to attract men who were, as she once put it to a curious co-worker, "Neanderthals of the lowest order." Ironically she had chosen to be a nurse, a profession that required intimate physical and emotional contact with patients. Perhaps it was her way of compensating for the voids that existed in her personal life. Perhaps it also accounted for the reason she seemed always to be working.

Nurse Fenstermaker's arms relaxed, then rose up to encircle the man she previously had planned on scolding. The movement was reflexive and offered immediate relief, like scratching an itch. She remained there until she felt her eyes begin to moisten at the edges, and then she stepped back. She was not in the habit of permitting emotions that warmed her spirit or anyone else's. But she was unable to suppress the pleasure that came simply from being known and appreciated. Her normally ruddy cheeks were aflame and her lips, while usually pursed, where relaxed and bore the tiniest hint of a smile. "Well," she said, not bothering to wipe her glistening eyes, "I guess we can let bygones be bygones then." After a moment she reached for his hand. "Thank you," she said softly. "I needed that."

Richard was about to speak when he saw her lips pucker and her eyes narrow, like she had flicked some internal switch hardwired to a still guarded and impertinent part of her. Abruptly, she straightened her dress and put on her best *you won't get another one past me* face.

"I'll be watching you Mr. Buell," she said, trying hard to convey sternness and indignation. But the aftereffects of Richard's hug and his kind words clung to her like a warm sweater. "And if I see any funny business, and I mean any at all, I won't hesitate to report you to Dr. Dorjee."

"Dr. who?" Richard asked in confusion.

"Dr. Dorjee," she said gathering steam. "You know, the person you and almost everyone else around here inappropriately refers to as Atty."

"Oh, Atty. Yes ma'am. I understand that."

"Good, I'll be on my way then." Nurse Fenstermaker whirled around and in a chilling flurry of white flew out the door, down the hall and into the ladies room. She bent downward at her waist and walked the stretch of stalls, looking beneath each door to make sure she was alone. Then she entered the last stall, closed the door, lowered the toilet lid and sat. She felt it begin to rise in her stomach the moment Richard had embraced her. By the time she had left his room it had pushed its way into her throat. Now the thing she had kept caged inside for so long was about to escape the windowless prison she had personally crafted over decades; a place where her emotions and desire for human connection had been kept captive, guarded by an icy resolve to never be hurt again and tightly locked in place by a stone cold tough exterior. She had not allowed herself to feel connected to others for so long, resisting anything other than casual, shallow relationships. It was, she had reasoned, simply the most effective way to protect herself. But years of loneliness had produced regret, and that regret had served only to gnaw at and weaken her fragile and ever diminishing sense of self worth. Amazingly, even miraculously, a simple act of kindness from a friend was all it took to break through the casehardened walls of her heart, allowing dignity and friendship to flow in and a torrent of heartache and tears to flow out.

* * *

Broward hospital was not a cheery place by any stretch of the imagination. Illness and dysfunction were palpably present in ways that could make even the most optimistic and upbeat person sick to their stomach. Richard was sitting in the day room of the Crazy Wing when he began to consider what he had told Esther when he was with her in heaven, how he wanted to help people to deal with their demons. He was among them now - the people and their demons. They overwhelmed his senses. The sights, sounds, and smells of illness were everywhere. Anguished moans and nonsensical chatter came at him from every direction, and the sickening smell of urine and feces hung in the air like an invisible vapor. An unshaven old man wearing a gray gown shook his fist and cursed at some phantom that only he could see. Another, with arms as thin as shovel handles, ran in place, glancing behind him as if trying to escape someone or something. A pretty young Asian woman sitting in a chair to his left, who up until a moment ago had been contently chewing on the sole of her slipper, began screaming when the chew toy was snatched away by one of the staff.

Illness pressed in on him from every side, and he began to feel overwhelmed and woefully unequipped to do what he had promised. Showing kindness to people like Nurse Fenstermaker was one thing. But this! This was like trying to solve world hunger! He buried his face in his hands and he began to wheeze against the pressure mounting in his chest.

"HOW CAN HE HELP ANYONE IN THIS PLACE? HE'S NOT A PSYCHIATRIST!" Author shouted.

"HE'S THE ONE PSYCHIATRISTS TALK ABOUT DURING STAFF MEETINGS!" added Melissa. "THEY ALL AGREE THAT BIGGER DOSES OF CLOZAPINE WON'T HELP! HE'S STILL GOING TO LOSE HIS MIND! WHO IS HE TO EVEN CONSIDER TRYING TO HELP ANYONE?"

Richard pressed hard on his temples and prayed for relief. Then, as if uncovered by a slowly thinning fog, the image of the swaying wheat field appeared behind his closed eyes. He saw the shining mountain and felt the warm wind.

"I LOVE YOU AND I AM WITH YOU," the familiar voice spoke, its booming baritone timbre accompanied by a sound like rushing water. "CHOOSE ME OVER THE OTHER VOICES. I WILL GUIDE YOU AS YOU DO WHAT NEEDS TO BE DONE."

Richard raised his head and looked around. Something inside him was changing. The people around him acted the same, but he saw them differently. Unlike before, their physical appearance and behaviors seemed unimportant. Instead he saw striking similarities of a metaphysical nature, on a level much higher and more meaningful than outward appearance or conduct. He saw patients and staff alike simply as human beings, intricately connected by flesh and blood, but most prominently by spirit. Unique but the same, perfectly designed yet imperfect. Each one struggling to make their way along the path of life, each one contending with screaming voices telling them which way to go, each choosing one voice over another and bearing the life altering consequences for better or worse.

For the first time he felt he belonged. He was one of them, wonderfully and tragically human to the core. He continued looking at the patients and staff around him and breathed in deeply, each inhale bringing a richer sense of connectedness. *How wonderful it is to feel something so different from paranoia*, he thought. *How perfectly sweet it is to be human and to think of others not as opponents but as pilgrims, as fellow travelers walking together through the turbulence of life.*

"DON'T BE A FOOL!" Author screamed, speaking directly to Richard for the first time he could remember since before Melissa had come along. Author's tone was accusatory and had a cutting edge. "I CREATED YOU! YOU WILL ALWAYS SUFFER! IT'S WHO YOU ARE, AND THERE IS NOTHING YOU OR ANYONE ELSE CAN DO ABOUT IT!"

Curiously, Melissa was silent.

Richard considered Author's vicious comment for a moment, and then decided to ignore him.

"Speak to me Lord," he said, naming the good voice for the first time.

He felt it welling up inside him, and then it began. "WHEN IT COMES TO THE EXPERIENCE OF SUFFERING, WHAT IS IT THAT SEPARATES THOSE WITH CLINICALLY DIAGNOSED ILLNESS' FROM EVERYONE ELSE?"

The answer came to Richard without conscious thought, and its impact was profound.

"A diagnosis. A diagnosis of illness is the only difference," Richard replied aloud.

"YES, ALL MY LOVED ONES SUFFER WHETHER OR NOT THEY ARE LABELLED AS ILL. LOVE ME, AND THROUGH YOU I WILL ALLEVIATE THE SUFFERING OF OTHERS," the voice said, fading like an echo and leaving Richard with his own thoughts.

Richard knew from personal experience that people with diagnosed mental illnesses almost always suffered more intensely than others. But where, he now questioned, should the line be drawn on suffering? *If human suffering were measured on a continuum,* he said to himself, *people with mental illnesses would rightly be placed towards the far end, the end holding extreme torment and agony. And those people need and deserve treatment. But what about all the others? What about the ones who are normal in the psychiatric sense of the word but still battle their own demons? And what about those who are ill, but have never been diagnosed? People like that are all around me!*

Richard thought about nurse Fenstermaker and Mark Valjean, two people who had spent a good part of their lives alleviating the suffering of the mentally ill. Ironically, in some cruel twist of fate, they suffered untreated from their own demons. He imaged that

Carl Maznik, a wonderful person by all accounts, had some difficulties of his own that had gone unspoken and untreated. Then there was Charles and Isabel, his sister Julia, his brother Edmond, and so many others in whom he saw pain and suffering that grew from countless and often unnamed places. *They all struggle with their own demons, their own voices*, he thought. *Their suffering might place them somewhere towards the middle of the continuum, but what does it matter? They still struggle! And they still suffer!*

"Author," he said aloud. "You are right, suffering is a part of life. But, you are wrong about one thing; we are not helpless, and we are not alone. There is a lot about life that we can't control, but that does not mean we should turn our backs on the things we can control. We will always have the ability to choose. And we all have the responsibility to care for each other."

It's sad though, Richard thought. *People's problems, whether clinically diagnosed or not, are often times not detected until it is too late; until depression caused by low self-worth drives them to suicide, until they overdose on prescription pain killers, shun friends and family only to live out their days in bitterness because some injustice has been done to them, or until they end up taking the life of a young girl in order to fill some perverse sexual need.*

The transformation Richard had dreamt about was happening. It was a strange but wonderful mixture of the supernatural power of God and his own desire to become something better than what he was before. He thought about the times he had made good choices, and he thought about the many times he had not. *When I cross the line from thought to action, be it good or evil*, he said to himself, *the whole world changes. But I don't have to try and change the world by myself. I just have to love God, try to make choices that please Him, and do what I can to love those He puts in my life. God will do the rest.*

Richard knew just where he needed to start.

Twenty-Nine

His injured arm beginning to heal, Richard reached for Charles and Isabel's hands as they sat across the table from him in the day room at Broward hospital. The rawness of their ordeal had weathered them. They didn't seem like a couple anymore. Instead, they appeared to be two disconnected people who happened to share a common pain.

His palms were wet and his tongue stuck to the roof of his mouth. The confidence he had gained by rehearsing what he would say to them vanished as he looked into their eyes. "I have something to tell you," he said, disappointed that he still felt the knot in his stomach he had prayed would go away. He let go of Isabel's hand and took a sip from a water glass, the quivering contents of which splashed onto his chin and the tabletop. He wiped them both and took her hand again.

"Richie, what's wrong?" Isabel pleaded.

"Nothing is wrong," he said. "I just need to tell you about something that happened to me after I... after I died."

Charles squirmed in his seat, blank eyed, while Isabel blinked repeatedly, trying to reset her brain to process the absurd.

"After you died?" she asked hoarsely. "Do you mean just before, at the rock quarry when...when that man..." Isabel's voice trailed off.

"No. I mean after I died. Before I was revived. Something happened that I need you to know about."

Charles agitation spilled over and he tore his hand from Richard's grasp. "Oh Come on! What do you mean after you died! Dead is dead! Lights out! That's it!"

Charles' tone shook Richard and he shrank in his seat. Then, he drew a breath and willed himself to continue. "That's not what happened to me!" he fired back. Richard's fingers caressed his upper lip as he agonized over what to say next. "I was in a place, a beautiful place--"

"You can't mean heaven!" Charles screamed. His eyes had the look of a predatory cat; his body cocked and ready to pounce.

"Charles, let him speak!" Isabel yelled, her uncharacteristic scolding causing her husband to cast a hardened gaze at her. The biting glare she sent back left him unable to speak. "Go on Richie," she said.

"I don't remember falling into the quarry pond," he continued. "I only remember knowing, even before I opened my eyes, that I was in a different place. When I did open my eyes I saw that I was on a hill in the middle of a huge field of tall, golden grass. I was under a tree, the only tree around. I can't find the words to explain what I saw or how I felt." Richard shook his head in frustration, knowing that his attempts to describe the place fell far short of the actual experience. "The colors, the sounds and smells. Light was everywhere. I felt...I felt peaceful."

Charles' eyes connected with Richard's. The only time he had ever heard his brother utter the word "peaceful" was when he was lamenting the absence of it. A moment later his eyes fell blankly upon the tabletop. He looked like a man enduring a long-winded sales pitch for a time-shared vacation spot, dragged there by a wife who longed for rest and peace.

"Charlie, I can't prove the existence of God to you any more than you can disprove his existence to me, so let's not bother with that. But if you are right, if we die and the lights go out and we cease to exist then I have lost nothing. What I thought was true would simply not be true. But I have not suffered because I was wrong. If I am right and there is a God who cares for us while we're here and wants us to be with him in heaven after we die, and you choose not to believe that, then you have lost out on all the goodness of this life and the next."

The words he spoke added fuel to the fire smoldering inside him, and his confidence grew as he continued. "I was there! I was with God in heaven! It's something I believe to be true! NOT telling you would be like withholding the fact that you won the lottery. And, TELLING you is no more irrational than it would be for me to steer you away from the edge of a cliff. I love you both and I want the best for you. That's all."

Isabel's face softened. Her eyes were open a little wider than before and they held a sliver of promise, as if she had found a delicate branch to cling to on her slow and agonizing descent into the hell that had unfolded since Esther's death. Charles mouth hung open and he looked puzzled, as if he didn't know the person who was sitting across from him. Neither he nor Isabel had ever heard Richard speak so articulately and confidently.

"There's more I need to tell you about heaven," Richard said before taking another sip of water and setting down the glass. He looked at Isabel and then at Charles. "I wasn't alone."

Charles vaulted from his chair, which slammed to the floor behind him. "Damn you. Don't do this!" he screamed.

Isabel rose beside him and cupped his face in her hands. Her eyes grew wide, and for the first time in a week they held tears. "Charles. My love," she choked. "We've been through so much. I beg you. Please let him speak. I need to hear this."

Charles looked into Isabel's eyes and saw the thing he feared would only bring more pain to them both. He saw hope. And while he was not prepared to accept it, he could not bring himself to deny his wife the temporary comfort it might provide. He closed his eyes, dropped his head and limply nodded for his brother to continue.

"Please. Sit." Richard motioned to the chairs. Both sat, but only Isabel looked at Richard. "Look at me," he said to Charles, who remained inattentive. Richard's need to make his brother face the truth came through forcefully. "Look at me!" he said boldly, slamming his fist on the table hard enough to make the water glass jump. Never in Charles' life had his little brother spoken to him the way he spoke now. He commanded his attention. And by God he got it.

"I have been racking my brain trying to find a way to tell you that your little girl is there! She's there Charlie! Esther is in heaven! With God! I saw her and I spoke to her! I held her! Whether or not you believe it is up to you. But I hope for your sake that you do. It's real and it's true. I know it." He paused and placed his hand over his heart. "And so does Esther."

Charles and Isabel sat in stunned silence. Richard drew a breath and leaned back in his chair. He reached into his shirt pocket, removed a folded scrap of paper and slid it across the table between the two. "I've been keeping this in my Bible. This is the place," he said, pointing to the paper. "This is the place I was at. This is the place where Esther is still. Open it."

Isabel unfolded the wrinkled paper and gasped when she saw what it contained. Having forgotten about the picture, Charles closed his eyes and then opened them again, straining to see through the wetness that clouded his vision. It showed Esther and her beloved uncle standing hand-in-hand beneath a tree on a hill overlooking a field of gold.

"You've seen this Charlie. Esther gave it to me at mom and dad's anniversary party. It's what saved me when I was going to kill myself at the cabin," Richard reminded his brother. "She said it was a resting place. I didn't know what she meant then. Now I do."

Charles hand shook and he retracted it once before reaching again for the drawing. He held it in front of his face as if it were Esther herself. He wanted to believe in heaven. More than that, he wanted to believe his little girl was there. His defenses cracked when he eyed the crudely drawn stick figures etched by his daughter's own hand. They crumbled and crashed to the ground when he realized that his five-year-old little angel, an untarnished and innocent child by any measure, had possessed insights into life and death on a level that he hadn't even come close to grasping. He was humbled, and he felt more than a trace of shame for his lack of faith.

There were rational explanations against the idea of God and life after death. Charles had, over the years, issued them all to the people of faith in his circle of family and friends. But they left so many big unanswered questions; questions he now knew could never be answered by applying scientific methods or logical thinking. Many would think him a fool for taking the easy path, for filling the void left by science and logic with faith, for believing that humans couldn't possibly know all the answers simply because they are not God. But that, to his way of thinking now, was plausible. Yes, it defied rational explanation. But life was full of things that defied rational explanation, things for which science had no answers and probably would never have answers. Besides, believing in God and an afterlife comforted him and his loving wife. So, for the first time since his childhood he chose to believe it.

"Charlie. Isabel," Richard said, reaching for both their hands. "God knows what it is to lose a child. And I know with all my heart that if you love him you will see Esther again."

With those words, Charles and Isabel could do nothing but embrace each other and weep. Their tears were stained with sadness from losing Esther. But for the first time they wept with hope - hope that they would one day see their little girl again.

Knowing these things comforted Charles. But the realization that he would have to live without her in this life once again flooded his entire being. His heart ached for her. Picking up her drawing, he pressed it to his face as if an essence of her had been left on the paper and would somehow mingle with his flesh and bring a small part of her back to him. Wanting more than anything to be a family again he reached for Isabel, wrapping his arms around her and pulling her close.

Thirty

Malcolm stopped by Richard's room to inform him that Sheriff Langford had come to visit. Richard hobbled on a crutch to the nurse's station to say hello to Nurse Fenstermaker before going to meet the sheriff in the day room. Uncharacteristically, she had taken the prior week off from work and was busy writing when he walked up and stood in front of her.

"Nurse Banff," she chirped without looking up from her work. "I don't see a record here for Mr. Gansberg's meds from the 3:00 PM distribution last Friday. Why is that?" Hearing no response she raised her head, ready to bark an order at the nearest person who could find the heedless delinquent and return her to her post. Then she saw Richard. "Oh, Mr. Buell," she said, her furrowed brow now relaxed. "How are you getting along?"

"I'm doing well, nurse Fenstermaker. I was just on my way to the day room and I thought I'd stop by to see how your vacation went."

"My vacation went quite well, thank you," she smirked, not having used the words "my vacation" in years.

Richard was prepared to ask her for details, but to his surprise she volunteered the information. "I went to visit a dear old friend I haven't seen in years and mend some fences," she said, knowing that Richard would not be so rude and intrusive as to ask which fences needed mending.

"I'm glad for you," he said extending his hand for a shake. "You deserve a dear old friend." She got up from her chair and returned the gesture. "I'm on my way to meet an old friend myself," Richard said. "So I'll leave you to your work."

Richard saw the Sheriff sitting at the same table that he, Charlie, and Isabel had sat at during the heart wrenching and life changing conversation they had the day before. The sheriff rose when Richard approached and they exchanged pleasantries. Not knowing why the sheriff had requested a meeting, Richard quickly got to the point. "What's up, Jim?" he asked.

"Well this may sound a little strange, but Mark Valjean made a request to talk with you. I guess he has some things he wants to say about what happened."

"Um. OK," Richard responded hesitantly.

"The request was denied, but an audio taping of his statement was approved. I can't leave it with you," the sheriff said, holding up a small plastic cassette. "You know the restrictions around here. But you can listen to it now if you like."

Richard took the cassette from the sheriff and turned it over in his hands. Valjean was a sexual deviant and a child killer who, if justice were served, would spend the rest of his life behind bars. The thought of hearing him speak was repulsive. But Richard knew that if he didn't listen to the man who killed Esther it would haunt him forever.

"Yeah. Let's hear it," he said.

The sheriff placed the cassette in a tiny black playback unit and pressed the play button. A few seconds of soft hissing came through the speaker, followed by scraping and rustling sounds Richard imagined were caused by Valjean jockeying a chair into position as he situated himself in front of the microphone. After a loud throat-clearing grunt he began.

"This recording is for Richard Buell. I am Mark Theodore Valjean and today is December the 20th." There was a long pause and another clearing of his throat. "I know what you did for me. I know what you did, and for the longest time I could not understand why you did it. I hated you for it - I truly hated you. I spent days and nights cursing you for saving my life. I wanted to die. For years I've wanted to die. I tried to do it, but I was afraid," he said, chuckling sadly. "I thought my life was worth nothing, yet I didn't have the courage to end it." The recording went silent for a few moments.

"I know why," Valjean started again. "I was afraid to die because of what was waiting for me on the other side. I was afraid if I didn't make amends that I would end up in the same place as I am here - in hell. When I finally gave myself up after you fell at the quarry, I felt... I felt relieved. I fought with you because that's what I've always done - fight to stay alive because I was afraid of death. But when you were holding me over that cliff a part of me hoped you would just let me go. I even hoped I'd feel the pain of death. But I also hoped that at some point the pain would go away and I would just slip away into a deep sleep and never feel anything ever again. I wanted to be free of this thing that I had become, and death seemed like the only way out." It frightened Richard to admit it, but he identified with everything that Valjean was saying.

The penitent killer continued. "Your probably thinkin', so did he want to live, or did he want to die? Well, neither really! At least not at that time. But now I'm glad to be alive 'cause I feel like maybe there's hope for my soul." A heavy sigh and several deep breaths followed another moment of silence. "That wouldn't be possible if you hadn't saved me from falling into that pit. You took the fall for me even though I deserved to die. I can't wrap my mind around that completely, and I can't come up with the words to tell you how it's changed me. All I can say is that over the past few weeks I have been sad, the saddest I have ever been for all the things I've done. There's a large part of me that feels I shouldn't say this because of what I did to you, to your brother and sister in law, and especially to their little girl."

Another long pause was interrupted by the sound of the device being turned off, and then back on again. There was no way to tell how long Valjean had been away, but Richard got the sense that he had stopped to gather his emotions so he could continue. It was apparent he had been crying. His voice was raspy and he sniffled between words.

"What I did is unforgivable...but I want to ask your forgiveness. I don't expect you'll offer it. But I need to ask for it. I'll probably spend the rest of my life in prison, and I'm OK with that. I deserve it. Justice demands it. This statement to you has nothing to do with that." Valjean cleared his throat again, and there was a raking sound, probably Valjean scratching his unshaven face. "I'm thankful for the mercy you showed me. It was undeserved and I won't ever forget it. I just needed to let you know these things." Another click was followed by a lasting silence.

The sheriff watched Richard without speaking. He was deep in thought and the sheriff could tell by the look on his face that the wheels of his mind were spinning. Richard nodded his head as if agreeing with someone who was talking to him. Then he asked to be excused and got up without waiting for a response from the sheriff. He hobbled over to the nurse's station and returned moments later with a pen, paper and envelope and began to write.

It seemed to the sheriff that Richard had forgotten he was there. At one point the sheriff started to say something and Richard, without looking up from his paper, held up his index finger as if to say, "Kindly wait until I'm done." Begrudgingly, the sheriff settled back in his chair and paged through emails on his smart phone. Minutes later, the sheriff looked up to take in the amber colored light of the sunset streaming through the windows of the day room. Then Richard spoke. "Sheriff, thanks for dropping by with the tape. I really appreciate you taking the time for this. Please give this to Valjean," he said, extending the letter he had just written.

"May I ask what's in it?"

"Would I be breaking the law if I didn't tell you?" Richard asked politely.

The Sheriff hesitated, scanning his brain for the answer. "I don't think so."

"Then, respectfully I'll keep it between me and Valjean."

The sheriff smiled, took the letter and said goodbye.

***

"How dare you give that smug son-of-a-bitch the satisfaction of a reply."

Richard whirled around in the mostly vacant hallway where he was strolling after the sheriff's departure. Mr. Lazarus looked like a black suit with nothing but a pair of fierce blue eyeballs suspended above the neckline, his ashen skin and hair blending with the gray walls.

"What do you expect to gain from this foolishness?" Lazarus asked.

Richard turned away from him and continued to walk without offering a reply.

"Do you expect him to ask God for forgiveness?" Lazarus continued, stepping out to catch up with Richard, who was quickly putting space between them. "What kind of god would sentence that innocent young girl to such torture? Does it mean nothing to you that he killed her?" Lazarus asked, stopping his rant and waiting for a reply. When he got none, his lip curled upwards. "Don't ignore me boy! Your pathetic life depends upon it!" he screamed. Richard continued moving forward without even a backwards glance. "I'm talking to you! You have me to thank for saving your sorry ass on more occasions than I can count! I demand an answer!"

Richard stuck his hands in his pockets and began to whistle the melody from "God Bless the Child," the Billie Holiday tune from his CD collection at work, which for some reason had popped into his head. Lazarus stopped in his tracks. His puckered face jutted forward in disbelief as he watched Richard turn the corner leading back towards the day room, never even giving him the satisfaction of eye contact.

Thirty-One

The floorboards inside the front door gave a familiar groan as Richard stepped inside Alpha House's main hallway. The rich, sweet smell of some baked delicacy wafted from the kitchen and the day room was full of conversation and activity that was intimate and friendly. It was a refreshing change from what he had experienced at Broward.

He was home.

Four months had passed since Richard had been sent back to Broward after the incident. During that time his wounds had healed and he had been a near model patient as far as the staff were concerned. But there were things that tested him. A patient the others had nicknamed "Squishy" had, for no apparent reason, spit on him and dumped a bowl of soup over his head while he sat in the cafeteria during lunch. And his copy of "The Big Book of Bugs" had mysteriously disappeared.

But his worst day was when he learned that Carolyn Barry had killed herself. Authorities determined that she had torn old pairs of white socks into strips and tied them end-to-end until the fabric rope was long enough to do the job. She secured the loose end to a bedpost and leaned into the noose until she lost consciousness. Piles of pillows, bed linens and clothing were mounded at her sides to ensure that her limp body would not fall to the left or right and loosen the tension of the noose around her neck. The night nurse found her during 2:00 AM rounds. A ponytail-sized crop of hair was found in her hand.

The bad voices were still present, and sometimes they were exhausting. It seemed that they had adapted to Richard's new outlook on life. The tone and content of their rhetoric was different. Their comments felt less viscous, a little softer and a little more palatable - more like the voice of God. Fortunately, Richard caught on to the ruse and was able to distinguish between the two.

Mr. Lazarus had shown up a few times, but he never spoke. He only observed in his arrogant, self-important way, as if to let Richard know that he was still there and if asked nicely would consider making himself available in situations demanding a sharp wit and cunning intellect. Richard took his silence to mean he was trying to appear restrained, but his body language revealed something different. His harsh blue eyes went wide in disbelief when Richard did something like tell a tech about his plans for the future, and they always narrowed whenever nurse Fenstermaker was around. Lazarus' mouth was as telling as his eyes, half open and gasping for air, alternately sagging, curling, and quivering. It got to the point where Richard actually enjoyed watching his facial contortions and would do things just to get a rise out of him.

Lazarus' countenance changed when he learned that Richard had earned the right to return to Alpha House on house arrest. He stood head down, leaning against the doorframe of the hospital's main entrance when Richard walked by him on his way to Charlie's car. No words were exchanged, not even a sideways glance was offered. But Richard knew that Lazarus felt dejected and wounded. Once inside the car, Richard looked back briefly as Charlie pulled away, but Lazarus was gone.

He was home now. And home held so many comforting things, not the least of which was Judith. She seemed always to be just a step behind him, following him from room to room and even to the smoking table. She was even allowed to accompany him into his apartment between the hours of 10:00 AM and 2:00 PM, as long as the door was kept open and she and Richard remained visible to the staff.

Things were different – better in many ways, but mostly different. Richard had decided that the quality of his life was due, in large part, to the choices he made. He chose to believe in God and listen to God's voice above all others. He chose to believe that most people were not bent on causing him pain and suffering. And he decided that all God wanted from him was to know that he was loved, and to give that love back to everyone in his life. God would, in His own time and in His own ways, do the rest to heal whatever wounds they may have and make them whole again.

Most times Richard was aware that he had a mental disorder called schizophrenia, and he regularly took his medications. But he thought the name applied to his illness was inadequate, like assigning the term "tornado" to an event that violently takes lives and causes unimaginable destruction. It failed to fully define his experience, and it surely did not completely define him as a person.

"Hey buddy, how's it going?" Carl asked as he emerged from his office, embracing Richard for the first time since his return. He noticed that Richard's body lacked the rigidity he normally felt when he went in for a hug.

"I'm good. It's good to be home."

"It's great to have you back," Carl added. "Hey, Nurse Fenstermaker called me from Broward." Out of habit Richard's body tensed a little upon hearing her name. "She said you've been transformed. That's the word she used – transformed." A smile lit Carl's face and he placed a hand on Richard's shoulder. A stack of papers he held in his other hand slipped out and fell to the floor, strewn about their feet.

"Aaah," he sighed as he bent down to pick up the mess. Half way down he lost his balance and threw his arms out to prevent from being completely splayed out on the floor. Richard quickly reached down to help.

"I'm fine! I'm fine!" Carl said, quickly gathering the papers and rebounding. Clearing his throat and composing himself, he started again. "I'm so proud of you for how you've handled things these past few months. I can't wait to hear about everything that's happened."

"We can talk in your office if you'd like," Richard replied.

"I'd like that very much," Carl said, motioning towards his office door.

The chair behind Carl's desk issued its signature groan as he leaned back. He glanced momentarily at the locked desk drawer holding his pills. His mouth went dry and the smile on his face slowly dissolved as the familiar pulsating throb emanated from the center of his body, announcing the need for relief. He looked up to see Richard sitting in the same chair Charlie had sat in only a few months earlier, pouring out his heart about the pain he felt for his brother. Carl placed his hand on his pant pocket and felt the outline of the key. Tiny droplets of sweat hung on his upper lip like condensed steam seething from the mouth of a kettle. He began to slide his hand into his pocket but stopped abruptly when Richard spoke.

"Mark Valjean asked for my forgiveness," Richard said.

Carl winced. He knew that they had to talk about Valjean; after all he was an Alpha House employee. But Carl felt somewhat responsible for what had happened. And he felt shame and sadness for not seeing the kind of man Valjean was.

"I told him that my forgiveness was not as important as God's forgiveness," Richard continued, shifting in his seat and hoping that repositioning himself would lessen the discomfort he felt rising inside him. "I told him that I understood something about what had happened to him, but that I wasn't ready to forgive him yet. I'm still working on that, but honestly I don't know if I can."

"I understand that," Carl said, hesitating. "I'm so sorry for what he did. I only wish I would have known he was that...that sick." A question badgered Carl, a question that had been voiced in his mind many times since Esther's death. *Could my little white pills have clouded my judgment*? he asked himself.

"I believe the trials we face teach us, and eventually they lead us to our purpose," Richard said, looking peacefully at Carl. "Do you know what I mean?"

"I...yes. I think I do," Carl replied, unable to say anything further, afraid to give voice to what he was thinking. Namely that he was sitting with a man whom he was charged with caring for, a man who was by all accounts severely mentally ill and delusional, yet had the presence of mind to try and do what was right. More than that he was wise enough to turn a terrible situation into something positive, and thoughtful enough to share it with a friend. Carl felt humbled and undeserving of the wisdom Richard offered. Still, he found a way to open his mouth and state what was foremost in his mind. "You are a good man Richard Buell. You're a good man. And I'm glad to have you back," Carl said, looking at his watch. "I'm sorry to have to do this, but could we continue our conversation later? I just remembered that I have a phone call I have to make."

"OK, no problem," Richard said, rising from his chair and walking to the door. He turned around before opening it. "You're a good man too Carl Maznik. You've been a great help to me, and someday I hope I can return the favor."

"You already have buddy. You already have."

When Richard had closed the office door, Carl placed his shaking hand over the key in his pocket. Relief was only moments away. Then he closed his eyes and willed his hand upwards to pick up the phone and dial for help.

Thirty-Two

Spring had arrived. Patches of bright green peeked out from the brownish winter carpet that covered the front yard at Alpha House. The oaks towering overhead bore thousands of newly sprouted miniature leaves, each holding the promise of the fullness of summer. The tulips Judith had planted at the base of each tree in the fall were in full bloom, like red, yellow and purple cups stretching upward to catch the suns rays and then drink them in.

"You can't do that! You can't crown your checker before it reaches my end of the board!" Sam objected. Booger reached over and moved his piece to a crowning square. "You can't do that! You can't jump over three squares. It's not even your turn!" Sam continued, shoving his chair back, standing and glaring wide-eyed at Richard. "Can you please teach him how to play this game? He doesn't listen to me, and we are out of options! We can't play Parcheesi anymore! The last time we tried Monopoly he actually told me that the rent on his hotels had doubled because he added casinos!" Sam glared at Booger, who was gleefully gyrating to some tune playing in his head and sipping iced tea from a glass shaped like a cowboy boot. "You can't do that!" Sam objected again. Booger smiled and crowned another checker.

Richard turned to Judith, who was sitting next to him on the porch swing. "Those two are like an old, really dysfunctional married couple," he chuckled.

The corners of her mouth turned up. "Yeah, but they need each other… just like I need you."

Richard took her hand and caressed it with the tips of his smoke stained fingers, then he raised it to his lips and placed a soft kiss.

"The stain on your fingers is getting lighter," Judith said, stroking the brown colored blotches. "How long has it been?"

"1 week, 3 days, 16 hours and 27 - no wait," he paused to peer at his wrist, which for the first time in decades actually held a watch, "and 28 minutes."

Her elbow jabbed his side. "You're making that up," she said.

"OK, one week and three days."

"I'm proud of you," she added, resting her head on his shoulder.

"Thanks. Oh look, Charlie is here!" Richard exclaimed when he saw a car pull up to the curb. Charles popped out and waved. Rounding the front of the car, he opened the passenger door and extended his hand inside. Isabel grabbed the top of the open door and stood up with Charles' help. Her blue and yellow sundress ruffled in the breeze. Ringlets of gleaming chestnut hair flowed over her shoulders and moved with her dress.

The curve of her belly seemed more pronounced than the last time they had seen her. Stepping forward, she placed her hands on both sides of her tummy and caressed the little person growing inside. She smiled warmly and waived to Richard and Judith. It was so good for her to see them together.

Judith and Isabel talked about bassinettes, and strange food cravings, formula versus breast milk, knitted swaddling blankets and a number of other things occupying the thoughts of the mother-to-be. Judith thought about consulting the family when Isabel asked her to recount some of the good memories from her childhood, and she took hold of the hand-held transistor radio tucked into her sweater pocket. But she decided that she knew the answers on her own and she never took it out.

Charlie showed Richard a picture of a trophy bass he had landed while he and Isabel were at the cabin. He and his brother made plans for a weekend of fishing and eating the bountiful mess of trout they would surely catch in the shaded cove by Sayer's Rock. They even decided to cut down a teetering aspen tree that seemed to be on the verge of falling onto the barbeque pit. They would split it into firewood for the coming winter.

When asked if they had named the baby, Isabel looked at Charlie and he nodded his approval. "We're going to name her Richenza," she said, extending her hand to her brother in law. "We want to honor her with the name of a great man."

Richard smiled in amazement and then shook his head as if something was wrong. "Are you sure you want to do that?" he asked. "She might get teased a lot."

"It's a beautiful name and she'll be proud to have it," Charles added. "Besides, the other options we had were Richardella, Richmal, or Richilda. Now how do you feel about Richenza?"

"Pretty good when you put it that way!" Richard said, his laughter echoing from the porch and into the sunlit yard.

"Esther would have loved her little sister," Isabel chimed, smiling as she imagined her little girl fussing over the baby. "Hey! Pancake knows there is a new little one coming!" she beamed. "She's been sniffing my belly, and last night she slept in Esther's room. She never does that!"

"I'm surrounded by hormonal females!" Charles joked. "Little brother, you're all I've got! It's you and me! You and me!"

For a moment Charles felt a tinge of guilt for the high spirits and laughter he was sharing with his loved ones, as if he was not allowed any reprieve from the pain of losing Esther. But, for reasons he didn't understand, he was in the midst of a moment of bliss. He had not experienced anything remotely close to it since Esther's passing. He had lost his little girl, and that hole would never be filled. But he still had Isabel, their soon-to-be-born daughter, and Richard. And Richard now had Judith, which in itself was enough to bring Charles unspeakable joy. Amongst the chatter he glanced at the bulge on Isabel's stomach, silently giving thanks for the little person that would soon fill his life with a new joy.

"I'm going to get some cookies. I'll be right back," Richard interjected, unable to help himself from thinking about the piles of freshly baked goodies that waited in the kitchen, just a few steps away. They would add even more sweetness to the moment.

He walked the hallway to the kitchen, thinking only about the good things in his life. He eyed the cookies, which were mounded on a large cake plate covered by a glass dome. He didn't bother flicking the light switch. Instead he opened the cupboard, retrieved four glasses and headed to the refrigerator for milk. When he closed the refrigerator door a shadowy figure stepped forward from behind it.

"You've been talkin' up a storm, haven't you?"

Richard turned away and placed the milk on the counter next to the glasses. He unscrewed the top and began pouring as Lazarus continued. "You managed to get out of the wacky shack, I'll give you that. But you don't seem to understand that you are putting yourself at risk. All this loose talk about learning from your failures and helping other people - you are making yourself vulnerable! Don't you see that?"

Richard remained silent as he reached into the cupboard and grabbed four ceramic plates. They rang out as he laid them on the marble island on which the cake plate sat.

"Becoming intimate with others will only make matters worse! Stay away for god's sake! They will end up hurting you, I can promise you that!"

Richard stacked the cookie filled plates one on top of another and turned to look Lazarus in the eyes for the first time since he began speaking. And for the first time since they had known each other, the weight of Richard's stare caused Lazarus to look away.

Richard waited until Lazarus found the courage to look back. "Our lives are not our own - those of us who are real," he said, pausing to let his words sink in. "And we are bound to each other in ways you will never understand." Richard glanced away, certain that he had spoken the truth. He waited until Lazarus started to squirm, and then he looked at him again. "I'm not the person I was before. I found a part of me that's real, a part I lost touch with a long time ago," he added, the corners of his lips turning up slightly as he thought about everything he had gained. "I don't need you anymore!"

Lazarus's lips quivered uncontrollably until he forced them into a counterfeit smile. "It's OK. I'll see you around," he replied, his voice as desperate and uncertain as the dying flame behind his eyes.

"Well then," Richard said, returning the smile. "I very much look forward to ignoring you."

About the Author

Mitch Davis lives with his wife in Round Lake Beach, Illinois. Finding Richard, his first published novel, was inspired by personal experiences with members of his family who suffer from mental illness. An avid reader, Mitch facilitates a guy's-only book club called "Books & Beer," which he jokes is just an excuse to have a few drinks with his buddies. He enjoys spending time with his granddaughter, woodworking, hiking, canoeing and being with family and friends at his log cabin retreat in southwestern Wisconsin.

For additional information about the author and his work visit www.MitchDavis.us.